**"If you or anyone in this congregation knows of any impediment, why they may not be lawfully joined together in matrimony, you should now confess it..."**

There were the rumblings of a skirmish at the chapel door, and the priest halted his words, looking up, past Ædwen, over her shoulder. She turned around and her breath halted as she saw a contingent of royal guards piling into the back of the church.

Strange. Why would the king's men descend on her wedding?

And then she saw him.

A tall, dark warrior who had to stoop to enter. Once inside, he raised his shoulders and head to his full, imposing height, and his blistering blue gaze came to settle on her.

"I do," he announced, his heavy brow forming a dark line.

*Stefan.*

Her first love.

The father of her child.

For a fleeting moment, her spine straightened in awareness as she felt the traitorous surge of elation soar through her.

He was here.

He had come back.

Her heart leaped with unex

She had thought she'd nev

## Author Note

All my stories begin with a tiny spark of an idea, and this one was no different. A Viking boy wounded and left for dead. A Saxon girl who rescues him. Might he be suffering from amnesia? And what would happen if these two fell in love, despite their different backgrounds? I do love a forbidden romance! And so *Her Secret Vows with the Viking* began.

Knowing her father would never allow her to marry a Dane, my heroine, Ædwen, and hero, Stefan, say their vows in secret. But when Stefan's memories return and he remembers that Ædwen's father was one of the men who killed his family, he cannot forgive her for hiding the truth, so he leaves.

This story starts almost two winters later, when Ædwen is distraught to be marrying the hateful Lord Werian. Her father has convinced her that her previous, clandestine union was invalid. But even though Stefan abandoned her, a day hasn't gone by that she hasn't thought of him.

Anger has kept Stefan away. But upon hearing about Ædwen's impending wedding, his unsatiated vengeance and desire burn. So he interrupts the wedding ceremony, announcing to the congregation that Ædwen is already married—to him—and he's returned to claim his wife.

I loved writing this book. These two may have made secret vows, but also a secret baby, which all added to my enjoyment of sending them on their path to an eventual happy-ever-after. I hope you enjoy it.

# HER SECRET VOWS
# WITH THE VIKING

**SARAH RODI**

**Harlequin**
**HISTORICAL**

# Harlequin®
## HISTORICAL

ISBN-13: 978-1-335-53971-7

Her Secret Vows with the Viking

Harlequin Enterprises ULC
22 Adelaide St. West, 41st Floor
Toronto, Ontario M5H 4E3, Canada
www.Harlequin.com

Printed in U.S.A.

Recycling programs for this product may not exist in your area.

**Sarah Rodi** has always been a hopeless romantic. She grew up watching old romantic movies recommended by her granddad or devouring love stories from the local library. Sarah lives in the village of Cookham in Berkshire, where she enjoys walking along the River Thames with her husband, her two daughters and their dog. She has been a magazine journalist for over twenty years, but it has been her lifelong dream to write romance for Harlequin. Sarah believes everyone deserves to find their happy-ever-after. You can contact her via @sarahrodiedits or sarahrodiedits@gmail.com. Or visit her website at sarahrodi.com.

### Books by Sarah Rodi

#### Harlequin Historical

*One Night with Her Viking Warrior*
*Claimed by the Viking Chief*
*Second Chance with His Viking Wife*
"Chosen as the Warrior's Wife"
in *Convenient Vows with a Viking*
*The Viking and the Runaway Empress*

#### Rise of the Ivarssons

*The Viking's Stolen Princess*
*Escaping with Her Saxon Enemy*

Visit the Author Profile page
at Harlequin.com.

For Charlie, for always being there
with your love and support.

And to the rest of the Dawsons,
for all the fun and laughter.

# Chapter One

1017—England

'*You can do this,*' Ædwen muttered under her breath, as she forced herself to walk slowly up the aisle. '*The worst has already happened.*'

It was her wedding day. She should have been feeling joy, yet instead she felt an overwhelming sense of dread, the church bells chiming dully along with the heavy thud of her heart. For this was what her father, Lord Manvil of Eastbury, had forced her to sacrifice everything for— an arranged, loveless marriage. An alliance deemed so crucial to him that her happiness and all she held dear had been surrendered.

She focused on putting one foot in front of the other, trying to block out the sea of Saxon faces in the congregation, their appraising gazes following her as she made her way to the altar. This church inside the monastery, the familiar wooden beams, the pews she had sat in so many times…they had been her refuge these past years. Yet today, it was as if she was being incarcerated for her past mistakes.

Beneath her fixed smile and blue silk tunic, she felt

utter despair, distraught to be finally bowing to duty and marrying Lord Werian, so her father could gain more power—more soldiers to protect his lands and build up a bigger force against Canute, the new Danish King of England.

She couldn't even bring herself to look at her intended as she drew closer to him. He was double her age and almost twice her size. And as if sensing she might have a last-moment change of heart and rebel against him in a final act of defiance, her father gripped her arm tighter, thrusting her forward, faster, to a future she didn't want. There was no chance of escape.

But she knew she wouldn't run. She needed this union to go ahead, because if it didn't, her father had threatened she would never see her child again.

'We are gathered here together in the sight of God, and in the face of this congregation, to join together this man and this woman in holy matrimony...'

Ædwen tried to focus on the priest's words, but it was all so absurd, as if this was happening to someone else. But then, she'd been living half a life for some time. Since her daughter had been cruelly taken from her as she slept and handed over to another family to raise, without her consent. Her heart ached.

Suddenly, a ferocious galloping of horses coming from beyond the walls drowned out the holy man's voice and the ground shook beneath her feet. The congregation stirred, looking around at each other, questioning the disturbance. The hammering of hooves stopped, replaced by the sound of men barking orders and then heavy footsteps running.

The hairs on the back of her neck stood on end. Something was wrong.

'I charge you both, as you will answer at the dreadful day of judgement, when the secrets of all hearts shall be revealed, that if you or anyone in this congregation knows of any impediment, why they may not be lawfully joined together in matrimony, you should now confess it...'

There were the rumblings of a skirmish at the chapel door and the priest halted his words, looking up, past Ædwen, over her shoulder. Turning around, her breath halted as she saw a contingent of royal guards piling into the back of the church.

Strange. Why would the King's men descend on her wedding?

And then she saw him.

A tall, dark warrior who had to stoop to enter. Once inside, he raised his shoulders and head to his full, imposing height and his blistering blue gaze came to settle on her.

'I do,' he announced, his heavy brow forming a dark line.

Her body baulked, reeling in recognition and the most disturbing shock, and she let out an involuntary gasp of surprise. She raked her eyes over his stark features, drinking him in, for she knew those intense eyes and that hard, handsome face... She hadn't seen it this past winter, but it was one she would never forget.

*Stefan.*

Her first love.

The father of her child.

For a fleeting moment, her spine straightened in

awareness as she felt the traitorous surge of elation soar through her.

*He was here.*

*He had come back.*

Her heart leapt with unexpected delight.

She had thought she'd never see him again.

And then, like the crashing of a wave on a rocky shore, she remembered…and her joy shattered.

Hurt and rage exploded inside her chest, taking over, crushing any spark of pleasure she had fleetingly felt upon seeing him. The faces in the church began to blur and she faltered, reaching out her hand to support herself on the wooden pew.

Memories floored her of the last time they had seen each other—the morning after he'd taken her virtue. It had been the best evening of her life and she had often wondered, in the months since, how they had gone from that—unable to wait, incapable of keeping their hands off each other—to him backing away from her in disgust and anger. A huge chasm had opened between them and the words he had hurled at her had been ugly and unforgivable. He had removed himself from her life so fast, but what had been a brief fling had a long-lasting impact.

Seeing him here now shocked her to the core. Her stomach roiled, her heart pounded in alarm and the walls of the church began to spin.

Where had he been these past fifteen months? And what could he mean by coming here today, bursting in on them like this? Her thoughts scrambled to understand, unable to make sense of it. It couldn't mean anything good, for he despised her. His presence here was dangerous—it threatened to ruin everything.

Fear stalked her veins, making her hands tremble, as Stefan began to stride purposely towards her, his men tussling with her father's guards behind him and the congregation whispering in a mixture of concern and excitement. There was nothing Ædwen could do but hold her breath and watch his dominating approach, his huge, fierce frame bearing down on her.

'Under the command of the King's guard, this marriage cannot go ahead,' he said, his deep, authoritative voice resounding around the church.

Ædwen's heart momentarily stopped beating. The people in the church fell into an awed hush. Lord Werian and her father lurched forward.

'Why ever not?' the priest asked, lowering his Bible.

'Because it would be unlawful, Father,' Stefan said, reaching Ædwen's side, stepping into the shaft of sunlight streaming through the window. He looked like a dark angel—or the devil—sent to torment her. His eyes were smouldering like embers, hinting at the anger beneath, and his scathing stare looked down into her face. 'For the lady is already married. To me.'

Appalled gasps rippled around the church and Lord Werian visibly recoiled. Ædwen felt herself sway, Stefan's announcement rushing in her ears.

Why was he doing this? They'd all be ruined!

'It is a lie!' her father roared, his face turning puce as his grip tightened around her elbow. She was almost glad of his hold, for without it, she might have fallen.

She had dreamed of a moment like this, often. For a long while, she had yearned for Stefan to return, of him coming back to claim her. Of him telling her he hadn't meant the things he'd said.

But not any more.

Too much had happened. Things that could never be forgiven. Things that would never have come to pass if he had remained by her side, as he'd vowed he would. He had said they would be together for ever, but instead, it had been just one final day. He had forsaken her when she'd needed him most and the bitterness of blame burned her throat.

He couldn't be here in Eastbury. Not now. Not today. If he broke up this union, she would never see her child again.

*Their* child.

A daughter he knew nothing about.

'It was a clandestine marriage, Father. We said our vows in private,' Stefan said, his distinctive, velvety voice stirring her blood, and images of that morning rose up before she could crush them…of her lying naked in Stefan's arms, her head resting on his shoulder, as he gently wound a thin silk thread around her finger. He told her it signified their lives were bound to one another.

Her face flamed.

'This is a serious accusation indeed, my lord,' the priest said, moving his gaze to look at her. 'Lady Ædwen, can this be true?'

All the eyes of the congregation were on her and the mortification was great.

'*Do* you know this man?'

As she glanced up at Stefan, her response to him was instinctive, as it had always been. Just looking at him still made her pulse beat so hard she thought everyone could hear it. And he was standing so near to her, she could feel the heat radiating from his magnificent body, warming her blood. She was so close she could breathe in his intoxicating, familiar scent of leather and spice, making her feel heady, luring her in.

She did know him, although he looked different to the man she had once known. He was even more attractive, if that was possible. The last time she'd seen him he'd been muscular but lean, still boyish, and dressed in the plain clothes they had found for him in the monastery. Now his frame was broader, much taller, and he was wearing the formidable mail coat of the King's guard. He was carrying a sword. Had he become one of Canute's men? That would make sense—after all, like their new King, Stefan was a Dane...

That day the Northmen's foreboding fleet had been spotted off the coast of Eastbury, the air had felt unnaturally calm, the waters still. She had been standing on the steps of the monastery where she spent her days, watching the intimidating dragon ships advance over the sea towards them. The ox horn and church bells were pealing out, warning the people of her father's settlement that they were under attack, and as the men had prepared to fight, lining up on the beach, the women had rushed around in terror, trying to find places to hide, sheltering their children and livestock.

But Ædwen hadn't felt fear—not for herself anyway, as she had known the wrath her father's men would unleash on their foe. Her father had called the men from the north heathens. Ungodly. He had been preparing for their arrival for some time.

Despite not knowing if the Danes were coming to their shores to plunder their lands, or in peace, Ædwen had wanted to warn them not to come, knowing what brutality lay in store for them here. She had pleaded with her father to be merciful. But in the end, he hadn't given them a chance. And by the look of the desolate scene afterwards, it hadn't been a battle, but a massacre.

When the slaughter was over, farmsteads had been left burning, lifeless bodies strewn about, the shallow surf stained red, and the Saxons had retired to her father's Great Hall to toast their glory, uncaring of the devastation they had left in their wake. But she, along with the monks and nuns from the monastery, had tentatively made their way out to the beach to help the Saxon wounded. Instead, she had found Stefan…

Looking at him now, his hair was still dark, but slightly longer—a bit dishevelled, as if he'd recently raked his hands through it, as she had once done. She knew the feel of that strong jaw under the palm of her hand, but now it was covered in a neat, thick beard. She remembered how it felt to be held in his sturdy arms and to bask in the warm glow of his affection…but those translucent eyes that changed colour with his mood were now dark with ire.

Did she know him? She thought she had once. But there had been times when she'd wished she had never found him that day on the beach. Wished she had never called out to her fellow novices and begged for their help. But he had been just a young man of a similar age to her and he was wounded, but still breathing. They couldn't have left him…

Now, he looked more Dane than ever. Fierce. The prominent silver scar on his forehead was a stark reminder of all that had passed between them. There was a controlled wildness about him. He was fascinating. Intimidating. And she wondered if her father had been right all along: that all Danes were cruel. For Stefan had broken her heart and shattered her dreams, destroying her life.

No, she didn't know this man any more,

'Lady Ædwen?' the priest pressed.

Her throat felt dry, her face hot with the indignity of the situation. And then she realised… *That* was why he was here, now, after all this while. Stefan hadn't come to claim her because he cared for her, because he wanted her back. He had come for revenge, as he'd said he would. And what better vengeance could there be than to accuse her of adultery, even bigamy, disgracing her and her father in front of everyone they knew?

But she would lose her child for ever… She could not let that happen.

Fuelled by her resentment and determination, she raised herself taller, tipping up her face in defiance. She forced herself to speak, trying to block out the stares of the wide-eyed Saxon nobles lining the pews. 'I did know him, a long while ago. But it is irrelevant. It should have no bearing on this ceremony here today.'

'But can it be true, Lady Ædwen…what this man is saying? *Are* you already married?' the priest asked.

'Of course it isn't true!' her father bellowed, trying to take back control of the situation, a vein throbbing in his forehead. 'This heathen should be thrown out of here at once.'

Stefan's eyes narrowed on them. He put his hands on his hips and took an imposing step towards her, seeming immovable, making a mockery of her father's words. 'She gave her consent willingly. All that is required are the words of the two people involved, is it not, Father?'

Ædwen shook her head in disbelief. Nothing had changed. Stefan was still as hateful as the day he had left her.

'*Did* you give this consent, Lady Ædwen, without the approval of the church and your father?' the priest said. 'Did you marry this man? I need to know.'

Ædwen felt the four walls closing in on her, her father's fingers digging into her skin as a warning not to say anything. Panic clawed up her throat.

Was Stefan really going to make her admit to it, in front of all these people, shaming her and her family?

There was a great hushed reaction in the room, as if each person was holding their breath, not wanting to miss her answer, and they seemed to lean in closer in the small, cloying space.

'Surely you would not lie in your house of God?' Stefan urged.

And her heart sank with resignation, for he was right. He knew her belief was strong and she couldn't lie. Not in here.

*The secrets of all hearts shall be revealed...*

Yes, she had once said her vows to this man—and in secret, because she had known her father would never allow them to be together. She was a Saxon and Stefan was a Dane—but she had been so in love, so sure of him, she had been prepared to go against her father's wishes and incur his wrath, feeling brave enough to do so with Stefan at her side.

That morning after they'd made love, Stefan had traced his finger from her makeshift wedding band over her body to her heart and asked her to be his wife. But she had sat up and told him she must tell him something before they wed… If only he had let her. Instead, he had said there was nothing she could tell him that would make him love her any less, planting little kisses along her bottom lip, her jaw. He had said the words *'I take you as my wife'* and she had repeated them, taking him as her husband.

She swallowed. 'Yes,' she whispered now, her voice strained. 'But it was just words. Not a real marriage…'

Because when he'd found out what she had been keeping from him, less than a day later, he'd turned on her. It had been the shortest marriage in history.

The congregation were now up out of their seats, shocked, talking between themselves, the noise in the church deafening.

'Due to the absence of witnesses, this will be difficult to prove,' her father intervened. She could feel the anger vibrating off him. 'And you are a pagan,' he shot back at Stefan. 'I believe that invalidates any union.'

Ædwen looked up at the elderly man beside her, who would use her for his benefit, who held the key to her future happiness. He had convinced her of the same— that the vows she had taken before were discreditable, that they didn't mean anything. She would not be here otherwise.

'It was illicit, not illegal,' Stefan said, his eyes flashing in fury, and he crossed his arms over his chest. 'Besides, if it is my religion you take offence to, I believe taking her to my bed created a legally binding marriage.'

Tremors of shock rippled around the room and Ædwen felt the gut-punch of humiliation. How could he? He was destroying her father's name—and disgracing her beyond redemption.

His searing gaze burned into hers, forcing her to remember. But how could she ever forget? She felt her face heat with the recollection of their bodies entwined…his hot, open mouth pressed against her skin. The intimacy and the pleasure he had given her had been like nothing else she had ever experienced. And then he'd taken it all away.

She shook her head, as if to rid herself of her thoughts. She didn't want to think about him like that. Of what happened that night and how it changed her life. Her arms wrapped around her stomach as she tried to hold herself together.

But he didn't know about the consequences. He had long been gone. He wasn't aware he had left her with a constant reminder of him, growing in her belly. But what had it all been for—those nine months of confinement, the secrecy to protect her father's reputation, if Stefan was determined to ruin it all today? *Ruin her*, once more.

'Tell me, did she sleep with you the night before your wedding, too?' Stefan said to Lord Werian, but the reproach in his eyes was directed at her and she shivered. How could he be so cruel?

Lord Werian's lips curled. 'Did you know about this?' he asked in indignation, turning to her father, against the backdrop of the people moving, piling out of the pews, in outrage at the scandal unfolding before them.

Blind panic rose inside as Ædwen realised Lord Werian was also retreating, taking a step back in revulsion. The wedding was over. The union wasn't going to take place today.

Her daughter would be lost to her…

'I'm sure this can be settled quickly. Quietly,' she whispered to Lord Werian in desperation.

'I don't think so. I don't want you now...' he said, shaking his head in disgust. 'You've been tarnished by the touch of a Dane.'

She felt ill. If the wedding didn't go ahead, would her father be merciful? She had given birth to the most beautiful baby girl and at first, she had nursed her, looked after her, in the seclusion and solitude of the monastery walls. But one morning, she had awoken to find her daughter gone, taken, and she had been forced to return to her father's fortress to prepare to be married. She had been distraught, inconsolable, as if she had lost a piece of herself.

Her father had promised her the child had been placed with a noble family and would have a good life. But Ædwen hadn't wanted to live without her...she had gone without food in protest; she had threatened to expose him. So he had made her a deal. If she went through with this union, securing his alliance with Lord Werian, he would arrange for her to see her daughter again, in secret.

It had been an agonising month of waiting for this day to come. She needed to see her child again, to know that Ellan was safe, to hold her in her arms once more. But now... Her chin began to tremble as the last of her hope began to slip away.

'I could kill you for all you have said. Instead, I shall be merciful and give you coin to leave, so as not to destroy my daughter's happy day any further...' her father bit, turning to Stefan, seemingly as frantic as she was, not wanting to lose all he'd negotiated for.

But Stefan stepped closer, staking his claim on her. He gave a sharp shake of his head, determined. 'I don't want your coin,' he said, his voiced laced with scorn. His hand wrapped around the hilt of his sword. 'I want my family back, whom you took from me. So instead, I shall take yours. Your daughter. *My wife.*'

Ædwen swung to look at him, her heart thumping in shock. Did he actually intend to claim her once more for himself? She was horrified. She had thought he had come here to shame her, to break up her wedding, not to take her with him. Alarm tore through her. Why? He loathed her and she him. The time had long passed to make amends, there was too much hostility between them—and a secret much too great.

'This is me being merciful,' Stefan continued. 'This church, your soldiers, are surrounded by the King's men. Are you prepared to go up against your monarch today?'

Hot tears burned behind Ædwen's eyes. She did not want there to be any bloodshed over her.

She pinched the bridge of her nose and pushed out a slow, deep breath to calm herself. 'My lord... Stefan... please...' she said, speaking to him directly for the first time, trying to appeal to the man she once knew and cared for. 'Why are you doing this?' She lowered her voice and spoke slowly, her hands spread. 'You don't even want me...'

'No. I don't,' he retorted, his voice like ice. 'But nevertheless, we are joined in marriage under the eyes of your God—and mine. And as my wife you'll respect me. You'll do your duty. You *owe* me that.'

Stefan unsheathed his sword, at the same time as his men at the back of the church raised their own weapons, and the congregation shrieked in unison, huddling together, afraid. He looked like his father, Ædwen realised—the man she'd seen fighting on the beach that day. A cold, ruthless Danish warrior. Had his need for vengeance changed him beyond recognition?

'By order of the King, this ceremony is dissolved,' he said. 'We will now take our leave and Lady Ædwen, too. Anyone who dares stand in our way will be cut down.'

Ædwen felt her father's fingers drop from her elbow, relinquishing his hold on her, knowing he had lost. So he wasn't prepared to go against Canute's word, or fight the King's men—not today. He would need to rally support to go up against the royal army...

His touch was replaced by Stefan's large hand, which wrapped around her waist, taking control, holding her body upright. The heat of his touch through the silk tunic seared her skin as he led her to the door, past all the gaping people, her father's barks of fury reverberating around the church, and she willed for the agony to be over.

# Chapter Two

Stepping out into the daylight, the heat of the afternoon sun matched Stefan's seething anger as he gripped Ædwen's waist, tugging her towards his horse.

She had allowed him to lead her out of the church, perhaps in shock about what had just happened, but when she saw more of his men, his horse waiting for them, he felt her change her mind, hesitate and try to pull away.

He seized her wrist and their skin touching sent an unwanted spark up his fingers. He had hoped that when he saw her again, he would look into her eyes and feel nothing. Instead, when her expressive blue gaze had lifted to meet his across the room, his heart had jolted with awareness. Now his skin was burning. *Helvete!* He didn't want to still be attracted to her, or feel so possessive of her. He resented her.

*The woman who had borne his child and then given her up.*

Ædwen wore her long blonde hair loose and uncovered, and his jaw clenched in distaste. It was inappropriate for married women to have their hair down and on show. Something he intended to rectify before they reached the next settlement. She was wearing an exquisite bridal tunic in blue, the colour of purity—but he had already exposed that to be a lie. She looked stunning, like a true noblewoman, and yet she had kept her highborn blood from him. In the end, she hadn't been honourable at all…

'Come with me,' he said, dragging her over to his trusty steed.

He released her for just a moment, so he could grip the reins to ascend the animal, and quick as lightning she turned and began to run. Her refusal to co-operate made his irritation soar. He swung himself up into the saddle and dug his boots into the side of the horse, spurring the animal into action, charging alongside her, gripping her under the shoulders. He hauled Ædwen up to join him, pulling her back against his chest, and she gave a strangled cry of protest. She struggled, her bottom wiggling between his thighs.

'Stop it!' he said, his voice lethal, drawing the reins either side of her, capturing her in his arms, tight, in case she had any further ideas of trying to get away. Damn, he was livid. 'Don't do that again. Don't even think about running,' he warned.

Stefan felt off balance, incensed by her behaviour and disturbed by their bodies colliding again after such a long time of being apart and the heated reaction it had caused. The amused glances of his men, smirking at the behaviour of his wayward wife, only infuriated him further. Her dramatics weren't helping the situation. But at least his men hadn't dared to ask why she was attempting to marry another while still wedded to him. The very thought of it wounded his pride.

He gave the instruction for his soldiers to set off and

forced himself to take a deep breath, to calm himself. He had made it. He'd got here in time. He had her and they were leaving this wretched place for ever.

He didn't want to be in Eastbury for a moment longer. Just seeing the familiar walls of the monastery standing on the cliffs, the stark mudflats and lonely creeks, and the vast shore where his father's ships had pulled up on the shingle all brought back a wave of unwanted memories.

He could recall the brutal battle now. He could almost hear the clashing of metal and wood as the Saxons' swords and axes hit their shields; the grunts of his father's men as they fought back, trying to defend themselves against a force double their size. He remembered the village people wailing in distress. He felt the smarting of his forehead as he recalled the blow he'd taken to his temple and he could still taste the metallic flavour of the blood in his mouth, before he had shut his eyes, willing death to take him…and then he'd seen her, leaning over him…

When a messenger had arrived last night, informing him of Ædwen's imminent wedding to Lord Werian, an incandescent rage had taken over and he'd known he had to come. He would not be dishonoured. Not again. For she was *his* wife. The woman who had conceived his daughter and carried her in her belly—and failed to tell him about it. He'd seen today as an opportunity to finally take revenge.

After a long, restless night's sleep, he'd left Wintan-caester with his men at dawn and ridden hard across the city, out into the undulating, patchwork countryside, not stopping until they'd reached the coast. This place once represented his rescue, his hope, but later, to use a Christian word for it, his hell. Rearing up outside the church, he'd descended his horse so fast and barged into the chapel with such force, everyone had turned to look. But he hadn't been prepared for the impact seeing her would have on him again. He'd felt a gut-punch of wrath tempered with relief.

To think what might have happened if he hadn't arrived in time to interrupt the service... Would she have gone through with it and said her vows to that man, the very same vows she had said to him? Betrayal ripped through him.

Ædwen gave another frustrated attempt to get away, writhing, struggling against his hold, but he was stronger; unmovable, his arms tightening around her.

'Stop fighting me. You'll fall and get yourself killed!'

He tried not to react, but his body had other ideas. He had strived to forget what it felt like to have her in his arms, of being this close to her, her warm, soft curves pressed against his chest and his groin, the floral scent of her hair drifting under his nose. And he grimaced, realising the forced intimacy was as much a torture to him as it was a punishment for her. He was shocked his body was hardening, still responding to her, despite everything...

'Why are you doing this?' she cried.

She gave one last protest and then slumped, giving up, turning her face away from him.

Anger whipped him, along with the biting wind. He couldn't understand it. Did she want to marry Lord Werian? Surely not. The man was almost twice her age!

'We must go back,' she pleaded, shaking her head, the sound of desperation in her all too familiar voice.

'Never!'

He wanted to get them far away from this place. He wanted to put as much distance between Ædwen and Lord Werian, and him and her father as possible.

'You've stormed in here and broken up my wedding. Shaming me. Why?'

His clenched his hands around the reins.

That night they'd spent together had been extraordinary, but tainted by the events of the following day. But she had still tied herself to him. And if he'd had to prove it, he would have. He would have gone one step further and told them of the birthmark above her left hip...the one he'd enjoyed discovering with his lips. And there was far greater evidence.

He would have told them that somewhere out there was a child. A mixture of Saxon and Danish blood. He would have stopped at nothing to achieve what he came here to do. He thought back to the look on the congregation's faces. They'd been shocked. Appalled. Had he ruined her? For anyone else, yes. He let out a slow sigh of satisfaction.

'Did you forget you're already married?' What was it with women thinking they could release themselves from their vows so easily? They could not be trusted.

'My father said I would have had to marry a fellow Christian for our marriage to be legal...that a union between a pagan Dane and a Christian Saxon would be condemned.'

He was incensed. She belonged to him.

'So you wish to be with him, to marry Lord Werian?

To lie with him, in his bed, tonight?' His stomach turned at the thought that she would choose that man over him.

'No!' she gasped, as if she was offended, disgusted. 'Of course not, but—'

Her answer appeased him a little and he forced himself to rotate his shoulders, to ease some of his tension, as they sped along the path. 'Then I did you a favour,' he spat.

She shook her head. 'You don't know what you've done.'

His eyes narrowed, her flyaway hair tickling his cheek. 'What? Destroyed your father's alliance? His honour? I should have done it a long time ago.'

'You've ruined everything,' she said bitterly, her voice a hoarse whisper.

He couldn't see how. And he wasn't sorry. He wanted her father to pay for his past wrongs. For all the pain he'd caused. And she should be thankful. He could have struck the man with his sword, or ordered his men to tear down the Saxon fortress, knowing Lord Manvil would use his force against the King given the chance...but he hadn't, for her sake. He'd restrained himself, kept his anger in check. And he'd saved her from a union she'd just admitted she didn't want.

Then he realised she was crying and it shocked him. Was she really shedding tears over not marrying that man? Over what had happened back in the church? He couldn't believe it. He had never seen her cry. Not even when he'd told her he was leaving her that bitter day the previous winter.

He softened his voice a little. 'Ædwen...'

She shook her head solemnly, uncontrollable, silent

tears streaking down her face, and he grew concerned. She had always been so stoic, so…joyful. It was one of the reasons he'd fallen for her. She had brightened his days when everything else had seemed so bleak.

Damn it. Her wilfulness and anger were preferable to this. He would much rather she stood up to him, argued with him, creating more of those sparks.

He released his grip on one of the reins, his hand smoothing down her arm, trying to calm her. 'Ædwen…' he repeated.

But she shrugged him off as huge sobs racked her body, her chest heaving.

He cursed, knowing they'd have to halt their journey, even though it had only just begun. He called to his right-hand man, Maccus, signalling with his hand. 'All of you, carry on. We're making a stop. Wait for us at the river crossing further up.'

Maccus nodded, taking the lead, but not before stealing a glance at Ædwen's forlorn face and it made Stefan feel like a brute. He veered off the coastal path, heading for an outcrop of large stones on the top of the next cliff, before slowing his faithful horse. He swung himself down, before gripping her arm and aiding Ædwen's descent. She was too upset to fight him.

He cast her down on to a rock and she buried her face in her hands, and he watched, confounded, as she sobbed until there were no more tears to come. Against his better judgement, he wanted to reach out and comfort her, but he knew he must stand firm. He mustn't be swayed by her tears.

He bunched his fists.

Yes, he had walked away from her when he'd discovered what she and her father had done. But despite them having spent all this while apart, he still considered their union as something they were both duty-bound to honour. When he'd learned of this illicit wedding, his jealousy had burned. He hadn't been able to bear the thought of Ædwen in the arms of another man. Her father's brutal ally. Not when she had promised herself to him. It just wasn't right.

He had anticipated her fierce resistance to leaving Eastbury and coming with him. He had expected a fight, but not these tears. They were far more disturbing. Far more dangerous, for they threatened to weaken him.

He told himself not to forget who she was and what she had done.

He pushed a hand through his hair and blew out a steadying breath, taking in the barren landscape dotted with scarce farmsteads—the desolate flatlands stretched out as far as the eye could see. It offered him a good viewpoint of anyone approaching and he was glad there was no sign of her father's men following them. Not yet anyway. That was something, at least. It shouldn't do any harm for them to stop for a short while.

He watched the surf tumble on to the shore down below. This vast bay, this beach, it said a lot about who he was. These waters had carried him to this place, away from his traumatic past to a new, promising future. But instead, what had been waiting for them when they'd arrived here had been much worse. This place served as an awful reminder of an attack that had left its mark on him, for ever. The sea was wild, like the battle that had been fought here. But it could also be tranquil, like those who now were at rest. The sand and stones were like the grief he felt, never to be washed away.

Once, a long time ago, he would have gone for a swim to try to cool his feelings, often his desire. But in Wintancaester, they were a long way from the sea. He hadn't swum in a while and he missed it. He suddenly ached to slice his arms through the cold water, to take his anger out on the surf, but he was well aware he was still in Eastbury—hostile territory—so they needed to press on.

He turned back to Ædwen. She was dithering, her plump bottom lip quivering, and he wondered if the shock of the day's events had now set in. He had expected her to be surprised at seeing him again, shocked at him breaking up her wedding. But there was a part of him that had hoped she might be relieved, even pleased to see him. Unfastening his cloak, he draped it around her shoulders, her fingers brushing against his as she gingerly took it from him, and his heart ridiculously skittered.

He caved.

'Are you all right?' he asked gruffly, drawing his hand over his beard. 'I realise it's been quite a morning.'

She looked up at him, her deep blue eyes swollen and red, her lovely face stained with silvery streaks—the same, beautiful face that had stared down at him in concern as he lay wounded on the beach that day.

The first time he'd seen her, he had thought her so striking, he'd wondered if she was a Valkyrie, sent by Odin to bring him to the Great Hall of Valhalla. But over the weeks that had followed, as he'd drifted in and out of sleep, unsure what was imaginary or real, he had realised she was in fact a young woman who had rescued him from the brink of death and brought him to a strange place where her people prayed to their God. The monastery.

Every day, she had sat by his side, reading to him, spoon-feeding him, changing his wound dressings, her gentle touch soothing him, until he'd regained his strength, if not his memories.

He had found contentment with her for a while, in this strange new place. A simple happiness.

The lay of the land here was similar to Denmark: a settlement surrounded by water. The people worked the soil, ate together and worshipped. But it was warmer here. Or he had just felt warmer with Ædwen in his life. She had quickly become his everything. His reason to live.

Fifteen months on, she looked the same—but also different. Her body had become more womanly, her breasts fuller, her hips wider—the result of carrying his child? Yet she was slim...too slim, he thought...her skin stretched over her prominent cheekbones. She was still stunning, the most beautiful woman he had ever seen—she took his breath away—yet he registered the dark circles under her eyes, the taut lines around her mouth. He noticed because he had once watched her, studying her face closely as she slept, and he had explored her body, intimately. She seemed different to the lively girl he had wed back then.

She pulled out a small scrap of muslin that had been tucked into the sleeve of her tunic. She brought it up to her nose and breathed in, before wiping it over her cheeks, mopping up her tears, pulling herself together. 'No, I'm not all right,' she said, squaring her shoulders, drawing her face up to his. He was relieved to see the fire and fight slowly return to her eyes. 'You've kidnapped me. Taken me against my will.'

'*Kidnapped* you? Ædwen, you're my wife!'

She reeled. 'How can you call me that? I haven't seen you in almost two winters! And now you think you can suddenly turn up, completely unexpected, and humiliate me in front of everyone I know, before forcing me to leave with you?'

He put his hands on his hips. 'You always cared too much about what others thought.' Wasn't that why she'd lied to him about what had really happened the day he had arrived here? Why she'd deceived him about who she was, wanting to keep her true self hidden from him? And why she'd kept their relationship a secret from everyone?

'Is it so wrong to want to be respectable? Isn't that why you strive for glory? Why you were so impatient to succeed in life?' Her tone was accusatory and he didn't like it.

'I'm just saying I would have thought me breaking up your wedding arrangements might have been preferable to you committing adultery and going to hell, spending a lifetime of unhappiness with a man you didn't want to be with.'

'What do you care about my happiness?' she said bitterly. She shook her head. 'How did you even know…?'

'What, that you were about to marry another man—while still married to me?' he spat out. He still couldn't believe she had been prepared to deny all knowledge of him and go ahead with it, as if she was denying there had ever been anything between them, erasing him from her life.

'Ours wasn't a marriage—it was a mistake!' she shot back at him.

He felt a muscle flicker in his cheek. 'Just as I said at the time.' The morning after the night they'd made love, when he'd found out he had married his enemy's daughter.

Had she thought having their child was a mistake, too? Is that why she had forsaken her?

'But it is a marriage, none the less. Whether you like it or not, you belong to me.'

She shook her head in despair. 'And yet you left me... you haven't wanted me all this while. You don't want me now. You said so yourself in the church. So why come back? What *do* you want? Is this some kind of punishment?'

He took a step towards her. 'I don't know. Is it?'

She shivered and rubbed her arms, turning her face away from him.

He did want to punish her, he admitted to himself now. For not telling him the truth from the start. For deceiving him about who she was—that it was her father who was responsible for the death of his family. Because that was unforgivable.

When he'd woken in the monastery, he couldn't remember who he was or where he'd come from. What he was doing there. He had a deep wound to his head and his shoulder. It had been disorientating. Daunting.

Slowly, his old memories had returned to him, like his name, his homeland of Denmark—and he could describe it to her in vivid detail. He could recall his happy childhood with his mother, his father and his brothers growing up. They had lived a nomadic existence, moving around the banks of the vast, beautiful fjords. He could recall how cold it was outside, but warm in their various homes, all huddled together round the fire, sharing stories.

The land had been unfarmable in places and they'd struggled for food, but they had always managed. But his more recent memories had been a mystery—shadows dancing on his periphery, just out of his reach. And the headaches had been severe.

She had tried to fill in a few gaps, telling him she'd rescued him from the beach, after he'd washed up on the shore. That perhaps he had fallen overboard, off a ship. And he'd been injured. But it was all a blur to him. He'd pushed himself to remember, frustrated with himself.

She had hinted at the animosity between his people and hers, telling him of Northmen like him coming to plunder their fortresses and monasteries for many summers, wreaking havoc on the people and the land. He had been horrified, yet listened with interest, trying to piece things together. Had his people come here to do that? But he could not marry up that image with himself, or his family. He felt sure whichever ship he had been on, they had come to the west in search of peace, perhaps looking for new, fertile lands to toil.

His heart had gone out to Ædwen that she had grown up seeing the worst of his kind, mistrusting them… and he had been determined to change her mind about Danes, wanting to show her he was a good man.

Slowly, he had recovered and grown stronger, and he'd begun to care for her, deeply. He had thought, out of all the confusion, he had found something good and, despite being unsure of his past, he had known he wanted her to be his future. Visions of her lying on animal skins, her hair and body splayed out on the furs beneath him, entered his mind before he could halt them. Damn. He tried to shake them away. He had made love to her and, wanting to make their union legitimate, to do things right, he had asked her to be his wife.

Then he'd seen her with her father and realised—it had all been based on a lie. His memories of the battle had come back so suddenly, so fiercely, all at once, over-whelming him, engulfing him in grief.

He remembered…

It had been a period of great despair in Denmark. Stefan had lost his first love and then his mother had died of the fever. It had changed him, changed his father beyond repair. It had prompted the older man to want to set sail across the ocean, leaving Denmark behind to explore the lands in the west. But when they'd reached the English shore, there had been a ferocious army waiting for them and his father had said they must defend themselves.

He remembered Lord Manvil leading the charge towards them, striking his brothers down, then coming for him, and his father stepping between them, trying to save him. Lord Manvil had plunged his sword into his father's chest, going right through him, and piercing his own shoulder, too, then he'd received the final blow to his head. They'd both been struck down, his father's lifeless body lying on top of him. And that is how Ædwen had found him on the beach.

Lord Manvil, Ædwen's father, had killed his family. And the sudden sorrow and anguish of all that he had lost had been too much to bear.

He'd felt sick.

Then he'd realised, Ædwen must have known. She had known what her father had done and kept it from him. *Lied.* And just like that, his trust was gone. He'd felt he could no longer be with her—the daughter of the man who had murdered his kin. It felt like too much of a betrayal. He had thought she was different. He had determined never to be gullible—ignorant—again when it came to women. But he'd fallen for someone, been hurt, once again. How could he not have seen the truth?

He ran his hand across his forehead now. His wound might have healed, but the scars ran deep.

He had thought about it often in the months that had passed. He had obsessed over past details, looking for clues he'd missed along the way. At first, he had been lost without Ædwen. She was all he had known here. But he had gradually found his place.

Yet when he'd learned about an even greater truth she'd kept hidden from him—his child—his bitterness had returned with force. How could she give up her child? *Their* child? How could she deny him the chance of being a father? Had she not wanted the responsibility of being a mother? Or did she think her prospects would be better if she cruelly gave the child away?

Whatever her reasons, he should have been part of that decision. He deserved an explanation. That was why he was really here, why he had broken up her wedding, what he wanted from her, he realised now. And he would only consider letting her go when he got the answers he so desperately needed.

She sighed heavily, drawing his attention back to the present. 'Stefan…you don't know what's at stake here.'

He crossed his arms over his chest. 'No? Then why don't you enlighten me.'

She turned away, shaking her head, her buttery blonde hair swaying.

'Go on. Tell me. What did your father or Lord Werian promise you in return for your hand in marriage?' He glowered at her.

'I can't,' she said, biting her lip.

His frown deepened, his brow furrowing as he fought for control. 'Something else you don't think I need to know, Ædwen?' he said coldly. 'I thought you would have learned your lesson about keeping secrets from me by now.'

He wanted her to tell him about the baby. He wanted her to confess she'd had his child. Admit she'd given it up. Would she ever? Once again, her actions were unforgivable, hard to comprehend, and disgust churned in his stomach. He would not abide her deceit. He took a hard stance on lying.

He could have forced the issue, outing it himself now, to see the reaction on her face when she discovered he knew the truth. How would she excuse herself? But it wasn't the right time, not with the furious wind whipping up around them, huge raindrops starting to pelt down. No, he would wait for the moment when it would have maximum impact.

He crouched down before her and took her chin in the palm of his hand, tilting her face up to look at him. 'When you're under my roof there will be no more places to hide, Ædwen. Nothing you can keep hidden from me.'

She shivered. 'What do you want from me?' she whispered. 'Where are you taking me?'

'To Wessex. To Wintancaester.'

'I have no choice…' she said, shaking her head sadly.

He couldn't understand her anger, or resentment. It seemed unjustified. He had every right to be furious— but why did she? His people had come here in peace— and been slaughtered. He'd lost his family. She had lied, tried to hide it from him. She had had his child and kept that from him, too. She'd given it up. Now he had saved her from an awful marriage…

'We always have a choice, Ædwen… It's those choices we make in life that shape us into who we are.'

And she had made her decision when she had lied to him and betrayed him over and again. Now he was determined she should face the consequences of all she had done.

# *Chapter Three*

Æ dwen had reasoned with him, pleaded and placated, but none of it had done any good. Stefan had been steadfast and now she was wrung out. Captive in his arms once more, riding away from Eastbury towards the river at a pace, she glanced around, trying to keep track of the route they were taking in case she should need to find her way back. She had walked the path along the coast many times, but she'd never been this far from home before.

She admired the tapestry of fields stretched out before them and felt the rushing of the wind through her hair. She lifted her face to the rain, which was coming down thick and fast now, and welcomed it washing away the salty stains on her cheeks.

She regretted letting Stefan see her cry. It had been a moment of utter hopelessness, thinking her daughter was gone, out of her reach for ever. The absolute frustration at the injustice of it all and the total shock of seeing Stefan again had wrought havoc on her emotions. But she wouldn't be that weak again. She knew she needed to gather her strength, to stand up to him and be strong, even in the face of her despair.

Ædwen was glad her anger was now taking the place

of her tears. It gave her something to focus on, other than her grief. She forced herself to remember how Stefan had let her down. How he'd abandoned her, just as her mother had done before him, reinforcing the fact that she couldn't depend on anyone, not even those she loved. Everything she had endured had happened because he'd left and she couldn't forgive him for it. She had hardened her heart against him.

It was a shock to be back in his arms again now. To be held so tightly. It was a cruel taunt—the thing she had once wanted most of all.

The silence between them was becoming more unbearable with every passing moment. The distance between them and Wintancaester stretched out with every thrust of her body against his as the horse galloped on and she searched desperately for something to say.

Everything was heightened. She could feel the graze of his beard against her temple as they sped along. And pressed against his broad, solid chest, his heat warming her back, she became excruciatingly aware of all the places they were touching. She felt the flexing of the muscles in his arms, his thighs, and it reminded her of when he had moved against her body once before, skin on skin, pressed into the furs, his hand wrapped around her mouth to muffle her cries of pleasure so no one could hear…

She squirmed, wanting to get away.

His grip tightened on her.

Perhaps this was a normal reaction to touching the man who had taken your chastity, who had given you a taste of sexual fulfilment and planted a seed in your body.

'How long will it take to get there?' she asked finally,

raising her voice to be heard above the roaring sea and the wind.

'Half a day's ride.'

He must have left early this morning...

She glanced down towards the tempestuous waves crashing on the beach below. If only she could get down and walk along the shore...breathing in the sea air always helped her to think more clearly. But then she noticed that the beach was crowded with seals, clustered together, their grey and brown fur damp from the icy water, and she gasped. It was an extraordinary sight.

'There are so many of them,' she whispered.

'It's their mating season. They've come to these shores to breed.'

*Just like him.*

'Oh.' She cringed, turning away. She wished she hadn't opened her mouth to speak. She didn't want to be discussing breeding or mating of any kind with him. It didn't help with her memories and her terrible, never-abating sense of loss for her child.

She wondered if she should just tell Stefan the worst of it. What she was keeping from him. Perhaps he would stop the horse and turn around. Send her back. But he was a stranger to her now. A dangerous stranger. And she couldn't bring herself to do it. She was afraid of how he might react. The enormity of what she might confess seemed far too immense.

No, some secrets could never be shared, for no matter how much they hurt to keep inside, they would cause far greater devastation if they were revealed. And deep down, she was ashamed. Not of Ellan, never, but of herself. Because her child had been taken on her watch.

Ædwen chastised herself once more for not being more vigilant, for thinking she and her daughter were safe in the monastery. She should have left with Ellan as soon as she'd been able to after the birth. But then she had never imagined her father would be so cruel as to take her child from her.

Now, she had no idea where her daughter was.

There was no way she could admit that to Stefan. She didn't want to see the disdain in his eyes, letting her know she was just as bad a mother as she felt she was. He would never forgive her, he would make her suffer further and she knew that for certain, because she wasn't sure she could ever forgive herself.

Was he right—had she made bad choices? In her desperation to get Ellan back, had she crossed her own moral boundaries? Should she have refused to marry Lord Werian today? Perhaps her turmoil had impaired her decision-making. But wouldn't any mother do whatever it took to find her child?

No, not all. Her own mother wouldn't have.

She almost wilted in relief when they heard the shouts of Stefan's men in the distance and glanced up to see them waiting on horseback on the other side of a bridge. She wouldn't have to be alone with Stefan any more.

'Everything all right?' one of the men asked, cantering forward, looking between them both. He was the one Stefan had called Maccus. He was a good-looking, fair-haired man, with kind eyes, but he was nowhere near Stefan's equal.

Stefan steadied the horse and she realised he had got better at riding. He had learned the basics at the monastery, but he had always struggled with balance because of his large frame. Not now. He was now in total control of the animal. In total control of her?

'Yes. Let's keep going to Herdbridge,' Stefan said, his breath warm against her cheek. 'We should make it by nightfall.'

'Any sign of soldiers from Eastbury?'

'Not yet,' Stefan said. 'But we'll keep an eye out. Be on your guard.'

Sitting upright, goose pimples erupted across Ædwen's skin. Did they think her father would come after her? They were probably right. Her father was not a man who gave up easily and she didn't know how she felt about that. Yet he wouldn't come out of affection for her, for he had never shown any. No, he would come for his own pride.

But did she really want to be rescued, to return to her father and incur his wrath for her foolishness? Did she really want to see Lord Werian again and deal with the fall-out of their ruined wedding? Or to be taken back to Eastbury to wed someone else of her father's choosing? No. Besides, would anyone even want her now? Yet if her father came for her, might he be persuaded to reveal the details of where he had sent her child?

They set off again, at a more moderate pace to keep the group together, and she wondered again why Stefan was doing this, especially when he had stated in the church that he didn't even want her. Ridiculously, she'd felt wounded. Was all this just for revenge on her father? Or on her, for concealing the truth from him back then? Did he not realise she had been punished enough?

Just being with him now was a painful reminder that she couldn't be with her daughter. Yet she was starting to wonder if going to Wintancaester might be a good thing. She knew Ellan was no longer in Eastbury and, if she was going to look for her child anywhere, it would make sense for her to start her search in the capital. Surely she had a better chance of finding her there than anywhere?

'Why Wintancaester?' she asked Stefan now, curious about his life and where they were heading. 'Is that where you went when you left the monastery? Is that your home?' Had he been living in Wintancaester all this time, serving the King?

'As much as it can be without my family here,' he said.

She noted the pointed comment and ignored it.

'When I heard Canute had taken Londen and then moved south to Wintancaester, I made my way there, to find people from my country,' he continued. 'When I came to the King's aid and he saw I could fight, he took me under his wing, making me one of his housecarls. Now he pays me for my services.' He spoke without emotion, his tone cool. Too cool. As if he was trying to mask his anger.

She let the information sink in, trying to picture what he was telling her. So he was a mercenary. A paid warrior. One of the King's private army of trained fighters. Had he killed many people? Many of *her* kind? She knew Canute had been ruthless when he'd first set foot on English soil.

She wanted more details, a breakdown of every day, every moment, every breath they had been apart. How that had all transpired. How he had felt. Instead, she had the feeling he was leaving out vital information. But then, she was guilty of the same and shame raced through her again at the truth she was keeping from him.

She couldn't marry up the man he was with her then, in the monastery—gentle and kind—with the ambitious, ruthless warrior he seemed to be now.

'I thought you might have returned to Denmark,' she said.

'I considered it, but there was nothing left for me back there. Everyone I cared about had crossed the sea with me to come here.'

When he had remembered—when his memories had finally returned—he had told her his people had come here in search of a better life, but instead they'd lost their lives that day in Eastbury, at the hands of her father. And she would never be able to make amends for that. For what he did.

She felt the need to steer the conversation on to less dangerous ground, away from old wounds. 'So, you live among other Danes in the city?'

'Saxons mix with Danes in Wintancaester, Ædwen. It is not like the remote Saxon settlements you know of, who are stuck in the old ways, trying to rally support against the King.'

Settlements like her father's, he meant.

'What is the King like?' she asked. She had heard stories of Canute. Everyone had. His reputation for being a formidable fighter and ruthless ruler had reached them on the coast.

'He is a man to look up to. A man of immeasurable power, but who wants peace, prosperity. He is fair...'

She turned to steal a glance at him. His eyes were full of admiration and she could tell from the way his voice had softened that he looked up to the man.

Would the King be fair to her, if he knew of her father's animosity towards him? she wondered. She had always longed to visit the city, but her father had never allowed it. She had lived a sheltered life so far. How would she be thought of in Wintancaester, if it was known she was her father's daughter? Yet she didn't think Stefan would put her in any real danger. She didn't think he wanted to cause her any real harm.

*'As my wife you'll respect me. You'll do your duty. You owe me that.'*

The words he'd spoken in the church kept echoing in her mind. And then a thought struck her, right in her chest. Her heart lurched. What would *he* do with her there? Surely he didn't expect her to actually live as his wife and all that entailed? Not if he despised her.

'What is your home like?' she asked and hated the quiver she could hear in her voice.

'The King provides all his housecarls with lodgings, in the palace grounds. How about you? When did you decide to leave the monastery?' he asked.

She hadn't decided. She hadn't had a say in the matter.

She had lived in the monastery since her mother had walked out of her life when she was nine, sent there to gain an education—and to be kept out of her father's way until he had use for her. She had spent her days teaching children, or looking after the sick, keeping busy so her thoughts couldn't drift to why her mother had forsaken her. That was, until that day the Danes had arrived. When Stefan had come, everything had changed.

That day of the battle, when Ædwen had first come across Stefan, she had found him buried beneath the body of an older man, who she had thought was his father. He had been left for dead on the beach. As she'd hovered over him, peering down into his face, checking for a pulse in his neck, he'd opened his eyes and gripped her arm, making her gasp.

She had been mesmerised by his blue eyes from that initial glance. They were the colour of the ocean on a crisp winter's day. On the cusp of becoming a woman, it was the first time she'd come into contact with a man she'd found so attractive. She couldn't bring herself to look away, despite the wound to his forehead and the injury to his shoulder.

Up until that moment, she had known her life was all planned out for her: that she would stay at the monastery, practising with the other novices, until the day her father found her a husband—someone who would advance his power, strengthen his fortress—and she was expected to obey him. But something had risen in her blood that day and, staring down at Stefan, she had made a decision that would change her life for ever.

They had struggled with his weight, carrying him over the rocky shore and up the cliff path to the monastery, but, knowing her father would never condone it, that he would order the man to be killed immediately, she had taken responsibility for him. Hiding him away in a small, unused room, she had felt strongly that they couldn't let him die. That, somehow, he was important.

Ædwen had known it was dangerous to bring a Northman into the monastery. She was putting everyone at risk, so to begin with, he had been bound, in case he woke and attacked them…and yet she'd had a feeling he wouldn't. There was something about him.

She had spent weeks at his side, offering him sips of ale and spring water she had collected from the well, feeding him spoonsful of pottage…and he had watched her from underneath those sleep-hooded eyes.

She had checked and cleaned his wounds, changing his bandages, making sure his injuries didn't get infected, trying not to stare at his fascinating bare chest and the strange ink markings and symbols decorating it. Miraculously, he had slowly improved.

She had found him sitting up in bed one morning and she'd gasped.

'*Hvem er du…?*' he'd said. *Who?*

'I'm Ædwen,' she'd replied shyly, patting her hand to her chest as if to explain.

'*Hamingia.*' He had smiled and her stomach had whooshed. It was the first time she'd seen his lips curl upwards, lighting up his face, and he was breathtaking. She had known then she was in real trouble.

There was a long moment while they stared at one another and the air between them had simmered with awareness—a connection that transcended their countries, language and faith.

She knew she shouldn't feel attracted to him. She knew her father had plans for her. But she was helpless against her feelings.

And so it had begun.

Back then, Stefan had picked up her native tongue quickly and she had enjoyed teaching him. In return, she had learned some of his words and discovered *Hamingia*, what he'd called her, was a guardian spirit to the Danes, bringing luck and happiness. Finally, his injuries healed enough for him to walk around. It was his memories that had suffered the most damage, something she had at first been grateful for. After all, why would she want him to remember who had been responsible for the massacre that day?

When he was up and about, living among them, they had to be separated. The monks and nuns lived apart, divided into two communities, which came together only to share the church and the hall where they would eat. She wouldn't see him all day long and she would be distracted from her duties and prayers, the days stretching out before her. But come their mealtimes, she would race to the hall, eager to talk to him and desperate to see his face. And by the way he looked at her, with a relieved hunger in his eyes, she had known he felt the same.

It was frowned upon, of course, and there were disapproving looks from the nuns about them engaging in conversation, about their proximity. She was excruciatingly aware of it—she'd been raised to conform—but Stefan hadn't seemed to care.

She shook her head to shake away her memories.

'Why did I leave the monastery?' she said bitterly in response to his question. 'You know purity was a requirement to stay there,' she said accusingly. 'And as I had come of age, my father realised he could benefit from marrying me off, so he requested that I move back to his fortress.'

'I see,' Stefan said and she noticed his hands tighten on the reins, his knuckles turning white.

Did he see? That she, too, had suffered at the hands of her father? At Stefan leaving her?

'But he did not know you were already married to me, did he? Perhaps you should have told him,' he said darkly.

She knew she was leaving out a huge chunk of information. But how could she tell him that she *had* plucked up the courage to tell her father. She'd had to, when she'd realised she had become one of those women in distress who were sent to the monastery for help. All because of Stefan and the intimate things they'd done together...

Those days in the monastery with Stefan had been heady, exciting. Slowly, Stefan's memories of his upbringing had returned to him and she would ask him questions, to learn more about him, wanting to know everything. She loved hearing about his childhood, his likes and dislikes—she could tell he was fiercely proud of his home country.

And then one night, she had awoken with his hand over her mouth, his body leaning over her. He was in her room! She had been startled, yet elated at the same time.

'*Don't scream,*' he'd whispered.

And she'd nodded.

'*Come with me,*' he'd said, picking up her cloak and backing out of the door. Making her choice, she'd thrown off the animal furs and tiptoed after him.

They'd walked along the cliff in the moonlight and he'd told her he'd remembered something new. That he liked to swim. And he'd tugged her down to the shore, laughing. She'd stood there on the beach, transfixed, gripping his tunic tightly, breathing in the scent of him, as she'd watched him run into the waves and dive beneath the water.

Her heart had been in her throat at seeing his beautiful body again, his taut muscles rippling beneath those strange blue markings. And when he'd come out of the surf, shaking his wet hair, she'd been giddy with excitement. And love?

They began to sneak out after dark every night after that, wanting more time alone together. And he would take her hand, entwining his fingers with hers. The first time he had kissed her, they had been down on the shore, and he had picked up a shell, dusting it off with his fingers, before handing it to her.

*'For you,'* he'd said. *'It reminds me of your beauty.'*

And she had looked up at him. *'No, it represents you,'* she'd said, smiling. *'The remains of a life once lived... but still strong. Ready for a new adventure as something else.'*

Their eyes stared, drinking each other in. He had leaned in to press his mouth against hers, tenderly stroking her cheeks, encouraging her lips to part with his own. It had been her first kiss and it had been perfect. Gentle, yet potent, making her shiver. And she'd never wanted it to end.

*'No one can ever know...'* she'd whispered.

It had gone on like that for weeks, them both living for the nights when they could be together. She would sleep in his arms, down on the beach, nestled into his shoulder, clinging to him, not wanting the dawn to arrive, when they would have to part. Then one night, at the end of the winter, he'd said he should think about leaving—that he was a Dane, a pagan, and he shouldn't still be there, living in the Saxon, Christian monastery. He felt he needed to find his way elsewhere. He was ambitious. He wanted to make something of himself.

She had been devastated. She'd known they couldn't stay like this for ever, yet she had hoped...

*'I want you to come with me,'* he'd announced.

And her heart had lifted. She wanted that, too. She

had known her answer, instantly. Yes! She'd thrown her arms around him, frightened, but excited, pressing herself against him. And he'd groaned, holding her tight, then he'd kissed her, passionately, stealing her breath away.

'Let's go inside,' she'd breathed.

'Are you sure?'

'Yes,' she'd whispered.

She shivered in his arms now, just thinking about it, and noticed the night was drawing in around them. The horse was tiring and so was she. It had been a long day. Where were they? she wondered.

'Cold?' Stefan asked.

She shook her head. He'd already given her his cloak to wear and she was definitely not cold being held in his embrace, her heated memories warming her blood, her mind still racing about a wife's possible duties to her husband.

'Are you expecting my father to come after me?' she asked.

'Yes. I have no doubt that he will.'

'I think you're right,' she said. 'I don't think he will let me go without a fight. He stands to lose too much.' He'd come to see her as an asset. An object to be bargained over, to strengthen the position of his house. It was much better when her father hadn't cared at all.

'But it will take him a while to gather his forces,' Stefan said. 'He's already lost the army he was set to receive through your marriage alliance, has he not? One he would use against the King.'

So he knew about that.

'I'm guessing that was all part of your plan when you stormed into the church this morning,' she bit out.

'Of course.'

He hadn't just come for her, then. She'd thought as much. After all, he had left because he believed she'd betrayed him.

That night he had made love to her, they had managed to get back to her room without being seen. He'd tugged her down the warren-like corridors, laughing and gasping between kisses. But once they were through the door, he had pulled her to him in serious, savage urgency. Their mouths had clung, and their touch had become more frantic, almost desperate, their hands suddenly all over each other.

She had writhed against him, unsure what she was doing, but wanting to feel the hard ridges of him, the reaction she was causing giving her confidence. Her hands had roamed up over his chest, his shoulders, delving into his hair. And his large hand had come down to cover her breast, the other cupping her bottom, tugging her towards him as if he, too, wanted them to be touching everywhere.

It was all a hazy blur…the removal of their clothes… their mouths clinging, hands exploring naked skin… And then he was above her, his knees parting her legs and suddenly she had felt him right there.

'Is this what you want? To be joined like this?' he'd whispered.

'Yes, I want to be one. I want you inside me,' she'd said.

And with a gentle thrust, he was.

*'Jeg elsker dig, min skat,'* he'd whispered. *I love you.*

It had been incredible. Everything she could have hoped for. But she could recall the exact moment the next day when those feelings of love had shattered and turned to hate.

She had been standing in the gardens of the monastery, talking to her father. He had made a rare stop off at the monastery on his way home and she'd known it couldn't mean anything good. He'd told her she should prepare herself to marry. That he had found her a match. And she couldn't believe it. She'd floundered. Because that morning, she had said her vows to another.

Standing alone, just the two of them, she had been wondering how she was going to break it to her father, when the monks had started to walk through the grounds on their way to the church, and she'd turned around to see Stefan among them, staring at her. He'd stopped dead on the path, his body stock-still, his face ashen and his eyes the colour of thunder clouds.

It was a look that made her wither inside and the trembling had started in her legs.

For in that moment, she could tell he knew. He had remembered it all. All she'd tried to keep from him, to protect him from his hurt and grief. To safeguard what they had together.

That night she'd waited, wondering if he would come to her. Finally, he had. She'd had his father's sword ready to give him. To help her explain what had happened.

'Stefan—' she'd started to say, rising off the bed, going to explain.

But he had held up a hand to halt her. 'Don't say anything. I don't want to hear it,' he'd said coldly. 'You lied to me. Kept the truth from me. Tell me, did you know what kind of man he was? What he was capable of? Did you see him plunge his sword through my father's heart, before you tried to wreak havoc on mine?'

She shook her head. 'Stefan—'

'You *knew* your father had killed my family, tried to kill me, and yet you never said anything. Not one thing.'

'You said there was nothing I could tell you that would make you love me any less…' she whispered, trying to reach him, but he baulked, stepping away, not wanting her to touch him.

'Then I guess we both lied. Because this changes everything.'

And then she'd noticed his satchel on his shoulder. He removed his father's sword from her grasp. He was leaving the monastery. He was leaving her. And she felt the pain of rejection tear through her, her heart crumbling.

Ædwen rubbed her chest where it was aching at the memory.

'My father will see what happened today, you taking me and ruining the wedding, as a slight on his reputation. He will want revenge,' she added now, weary from the day's ride.

'Don't we all?' Stefan said darkly.

'But what if he comes to Wintancaester?' She shook her head sadly. She didn't want there to be any more death. She'd seen enough to last a lifetime. And especially not over her. 'Are you prepared to bring a fight there? To put innocent people at risk?'

'Wintancaester is a fortress. It will take a lot for him to get through the city walls. But, yes, I am prepared to fight.'

Then perhaps they all were. Her father would regroup, she felt sure of it. And it seemed Stefan would prepare himself for an attack. For what? His own retribution? Surely not for her… But she realised now she would fight, too. When they arrived in Wintancaester, she would start asking questions. She would begin her search. She would use this as an opportunity. She would fight for her daughter. She would never stop looking for her.

# Chapter Four

Ædwen was relieved to finally see the straw-covered rooftops of a settlement in the distance. They'd been travelling all afternoon and she was hungry, soaked through and she couldn't wait to finally be released from Stefan's hold.

As he began to tighten his grip on the reins, slowing the horse, she realised they were making a stop outside a large building that looked to be some kind of barn. She saw men standing at high tables outside, the din of raucous laughter escaping from the door every time it swung open and revellers stepping out into the night, and realised they must be at an alehouse.

'Where are we?' she asked.

Stefan led his men into the stables at the back of the establishment and he jumped down, tethering his horse.

'We're at a tavern in Herdbridge,' he said. 'We need to rest the horses. We'll get some food and stay here for the night, then carry on to Wintancaester in the morning.'

She opened her mouth to protest, panic rising in her chest. Surely he didn't expect her to spend the night with him and his men here? Where would they sleep? It didn't look like the kind of place that had rooms. But then, being surrounded by people was a good thing, wasn't it? It meant the two of them didn't have to spend time alone. So she pressed her lips together, keeping quiet.

Might she be able to signal for help? Although, if she managed to get away from him, where would she go? The city would be her first choice.

'What is it?' Stefan said, looking up at her, as he stroked the horse's nose, his gaze raking over her face. 'Not where you thought you'd be spending your wedding night?'

She slanted him a look. She knew he was goading her, but the truth was, she had been prepared to suffer anything if it meant being reunited with Ellan. Yet she had to admit she felt immense relief that her wedding to Lord Werian hadn't taken place. That she didn't have to lie with that man tonight, or any night, and suffer him putting his hands on her. The thought had filled her with sickness and dread. But with her relief came feelings of guilt—that she had once again failed Ellan. That she hadn't done what she needed to do to see her child again.

She slid down the side of the animal without Stefan's help, feeling wretched, not wanting him to touch her, knowing the reaction it caused when he did, and he surprised her by pulling a piece of white cloth from his satchel and handing it to her.

'Here, put this on,' he said.

She looked at it, puzzled.

'For your hair,' he said. 'Married women are meant to keep their hair covered. It would be inappropriate for a woman to be seen here, travelling with all these men, especially an unmarried one. You need to wear this.'

She went to protest, then realised she ought to pick her battles and nodded, draping the large piece of cloth around the top of her head, covering her soaking wet hair, her neck and chin. He took a step towards her and, before she could stop him, he reached up and tucked a few loose tendrils into the material. His fingertips trailed against her neck, sending tingles down her spine, making her shiver.

'There. As it should be,' he said.

She wished he wouldn't touch her—whenever he did, it sent her body up in flames. But her wish was denied once more as he gripped her arm and led her and his soldiers into the barn. 'Keep your eyes down,' he said.

The heat of male bodies hit her as they stepped over the threshold and the noise of burly voices, all talking at once, over each other, assaulted her ears. Stefan guided her to a large bench and table up a corner, away from the lively antics of some of the more animated revellers, while his men fetched them some drinks. Ædwen sat as close as she could to the roaring open fire, staring into the dancing flames, hoping the mesmerising crackle and hiss would help to calm her.

She had never been anywhere like this before. It was a far cry from the quiet sanctuary of the monastery. So this was the type of place that men liked to while away their evenings? She wondered how else Stefan spent his nights, whether he'd met another woman after he left her, and instantly shook away the thought. She did not want to think about it.

Stefan followed her down into the opposite bench, his knees brushing against hers—was there no escape from him? She was almost glad when his men piled in after them, forcing her to shuffle up.

'I didn't get a chance to introduce you all before. Men,

I'd like you to meet Lady Ædwen, my wife,' Stefan said to the warriors round the table.

Her breath hitched. So they were announcing it, making this ridiculous sham of a marriage known now? Why, all of a sudden? He hadn't wanted to acknowledge her this past winter. He hadn't come for her before. And she hadn't even known where he was, or if he was even alive.

He had missed so much. He hadn't witnessed her body bloom and grow with his child, how huge she'd been, and then slowly return to normal again after the birth. He hadn't been there when she'd delivered their baby. He didn't know what pain, what trauma, she'd been through and she didn't know how to feel about it all—that he had come to fetch her now. It was so absurd. And the more people he told about them being married, the harder it would be to extract herself…

'*Estranged* wife,' she added and got a little satisfaction from seeing a muscle flicker in Stefan's cheek.

The men looked between them, amused.

She didn't know why she wanted to antagonise him. Stefan was certainly not a man you'd want to incense. He looked formidable, his dark blue gaze glowering at her.

'Ædwen, this is Maccus and the rest of my men,' Stefan continued, introducing them each by name, and one by one they nodded and said it was nice to meet her, before hiding their smiles in their tankards full of ale.

The talk quickly turned to the rain and the long journey, but they were polite enough not to mention her disrupted wedding ceremony and the reactions of her father, her jilted groom and the shocked congregation. As they began to break off and speak among themselves, she became acutely aware of Stefan sitting just across from her on the other side of the table, staring at her. She was aware of his sculpted body in his uniform and the way his large hands toyed with his cup.

'So you are their leader?' she asked, trying to think of something to say, to fill the silence, before taking a sip of her ale. It tasted good on her parched tongue.

'We all fought to be in Lord Stefan's contingent,' Maccus interrupted, elbowing her in good spirits. 'Your husband is the man to follow, Lady Ædwen.'

Was that right?

Stefan had clearly made a name for himself, she thought. She knew the housecarls were the most elite of the King's troops, the most-feared soldiers of his guard. Had Stefan ever been content with the much simpler life he'd lived with her before? Yet she had always known he wasn't a man who could stay confined within those walls, hidden from view for long. He was larger than life, a man who deserved to be seen. He'd had ambitions beyond the Saxon monastery and she had wanted him to achieve them. Only, she had always thought he would find success and she would be there by his side to see it. Now, he was a stranger and she was hearing about his triumphs from someone else.

She was relieved when a serving woman came over with a bowl of stew for each of them. As well as her stomach rumbling in response at the delicious smell of the food, she was pleased to see another female among all these men. But as the woman relinquished her heavy load, passing the steaming dishes around the table, she smoothed the material of her pinafore over her swollen stomach, showing off her bump, and Ædwen's face fell—in envy and total devastation. She turned her face away before anyone could see her torment.

For a while, when she'd realised she was with child, she had tried to keep her growing belly hidden beneath her tunic and pinafore. But she had known she couldn't hide it for ever. And she had determined that even when she had to confess, she would be safer inside the monastery walls than anywhere else.

How wrong she'd been.

The holy sisters had been compassionate in those early days and they had helped her through the long and tiring birth, and the days afterwards. But she had known she couldn't expect them to shelter her and Ellan for long, that she would need to face her father eventually. And when she had, his wrath had been great indeed. Far greater than even she had expected.

The woman passed a bowl to Stefan.

'Thank you. Though you shouldn't be doing this work in your condition,' he said.

Ædwen glanced up at him.

'And who's going to serve your food if I don't? I haven't got time to rest. Besides, I've got a child in my belly, I'm not ill,' the woman retorted in good humour, rolling her eyes. And then she fixed Ædwen with a look. 'Don't you let your husband get you with child, dear, you'll be stuck indoors. He won't let you lift a finger!' she teased, giving her a wink.

Stricken, Ædwen was too distraught to return her smile. She knew the woman was well meaning, but it didn't stop the pain of her loss consuming her again. There were reminders everywhere, she couldn't escape them, and she felt as if she was gasping for air through a thick smog of grief.

She could sense Stefan watching her, as if his assessing, penetrating gaze was aware of her every reaction, her body's every movement, and she knew she had to hold herself together. She couldn't afford to fall apart again, not in here, sat among all these men.

She smoothed her hands over her knees to give her fingers something to do, her eyes something to focus on other than him.

'I'm your husband's best man. Or he was mine at my own wedding recently,' Maccus said, picking up where their conversation had left off.

She turned to look at him, glad of the distraction. It seemed Stefan had made friends. He had a life she wasn't a part of.

'When we get back to Wintancaester I shall introduce you to my new wife. You two will get on, I think,' Maccus said. 'She will look after you. Show you around.'

'Thank you,' Ædwen whispered. But she wasn't planning on staying, or making acquaintances with Stefan's friends. She was determined to leave just as soon as she could get away. Stefan didn't want her—he had said so himself. She would be a burden to him and he'd soon tire of having her around. Given the chance he would abandon her again, just as he had before.

'Dark horse, your husband,' Maccus continued. 'None of us knew he was married up until today.'

She stirred her stew, taking some of the liquid on the spoon before letting it pour back down into the bowl again. 'It seems it's come as a surprise to us all, then,' she said, raising an eyebrow at Stefan.

So he hadn't talked about her to anyone. He'd kept their union a secret. He really hadn't missed her at all. It made all this seem so strange.

'Eat your food before it gets cold,' Stefan said gruffly, gesturing to her pottage. 'You must be hungry.'

It almost seemed like he cared. But she knew that he didn't. If you cared about someone, you didn't turn your back on them and walk out of their lives.

'You don't need to treat me like a child,' she whispered.

But he was right, she was starving. She'd not been able to stomach anything before going to the church this morning, so she hadn't eaten all day, and even though it was just watery meat and vegetables, when the first mouthful reached her lips, it felt good to have something warm, the gravy filling her hollow belly.

She took another few mouthfuls and then glanced back over at the serving woman carrying more bowls and collecting empty tankards. She looked exhausted. Ædwen remembered that feeling, although she had enjoyed being with child. She had been lucky—she hadn't suffered any sickness, but she had also resolved to savour each step, as she knew she would never go through it again. For she had determined she would never love again. Besides, she knew no man would want her, not when they discovered she was a single mother to a half-Dane.

She thought back to the words her father had told her the morning Ellan had been taken. Down on her hands and knees with grief, she'd begged and pleaded with him to bring her daughter back, to no avail.

*'It's better this way. No one will know about what has*

*gone before. And you can always have another child,'* he had said, matter of factly.

But she didn't want another child. She wanted her daughter. Stefan's child. She wanted Ellan.

She had wanted her from the moment she'd known of her existence, even though Stefan was gone. She knew there were tinctures she could have taken, herbs to put a stop to what was happening inside her, to prevent her fall from grace. But she hadn't wanted to take them— the baby was a part of him. All she had left of him. She hadn't wanted to get rid of it.

It had been daunting, terrifying at times, wondering how she would cope as a mother, raising her child alone, but it was also exciting, once she'd made her choice. With a fierce determination, she had decided she could do it. It would take hard work and sacrifice, but it would be worth it. She was bringing a new life into this world. And although hers and Stefan's relationship had ended badly, she knew their child had been created with love. On her side anyway.

Taking another mouthful of stew, her heart suddenly lurched with a thought. Had Stefan had another child? What if he had another woman waiting for him in Wintancaester? A family of his own. It would be more than she could bear...

She knew there must have been women before her. The way he had touched her, he had certainly known what he was doing. But had there been anyone since?

Her eyes returned to his across the table. He seemed more commanding, more serious than the man she knew before. Amber flecks in his blue gaze reflected the flames of the roaring fire. Beneath, they were the colour of the

turbulent ocean they had ridden past today. His scar to
his forehead had healed well, leaving only the faintest
of lines, and she liked to think she had a hand in that.

They had always understood one another, despite the
initial language barrier. And she cursed herself for not
telling him the truth from the start. If she had, if she'd
told him what her father had done right from the beginning, would things have been different? Or would
he have walked away from her before things had gone
so far?

But she had done it to protect him. And perhaps herself, at first. She hadn't wanted him to know her father was a monster and that she had his blood flowing
through her veins...

She had thought that lying was the greater kindness.

Stefan had been recovering from a trauma—a terrible injury—and struggling to regain his memories.
She had wanted to save him from more grief, thinking
that if he learned the truth about all his comrades being
slaughtered at her father's hand it would cause him unnecessary hurt. Yet she knew now that was wrong. Grief
helped you to come to terms with what you'd lost. You
couldn't run or hide from it.

She stretched out her hand to pick up her tankard at
the same time he reached for his and their fingers collided, making her snatch back her arm as if she'd been
burned. His hand wrapped around the vessel, his strong,
long fingers lifting it to his lips. Fingers that had once
caressed her skin so tenderly.

Her eyes trailed to the tanned skin at his wrists, which
were covered in swirls of dark ink. It was the same blue
dye that was sprawled over his chest and shoulders, hid-

den beneath his tunic and mail coat. She had been troubled, then fascinated when she'd first seen the patterns, but he'd told her it was customary for his people to paint their skin with totems or messages to their gods, to keep them safe. And she had grown to love them, to be fascinated by them, trailing them with her fingers.

But this one on his wrist was more recent. She hadn't seen it before. Her eyes narrowed, trying to work it out. Dark streaks seemed to flare from an inner spiral. Was it a sun, or the flames of a fire? She couldn't be sure without pushing the material of his tunic further up his arm.

She looked back up into his eyes and realised he'd caught her staring, his disconcerting gaze holding her own over the rim of his cup. His presence was stifling.

'That's new,' she said, blushing, nodding to the symbol.

'A symbol of light—and truth—to guide me in the darkness,' he said, before tugging down his sleeve to cover it up.

Ædwen had barely touched her food and it bothered him. As did her lack of reaction to the serving woman who was with child. She had turned away, as if it had no impact on her at all, as if she hadn't ever been in that position herself. As if their child was some sordid secret she did not want people to know about. Had she been ashamed of their daughter, as she had always been of him, wanting to keep him hidden and their relationship a secret?

'I didn't know you could have such a thing done here.'

'Such a thing?'

'The markings. The designs. Who did them for you?' she asked.

'A woman in Wintancaester. She is very skilled...'

Her beautiful eyes flashed. 'I'm sure.'

He cursed himself. He really should stop trying to get a rise out of her.

On the one hand, he admired her strength—the fact that she was putting on a brave face in the current circumstances, surrounded by his men in an alehouse. It had been a long day. Much had happened. And it was disorientating being back in each other's presence. But did she have no heart? How could the memory of being with child not affect her? It did him and he hadn't even been there to witness it.

He wished he had seen her with a swollen belly. In full bloom. He wished he had been there to share those moments other couples had experienced, like Maccus, when he'd pressed his ear to his wife's stomach in wonder to hear the baby's heartbeat. But he had been denied all of that. *She* had denied him all of that.

His hand bunched into a fist on the table.

Who was this woman sat across from him, who he was introducing as his wife? He knew she was strong-willed and stubborn, but she seemed a hard shell of her former self. So cold. And yet still warm and soft to the touch. The effect she had on him when their bodies bumped, their knees brushed, or their eyes met was concerning and he needed to regain his composure.

He felt as if his eyes were reacquainting themselves with her beauty, as they kept being drawn back to her face. It was hard to look away. Strands of her long, golden hair were coming loose from her makeshift wimple, and he itched to reach out across the table and tuck them back in again. But he didn't know how she'd react and he didn't want to cause a scene, not in front of his men. He needed to keep his control.

Yet she was his wife. He had every right to touch her. And why shouldn't he? He had suffered the discomfiture of having her in his embrace, between his legs, all day long. He'd wanted to reach Herdbridge so he could release her from his grasp, to get some distance. But now, disturbingly, he was missing the feel of her in his arms. What the hell was the matter with him?

He knew after a few jars of ale some of the men would find a woman and a secluded place to satiate their desires. And he had every right to take Ædwen to one of the back rooms and claim her tonight, yet he knew that he wouldn't. Because he knew what consequences it had had last time. Their first and only time.

'Where will we be sleeping tonight?' she asked.

And his spoon froze, suspended in mid-air. His groin tightened. He ignored the smirks and whistles of all the men at the table and instead tried to keep his body in check. Had she been thinking along the same lines as him? Did she want to lie with him, too? No... He took in her wide eyes and realised she looked uncertain, chewing her bottom lip, and her vulnerability struck him right in his chest.

'Where would you like to sleep, Ædwen?' he said, leaning back against the wall, giving her a slow, seductive smile.

But she tipped her chin up and glared at him. 'Given the choice? Back in my room, at the monastery.'

He grinned wider. 'That's out of the question.' Then he leaned in towards her, bracing his arms on the table, his face coming close to hers so only she could hear.

'There are rooms out the back here, if you'd like us to be alone.'

'I think you've had too much ale,' she said in disgust, pulling away from him.

He straightened. Too much of her nearness, her intoxicating floral scent, certainly.

He shrugged. 'I'm afraid no one gets much sleep here,' he said. 'Because this place serves all night.'

And before he knew it, his men were up, out of their seats, encouraging each other to down jar after jar of ale, seeing who could drink the fastest, and the most, drawing a crowd. Stefan shook his head at them, amused. It helped to release some of his pent-up frustration. At her. At the situation he'd put them in.

He didn't mind the men letting their hair down. He wasn't expecting any trouble from Lord Manvil tonight. Yet he would remain vigilant. From now on, he would be responsible for another person's safety. Plus, he really didn't want a sore head for the rest of their journey home on the morrow.

Ædwen was watching the men with interest, chewing on her nails, and he raised himself out of his seat and came round the table, sliding himself down into the bench to sit beside her. He wrapped his hand around her fingers, tugging them from between her lips. His eyes were drawn to her plump, bottom lip...her parted mouth. It was like the petals of a dewy rose.

'Tsk. Stop biting your nails,' he said, bringing her hand down on to the table. 'Worried about something?' he asked, smoothing his thumb over the top of her hand.

He noticed her breath hitch, her blue eyes widen, before she seized her hand back.

'When will we be leaving here?' she asked, glancing all around, as if she was worried someone had seen him touch her.

'At first light. Why? Are you impatient to leave?'

He could understand her trepidation. He didn't much like the thought of staying here tonight either, surrounded by strangers. He wanted to get her to Wintancaester, safe inside the city walls.

Tomorrow, they'd be back at the palace and Ædwen would have a nice warm bed to sleep in. His bed. Sunday was market day and it would be busy, the streets crawling with people wanting to trade their wares. He wondered what she'd make of the capital. And he realised, he was excited about showing her his home…

When he'd first made the journey to the city, people had whispered and cowered away from him, knowing at first sight that he was a Dane, but when Canute had taken the throne and begun to unite the Christians and pagans, he had no longer felt like an imposter. Now he commanded the people's respect. The Saxons and Danes of Wintancaester.

His eyes raked over Ædwen, taking her in. She had stopped dithering, and her cheeks were infused with a rosy glow from the food and the fire. Her bridal gown was beginning to dry out, although he knew it was ruined for good. Mud was splattered all along the bottom and there was even a tear in the hem. He hadn't been aware of when that had happened.

Not that she'd be needing it again. It was a beautiful tunic. It enhanced the full swells of her breasts and it had tiny, intricate buttons all down the front—buttons designed for another man to undo, he realised. And his envy threatened to bubble up inside.

'As soon as we get to Wintancaester, we'll need to find you some new clothes. You can't go around dressed like that indefinitely,' he said.

She frowned and brought her hands back up to her mouth.

'Something else bothering you?'

'Only that I'm in an alehouse surrounded by strangers, unsure what I'm even doing here, or why you're taking me to the capital,' she said. 'Now you're talking about getting me new clothes? But I don't even know you. Not any more.'

'Strangers?' he mused, his lips curling upwards again. 'I'd hardly call us that. There was a time we knew each other...intimately. I'm sure anything unknown between us can be rectified with a brief conversation. Why don't you tell me about your life since I've been gone? What have you spent your days doing?'

*Why don't you tell me about the baby...?*

She gave a little shake of her head, picking up her tankard and staring down into its depths, swishing the honey-coloured liquid about. 'There's not much to tell.'

*Liar*, he thought.

'If there's not much to tell, nothing much could have changed, since before. Since we were lovers.'

She looked up at him, stunned, confusion clouding her blue depths, perhaps wondering why he'd brought that up. He didn't know himself, only that he felt there was something unfinished between them he wanted to address.

He saw her swallow, her throat work. 'Once,' she said, turning away from him. 'We were lovers only once.'

Tension was strumming through his body. And once hadn't been enough. Damn, he'd gone too long without a woman, he realised. That must be his problem.

*Too long without this woman,* a little voice in his head mocked.

He still wanted her in his bed, he admitted to himself now. Despite it all. And although he despised himself for it, he realised there was at least something he could do about that. And once he'd had her again, perhaps he could finally put these feelings behind him. Perhaps he could finally move on.

The jeering of his men grew louder as Maccus drained another jar and Stefan's hand gripped hers again, tugging her with him. 'It's getting rowdy. It's too loud to hear yourself think in here. Let's get some air,' he said, draining his cup and setting it on the table.

She tried to resist him, but his fingers wrapped around hers, his grip on her too strong, and reluctantly she allowed him to lead her in the direction of the door and out into the yard. Once outside, he released her from his hold and she drew her arms across her chest. *A defensive barrier*, he thought. One he had a desire to smash down.

Now that the storm had cleared, it was a beautiful evening. The full moon lit up the surrounding buildings and trees in a pale, milky glow.

'Tell me what's on your mind,' he said.

'I don't know…everything,' she said, raising her palms, exasperated. 'I don't know what you want with me…why we're even here. You got your revenge today, on my father, on me, you ruined my wedding, our family's reputation, so why not let me go? What more can you want?' she said, dropping her hands.

He stepped towards her. 'What, indeed…?'

'If you're truly taking me to Wintancaester—why?' she said, her voice rising. In panic? In frustration? 'And how will we live? What will you expect of me, when we get there?'

He felt the flare of desire. Were her thoughts following the same path as his own?

'That's a lot of questions,' he said, his lips curling upwards. 'But don't worry, I won't make you do anything you don't want to do, Ædwen.'

'If that was the case, you would have taken me back already. You could take me back right now,' she said, going to walk past him and he caught her against him and swung her round, backing her against the wall of the alehouse. Anger, and need, pounded through him. He leaned his one hand on the wall above her head, the other taking her chin between his thumb and forefinger, lifting her gaze to meet his. Their bodies were mere inches apart.

'You keep saying you want to go back. But I don't think you mean it. Would you rather I was Lord Werian right now? Would you rather it was him, looking into your eyes, touching your skin?'

He watched her tongue dart out of her mouth and tentatively trail over her parted lips.

'No,' she said, shaking her head. 'But—'

'How can I be certain of that?' he said, staring down at her, his thumb delicately stroking the base of her throat. Her breathing was irregular, her breasts rising and falling unsteadily, and he stepped closer, his body almost pressing against her.

'Stefan—'

He lowered his head and captured her lips with his, controlled, testing her. He meant what he'd said. He wouldn't do anything she didn't want to do. But he had to know, one way or another, whether she still desired him, as he did her. She had lots of questions, but he did, too. And his kiss was one of them. A soft enquiry...

He waited for her to pull back, to push him away, but instead her lips parted willingly—instinctively—on a little gasp. She yielded, opening her mouth to allow his tongue's gentle caress, and her hands came up, her fingers delicately touching his chest, and a victorious surge soared through him.

He slid his tongue inside her mouth, carefully, coating hers, as his fingers twisted into her hair at either side of her neck, beneath her wimple. He drew her head closer, deepening the kiss, and he felt her entire body tremble.

His kiss had a purpose. He had wanted to brand her with his lips, claim her as his own again, to remind her who she belonged to. But what had started out as a proprietary display of domination had him now surrendering to his own need and he wanted more. He wanted to run his hands all over her, to learn the lines of her body again, to brand her as his.

He grazed his fingers down over the undulating curves of her collarbone, his thumb stroking the smooth skin of her shoulder. He could feel her heartbeat, hectic now, thudding against his chest as he continued to stroke her tongue with his own, taking total possession of her mouth. And her response was explosive. She pushed her tongue against his, pressing her body closer, moulding her curves to his hard ridges, arching into him, as if the insane need that was directing him was erupting inside her, too.

He wanted her. So badly. He had gone from being starved of her touch, deprived of seeing her face, having to hold his needs in, to an afternoon of having her back in his arms, between his legs, and it had sent him to the edge of reason. And he knew, if they didn't stop now, he would be lifting her dress and thrusting into her hard, right here in the courtyard of the alehouse, on show for every person walking past to see.

Where was his restraint? That cool control he was known for as commander of the King's housecarls? He needed to dig deep to find it. And with a resolve even he didn't know he possessed, he tore his burning lips from hers, getting the torture of pulling away from her over as quickly as possible, and he stared down at her, confounded, as he drew in some deep, ragged breaths.

He wondered how he could still want this, with her, knowing what had happened to his family. Knowing that she had lied. And knowing she had given up their child.

He *shouldn't* want this.

He watched as her own sanity returned and she let go of his chest in dismay, her face blushing a deep, beautiful red. She pressed her back further against the wall, trying to put more distance between them.

Her fingers came up to touch her lips, as if he'd scalded her.

'What do you think you're doing?' she gasped.

'I had some questions of my own. And I got my answer—you're just as eager as I remember,' he rasped. 'At least we know we're still compatible in one way.'

Her eyes narrowed on him. 'I was young. Foolish.

And only eager because you had convincingly made me believe you cared for me,' she said, straightening, in defence of her behaviour back then, her tone accusatory. 'You lied.'

'I did not know who you really were, did I?' he said, raking a hand through his hair. 'And I'm not sure I do now. But the truth is, this time I don't care. I've decided… I want you back in my bed, Ædwen. And when we get to Wintancaester, I'm going to have you. To release myself of this insatiable, burning desire I have for you, once and for all.'

'Do I have a say in this?' she said unevenly, thrusting her chin up, her beautiful, wide-eyed face still flushed from the heated passion of their kiss.

He stepped towards her, hooking his thumb under her jaw, his eyes focusing on her swollen lips. 'I think you just did.'

Suddenly, a thundering noise made the ground shake beneath their feet and he finally released her, whipping his head round to see the chilling sight of a group of men on horseback rearing up in front of them, surrounding them. Stefan recognised the leader immediately. Lord Werian.

He cursed himself for allowing Ædwen to distract him. That he'd let his men drink, as they'd now be oblivious.

As Stefan reached for the hilt of his sword, he realised there could only be one possible reason the Saxon man had come. To take Ædwen from him.

# *Chapter Five*

This couldn't be happening. Not after how far they'd come. But instinct had him tucking Ædwen behind him, sheltering her, as he faced up to the men.

'Lord Werian. I didn't think I'd be seeing you again so soon.'

The large, sweaty man removed his helmet and sneered. 'I could not let a heathen get away with humiliating me at my own wedding. After I had a chance to think about it, I realised Lord Manvil was right. That you pagans have no rights over these lands, or our women. And I thought as I've already paid for her, I might as well have her, even if just for one night.' He cracked his knuckles. 'So here I am. Come to claim my bride on our wedding night.'

Stefan felt Ædwen tense against him and anger and disgust churned in his stomach. His fingers flexed over the handle of his blade.

'So how would you like to do this?' Lord Werian continued. 'Will you hand her over, willingly, in the hope that I will spare your life? Or will you go down fighting? Although I can't promise I won't make you watch as I take her, before running you through.'

Stefan's eyes narrowed on him and he struggled to

contain his fury at the man's words. He wasn't one to shy away from a fight. He wanted to take them all on. He knew he was skilled and his rage would count for four of Werian's men, but he also had Ædwen to think about. How would he keep her safe, stop her from being taken, while he was busy fighting?

Ædwen stepped forward, curling her hand around his arm. 'Lord Werian,' she said, bravely, 'we do not want any trouble.'

'Perhaps you should have thought of that before spreading your legs for a Dane before marrying me.'

Stefan heard her sharp inhale of breath.

'If you believe I have already claimed her, then you know she belongs to me,' Stefan said, stepping in.

'Not if you are dead…' The man smirked.

'All right,' Stefan said. 'I see where this is leading. And I am prepared to fight you for her, in fair combat. Just you and me, a sword each. The winner takes the woman.'

He was aware Ædwen had swung to look at him, disgust in her eyes.

'And why would I do that, when I can have my men run you through right now?' Lord Werian countered.

'Do you not want to claim back some of that honour I took from you today?' Stefan said, goading him. And he knew he'd succeeded. The man's lips pressed together. 'Do you not want to go home and tell people you beat me, fairly, and retrieved your bride?'

The brute nodded slowly. 'Very well. We will fight. To the death.'

He swung down off his horse and spun his sword in his hand. 'Let us begin,' he said. 'My men could dig your grave while they wait for me to run you through, if you like.'

And his warriors cheered, their horses cantering forward, marking out the battleground.

'No need for that just yet,' he said, before turning to Ædwen. 'Stay well back,' he said, lowering his voice. 'If something should happen, you need to get inside. Stay with Maccus and my men.'

'Stefan…' she said, her eyes wide. 'Why are you doing this? You could just forget all of this. Hand me over…'

'Is that what you want?' he asked, incredulous. A possessiveness he didn't understand lashed through him. 'You want to go home with him? You want to be his wife, his lover?'

She shook her head. 'No… But I don't want anyone to die. There's been enough death already.'

Stefan had known by going to Eastbury today and taking her from this man, and her father, he was putting her, and himself, at risk. By bringing her to the city, he was leaving the people of Wintancaester vulnerable to attack. Lord Manvil wouldn't rest until he'd reclaimed his daughter. He knew the man couldn't stomach her being in the hands of a pagan. But he hadn't counted on Lord Werian wanting her back, too.

Looking at Ædwen, he couldn't blame the man. She was achingly beautiful. He'd already made his decision. He had got them into this and he would fight for her. He knew losing was not an option.

Stefan could hear the sound of the men roaring with laugher inside, unaware of what was unfolding out here. And he cursed himself, for not being more vigilant, for not predicting this might happen. For he should have known Ædwen was too great a prize for any man to give up. Wasn't that why he'd come back for her? One of the reasons, anyway.

Moving his shoulders, loosening up his muscles, he prepared to fight.

Lord Werian struck the first blow, but Stefan raised his sword, holding him off with his own blade. And then Stefan sliced his sword through the air, towards his opponent, but the man barely flinched. He was large, solid, and Stefan was weighing him up. How best to tackle him. Fortunately, he had speed on his side, he was agile…and he had a feeling he'd had a great deal more practice on the battlefield lately.

Lord Werian's sword caught his shoulder on his next swing and it smarted. But it was just a scratch. He retaliated, drawing blood from the man's arm, and suddenly the blows came thick and fast, from every which way. The clashing of metal reverberated around the courtyard and the thudding of their footsteps became more ferocious on the muddy ground, their breathing coming harder, faster.

He could hear Ædwen gasp and wince with each blow of the blades and he wondered…was she on his side, willing him to win? He could still taste her on his tongue…still feel her soft curves pressed up against him. There was no way he could let this man lay a finger on her. She was his to touch and his alone.

The fight wore on and Stefan was tiring, but so was his opponent. He took a quick glance at Ædwen, her eyes wide, her face pale in the moonlight, and he drew strength from his wrath that any man would dare to take her from him. With one final, brutal blow, he knocked the weapon out of Lord Werian's hand and the brute fell, heavy, on to his back in the dirt.

Stefan stood over him, the tip of his blade coming up under the man's chin.

The horses around him seemed to snicker, as the Saxon soldiers looked between themselves, horrified, watching on, unable to believe their Lord had fallen and waiting for Stefan to make the kill.

'Stefan…' Ædwen said, rushing forward.

He glanced up, through his fog of rage, his emotions soaring, to see her coming towards him.

'What? You want me to spare him?' he said.

'Perhaps…perhaps if Lord Werian agrees to let us be. To admit defeat and agree you have won… There is no need for more bloodshed.' She was a lot more lenient than he.

He pressed the tip of his sword in further to the man's skin and the brute winced. 'What do you say?' he asked the man.

The man swallowed, raising his chin to try to get away from the blade. 'I think I could return to my settlement and look for another bride.'

'You think?'

'I know.'

Satisfied, Stefan removed his sword and stepped backwards, and Ædwen, as well as all the men, seemed to release a collective breath.

'Leave this place. Leave us,' Stefan said. 'And tell Lord Manvil more of this will happen if he sends any other men after us.'

Lord Werian stumbled over to his horse, his shoulders slumped, and heaved himself on to it, before the men turned their animals around and began their retreat.

Stefan wiped off his sword and tucked it back into his scabbard, before turning to look at Ædwen, his gaze finding hers.

'I didn't know you could fight like that,' she said. 'So well... Without fear...'

He shrugged. 'There's a lot of things we don't know about each other.'

'Did your father teach you?'

He scowled. 'My family were farmers, not warriors.'

'But he fought just like that. Like you...' And then her voice wavered, as if she'd realised she had said the wrong thing.

His eyes narrowed on her. 'So you saw him? You saw what happened to him?'

She swallowed. 'Yes. He fought well.'

'He tried to defend himself. I told you my family didn't come here to cause trouble—'

'Maybe my father didn't know that.'

He took a step towards her. 'Are you defending him?' he asked, his voice lethal.

'No,' she said, shaking her head. 'I'm just trying to give you some context, of the raids we had suffered before you came. The ransacking of villages, plundering of our monasteries and buildings and the raping of our women. Why there is so much animosity. Why my father and Lord Werian might feel threatened...'

He glanced away. 'You told me already. But that wasn't us. There wasn't enough land in Denmark. It was leave or starve. My father said he had heard England was a place where we would be welcomed. Where we could start anew. Find land to farm. Instead, we found an army, waiting to kill us. My first memories of this place were bodies stacked up everywhere, buildings burning, people screaming.'

And her. Always her.

'I know…but that's no justification for acting in a similar way. At some point, it has to stop. Our people have to get along.'

'I thought we were getting along rather well, until he arrived,' he said, feeling the tension from the fight finally leave his body.

She rolled her eyes.

'Come on, let's get you back inside.'

# Chapter Six

Entering the old Roman walls of Wintancaester, the city was an assault on Ædwen's senses. She had never seen any place like it. Riding through the gates, the beautiful monastery dominating the skyline, she saw the narrow, bustling streets were overflowing with people, full of vivacious traders selling their vibrant wares, the smell of spicy foods wafting under her nose. It was captivating, colourful and so diverse, the grand opulent palace in the centre surrounded by people from all walks of life, speaking in various languages.

There was so much to see and take in. For a moment, she was in awe. And then she realised how difficult it would be to find someone here…where would she start? Could she question the soldiers on the gate, or the stallholders, who must see hundreds of people every day, or perhaps she could go and ask in the monastery?

She couldn't wait to reach their destination and extricate herself from Stefan's arms. Since that scorching kiss last night, she couldn't seem to catch a breath without drawing in his spicy scent, or coming into contact with some part of his muscular body. He reminded her of the city walls. He was imposing, impenetrable, like the stone. And she wondered at the defences he'd built up around his heart, as she had hers.

She couldn't believe he'd kissed her! And she couldn't believe she'd kissed him back. The moment his firm lips had touched hers, she had reacted with force, helpless to stop it, needing something from him, perhaps a clue as to what he wanted. A hint as to how much he still hated her...and desired her. And if he hadn't pulled away, she didn't know what she would have let him do. It was as if she lost all restraint when he came near her and the most mortifying thing was, now he knew it.

And then he'd fought for her. When he'd released her from his embrace and she'd seen Lord Werian and his men surrounding them, her heart had been in her mouth. Her fear had roared in her ears and she'd realised, she did not want to go back. But she hadn't wanted Stefan to fight. She had been terrified he might get hurt and it troubled her that she cared. And she couldn't understand—if he despised her so much, why had he fought for her, why hadn't he just given her up?

When they had returned inside the tavern and they'd told the men what had happened, the soldiers had put down their tankards. They'd stopped drinking, sobering instantly. They'd each felt bad they hadn't been there to help their leader and wanted to make amends, each of them heading out into the night air to keep a lookout and stand guard.

She had slumped back down on to the bench and felt her exhaustion from the day creep over her. She'd tried to fight it, knowing she should stay alert, and she had willed her eyes to stay open, but at some point she had given in and rested her head on her arms on the table, closing her eyes, just for a moment...

But this morning she had awoken to find she was nestled into something solid, but warm. Something rising and falling steadily. And as she'd lifted her head to get her bearings, she'd seen with dawning horror that she'd been asleep in the curve of Stefan's shoulder.

How had she got there?

She'd jolted upright, her sleepy eyes suddenly wide, only to look up into Stefan's bright blue mocking depths and she felt her cheeks burn.

'You looked uncomfortable sleeping on the table,' he said, by way of explanation. 'I thought I'd get you used to what you can expect when we arrive in the city.' He gave her that devilish side-smirk and her heart had clamoured.

She had been reluctant to ride in his arms again after that, but he'd given her no choice. It had been a very long morning and she was so desperate to get some space from him. He was all-consuming.

Ædwen almost wilted with relief when the men finally drew the horses to a stop in a large courtyard. Modest timber-framed huts with straw-thatched roofs were dotted all around the edge of the square and children were squealing, playing games in the middle of the wide, open space. Her heart twisted at the sight.

'These are the housecarls' lodgings,' Stefan said. 'The King keeps his men close to the palace, so we can be at his side when he needs us.'

She nodded, looking around, suddenly nervous, wondering which one belonged to him.

Once the horses were safely secured in the stables, Stefan thanked his men, and one by one they departed,

leaving them alone. Maccus told her again he was looking forward to introducing her to his wife and she decided she liked him. He had been kind to her.

'Come on,' Stefan said, taking her elbow in his hand
and leading her across the square.

Women were throwing open their doors, welcom-
ing home their husbands, and Ædwen glanced all about
them, taking in the happy scenes.

'The church is just through that archway over there,
next to the monastery, should you wish to pray at any
time,' Stefan said, continuing to stride out at a pace. 'But
I'll show you around the place properly later.'

Later? Why not now? What were they going to do
now? She panicked. And just how long was he planning
on her staying?

She looked up at the huts. They weren't grand, or formidable, like her father's fortress, but she was strangely
curious to take a look inside. Perhaps it would give her
some clue as to how Stefan had been living this past
winter. The man he'd grown to be... And perhaps it
would give her an idea of whether he was expecting her
to stay here with him, as if they were just meant to pick
up where they left off, as husband and wife. Lovers...
A knot tightened in her stomach. This was madness!

But Stefan continued out of the courtyard, leaving
the men and women behind, and into the elegant cloisters of the palace.

He nodded his dark head in acknowledgement to a
group of men walking in the opposite direction, who
all bowed their heads back in respect. They carried on
into the beautiful building until they came to a few steps
leading down into a corridor. Right at the end, they came

to a large wooden door and he unlocked it. He pushed it open and gestured for her to step inside. As she did, she raked her eyes over the room, taking it all in.

'What is this place?' she said.

'My rooms,' he said, throwing his satchel down on to the floor. 'I hope you'll find them to your liking.'

She swallowed. 'You don't live out in the courtyard with the other men?'

'No, the King brought me inside the palace a while back.'

She nodded. He really had done well for himself. She didn't know if that made her feel better or worse. That he had succeeded without her support. That now he had far more power and influence than even her father. It certainly didn't help to put her at ease.

The ground floor was a huge, open space, yet it was sparsely furnished. There was a large animal skin covering the floor, a bench strewn with fleeces and a long, central wooden table, but the rest was fairly empty, making it feel quite stark. There was a hearth in the middle of the room, which would make it cosier, she imagined, but the walls were bare. It needed a woman's touch. Perhaps some tapestries or animal skins on the wall.

'I don't need much.' He shrugged, as if he could tell what she was thinking.

Yet last night he had said he'd needed her—if only to release himself of his desire.

She nodded, her mouth dry.

She still couldn't believe he'd kissed her. She didn't know what she'd been expecting him to say or do when they'd gone outside, but she hadn't expected that.

He closed the door behind him, making her jump, and

she swung to look at him. He rested his back against the wood and a shiver of awareness edged along her skin. They were alone.

'Take a look around,' he said, his dark gaze watching her.

And she wondered—did it feel strange for him to have her here, in his home? Was he on edge, too, unsure of what she'd make of it? Did he want her to like it?

It gave her the confidence she needed to step further into the room. She had never been a guest at someone else's home before. Stefan's home. Let alone the King's palace. She wasn't sure how she should behave. Or what he was going to demand of her.

'You've done well for yourself,' she said, running her hands over some wooden figurines on a shelf. 'What are these?'

He shrugged, pushing himself off the door and coming towards her. 'Some carvings I made. They're of my Norse gods.' He picked one up and turned it over in his hand. 'This one's Odin, the All-Father...and this one is Thor,' he said, pointing to the markings on the sculptures. 'This one is Frigg, Odin's wife,' he said, moving the carving around in her hand, showing her the features, her skin tingling at their touch. 'A great Queen of Asgard. She reminds me of you.'

She looked up at him. He was so close. She could feel the faint tickle of his breath against her skin. 'Why?'

He seemed to lean in closer. 'Surrounded by an air of secrecy, she is thought to be a paragon of beauty... love...fertility,' he said, studying her face.

Ædwen realised she was holding a breath and she only

released it when he removed the figure from her hands and placed it back down.

Next, she picked up a wooden cross and gave him a questioning look.

'It was a pagan symbol long before a Christian one...' He shrugged.

She glanced around, taking in a kite-shaped shield with a metal boss in the middle. Perhaps she could use that against him if she must, she thought wryly.

'Where do you sleep?' she asked.

He nodded in the direction of a small staircase leading up to another living area above. A sort of raised platform.

'Up there.'

Now she'd walked further into the room, she could see there was a bed, covered in furs. She looked back at him. Surely he didn't expect her to stay here with him, to share his home? They would have to eat together... sleep together...there was nowhere else to be but together. Yes, it was spacious, but it still wasn't ideal, especially when he kept looking at her like that, like he was imagining undressing her. And why was her traitorous body responding, a coil of heat unfurling in her belly and lower?

'You want us to stay here, together?' she asked. 'To share this room? Your bed?'

He stepped towards her, barely containing his wicked smirk. 'What's the matter? It's not like we haven't done it before.'

'A long time ago. And thanks, but no thanks. Once was enough.'

His eyes narrowed on her.

Suddenly there was a knock at the door behind him,

breaking the connection, and Ædwen released a breath she hadn't realised she'd been holding.

Stefan hesitated before slowly walking over to open it. A young boy stood in the entryway.

'Sorry to disturb you, Lord Stefan. The King is very eager. He requests your presence at his feast tonight. He is impatient to hear of your trip and to meet your wife, Lady Ædwen.'

Stefan nodded. 'Thank you, Ethelred. Tell him we'll both be there and we're very much looking forward to it.'

'I am glad to hear it. I shall go and relay your message, Lord.' The boy nodded and left. But as soon as Stefan shut the door again, Ædwen snapped. This was absurd! She couldn't believe she was here, in Wintancaester. In the palace. In Stefan's home. With him. And now she was being invited to the King's feast?

She shook her head. 'You can't expect me to go to that,' she spluttered.

He captured her in his navy gaze. 'Why not?'

'I'm sure the King doesn't want me there.'

'Did you not hear you were just invited?'

'More like summoned.' She sighed. 'I'm tired. And in case you hadn't noticed, I have nothing to wear. I can't go in this tunic, splattered with mud. I would be seen as a disgrace. More of a disgrace than I already am, thanks to you,' she bit.

He frowned at her, his eyes raking over her.

'You're right. You can't.'

She couldn't believe he was agreeing with her and, for a moment, her heart lifted in hope. Would he let her go?

Then he moved towards the door. 'Stay here. Make yourself at home,' he said, gesturing with his hand to his lodgings. 'I'll go and see if Maccus's wife has anything suitable you could borrow, just for this evening. You can't get out of it that easily, Ædwen.' He retreated out of the door. 'I'll be back shortly.'

The door closed with a thud and she stared at it, unsure what to make of any of this.

She looked around her, soaking up the silence. It was the first time she'd been alone in days, and she suddenly felt a bit lost. But also…free.

She was on her own, at last. She looked around again, taking it all in. His scent surrounded her and all his belongings… It was a glimpse into a life she could have had with him. Her and Ellan…and instantly, she knew she couldn't stay.

She glanced at the door, which he'd pulled to close behind him. Was she really going to sit here and wait for Stefan to come back? After the things he'd said last night and what he wanted them to do together? So he could bed her and then leave her again? No…she knew she was helpless against his touch, yet she could not let him seduce her again. Not knowing that deep down he despised her. It might just destroy her.

And if he got too close, he would see how her body had changed…he would know what it meant, and what she'd kept from him, and she knew his anger would be great. She couldn't be sure what he would do.

This was her chance to get away. She had to think of her daughter, who was out there, somewhere. The days were slipping by so fast. She needed to feel as if she'd at least done something towards getting her back.

She had been forced to do the one thing she'd vowed never to do—abandon her child—and beyond her own pain of being separated from her baby, what was even worse was the thought of Ellan growing up despising her, feeling lost and alone, just as she had felt when her own mother had left her. She had to do whatever she could to find her.

She wrenched open the heavy door and with a furtive look up the empty corridor, she quickly made her way out of the palace, back along the path Stefan had brought her and out through the courtyard. Fortunately, there was no sign of Stefan or Maccus and the rest of the men. Stefan would not be happy if he saw her out here, not after he'd told her to stay. How would she explain it?

She headed out into the frantic thrum of people in the streets. She allowed herself to get swept along with the jostling crowd until she came to a few stalls selling spices and trinkets. She took a deep breath and began to ask the various vendors questions.

Did they speak English? Did they know any families who had just arrived in the city with a child? Any baptisms they were aware of? Any orphanages nearby? She was looking for a child around six months old...

But the stalls were heaving and she got pushed around, the delicious, spicy smells creeping up her nose, and she quickly began to lose hope. This was futile. What had she been thinking? No one had seen a baby. Or they'd seen hundreds. Everyone kept shaking their heads. No one had any answers. And she started to feel a bit desperate, panic clawing inside her chest.

She had just managed to duck out of the way as a horse and cart came rumbling past, when a large hand clamped around her mouth and she froze. Her body was hauled against a man's chest and he drew her backwards into the recess of a dark passageway.

Terror gripped her. She had heard of the gruesome crimes that took place in the city, but she didn't think they happened in broad daylight. Suddenly she regretted leaving the safety of Stefan's lodgings, the protection of his strong arms and watchful gaze. Because for all his faults, for everything that had happened between them, she knew he would never put her in danger. Not like she'd done herself. She was a fool!

'Give me your coin. All that you have. Now,' the man roared, the vile stench of stale ale on his breath.

She closed her eyes briefly and shook her head, unable to speak, fear cloaking her throat as his thick, clammy fingers covered her mouth.

He removed them momentarily, wrapping them round her throat instead, as he thrust her up against the wall, grazing her cheek against the stone, patting her body down with his other hand.

'I don't have any,' she managed to whisper. 'I don't have any coin.'

She had nothing, she thought with stark realisation now. Stefan had arrived back in her life again so suddenly, taking her away from her home and all her possessions. She had nothing but the items she was wearing. She was totally and utterly reliant on him.

A shiver shuddered down her spine as she heard the man unsheathe a dagger and felt the tip pressing into her back.

'Then I'll have to take the only thing you do have,' he sneered.

With brute force, he ripped off her gold necklace with

his other hand, shocking her. It had a cross on it and had been given to her by her mother when she was small. It was dear to her—not because of its value, but because it was the only thing she had to remind her of her.

She squeezed her eyes shut as he pressed his body against her, his knife coming up to her throat. She didn't dare move, feeling the blade cutting into the skin of her neck.

Next, he removed her armband, prising it from her skin.

She lifted her chin up, trying to hold her neck away from the blade.

She imagined Stefan, Maccus and his wife kindly searching for a fresh tunic for her to wear, then Stefan returning to his lodgings and finding her gone. He would be livid with her. She was livid with herself. Now she would do anything to be back in that room, waiting for him.

'Ring,' he demanded and she lifted her hand so he could wrench it from her finger. It was the band Lord Werian had gifted her. But she wasn't sorry to see it go. She had never cared for it, or him. She imagined it was worth a great deal, but the piece of thread Stefan had once wound around her finger had been much more precious.

'Get your hands off her!' she heard a familiar voice roar.

And she whispered his name in relief. 'Stefan.'

How had he found her?

The man sneered and pulled away from her, dropping the blade from her throat.

'What the hell do you think you're doing?' Stefan

said, and she turned to see his sword raised, pointed towards the man, a look of blinding rage on his face.

'I've got a family to feed. Four children. A wife. We're all starving,' the brute said in explanation, suddenly releasing Ædwen. But without warning, fear bulging in his eyes, he lunged, plunging his knife into Stefan's side, before trying to make a run for it.

Ædwen heard herself scream, but Stefan's reactions were quick. He didn't even seem to flinch at his injury, but instead grabbed the man's arm as he went to tear past him and swung him backwards into the passageway, ferociously slamming him into the wall, knocking his dagger out of his hand.

'You'll face the hangman's noose for this,' he bit out.

Her attacker slumped, winded by the force of the impact of his back hitting the stone, and Stefan pinned the man in place with the tip of his own blade.

His father's blade, she realised, noticing the familiar, knotted patterns on the hilt. She hadn't noticed it last night in the dark.

He grabbed the man's wrists and twisted his hands behind his back, turning him round, roughly pushing him up to the wall where she had been pressed against the stone just moments before. He bound him with the length of rope from his belt. And then he turned to her and he ran his hands over her bruised cheek, her arms, checking her over, his eyes wild, his breathing shallow.

'I'm all right,' she said, trying to calm him.

He gripped her jaw and tilted her face upwards, assessing the cut to her neck.

'Did he hurt you?'

She turned her face away, out of his grip. 'No.'

He drew in a sharp breath, but it was as if he wasn't really seeing her. He was thrumming with rage and raked his hand through his hair, pushing out his breaths as if he was trying to control his temper.

'Stefan, I'm fine,' she said again, trying to reassure him.

'I'm sorry,' the man stuttered, turning round, looking between them both. 'You can take back the trinkets. Just let me go. Please. My family. They're depending on me.'

'You should have thought about that before you attacked my wife,' Stefan said, his blade unwavering.

But looking at the scrawny man, looking as if he hadn't eaten in days, dressed in tattered, dirty clothes, Ædwen took pity on him.

She placed her hand on Stefan's arm. She was suddenly aware they had an audience—that a crowd had gathered at the end of the passageway, watching with interest.

'Stefan, it's fine. I'm fine,' she whispered again. 'Perhaps this man just needs to be shown there are other ways to feed his family other than through stealing. Perhaps if he vowed never to do it again…perhaps if he was given a second chance…'

Stefan looked at her, shaking his head, clearly not liking what she was saying. 'I'm starting to think you'd give anyone a reprieve, no matter what they did to you,' he growled. 'You're much too soft, Ædwen. I don't believe in second chances,' he said.

No, she believed that.

More of the King's men piled into the passageway, trying to break up the crowd, and Stefan handed the brute over to them, directing the men to take him to the cages.

'Stefan, he has my necklace. From my mother,' Ædwen said.

And Stefan ransacked the man's tunic until he found them.

'Thank you. So you see,' Ædwen said, 'no harm has been done here. More damage will be done if this man doesn't get back to his family, I'm sure.'

Stefan grimaced, still reluctant to do as she was asking, but Ædwen was steadfast. 'Please,' she said. 'Let him go.'

And then he sighed. 'Let this man sleep off the ale in a cell. Give him a warm meal before releasing him in the morning,' he said to one of the soldiers. And then he turned to the thief. 'I don't ever want to see you stealing again,' he said.

And the man nodded gratefully, before turning to Ædwen. 'I'm sorry, Lady. I meant you no harm.'

Ædwen stepped towards him. 'I forgive you,' she said and turned to Stefan and took the ring from his hand. She unfurled one of the man's bound hands and pressed the tiny gold band into it. 'Make sure your family is provided for.'

And then Stefan gripped her by the elbow and launched her forward, moving her out of the alleyway, pushing through the crowds of onlookers and down the narrow street. He was walking so fast she could barely keep up with him. He looked angrier than she'd ever seen him, the harsh lines of his face making him look forbidding. But as they reached the corner, the palace in sight, he stopped abruptly, releasing her, and leaned— no, sagged—against the wall.

'Stefan?' she asked.

He tugged up his mail coat and tunic to reveal a bloody wound just above his hip and winced.

She gasped. It looked deep. There was a lot of blood. Another scar to add to his many others…another scar caused by her.

He glanced up at her, his stare lethal. 'This is your chance to run if you still want to, Ædwen. I won't be able to chase after you now,' he spat out.

She bit her lip. He was mad. And rightfully so. She deserved it. This was all her fault. This had only happened because she'd been foolish enough to leave his room. In her desperate attempt to find Ellan, she had put herself in danger. She had made another terrible decision and now Stefan had been hurt because of her.

Hot tears burned her eyes and she shook her head. 'I wasn't running,' she said.

'No? Then what the hell were you doing?' he roared. 'I told you to stay put.'

'I was just taking a look around.'

'Without telling me? Without my permission?'

'I didn't know I needed it,' she bit.

'I didn't know where you were. Where you'd gone. How can I protect you when you go off without telling me?' he said, his dark face furious. 'It's not safe. You want to go somewhere? I'll take you. You want to do something? You ask.'

'I thought I was your wife, not a prisoner!' It was the first time she'd used the term, acknowledged being his… and the word felt strange on her tongue.

'You are. And you'd better start acting like it. Start obeying me, as you promised you would when you married me.'

She reeled and he cursed.

'Why have you brought me to such a place? Where such things happen,' she accused, although she knew her argument was weak.

'I did not know you'd go off wandering the streets by yourself, did I? What were you even doing out here, Ædwen? Haven't you had enough adventure this past day?'

She bit her lip, knowing she couldn't tell him. 'I'm sorry,' she said, relenting, suddenly wanting him to drop his line of questioning. 'You're right. It was reckless of me. I won't do it again.'

He stared down at her in disbelief. 'I'm right?' he asked, raising an eyebrow. 'Now I know you're hiding something.'

He drew her closer, wrapping his arm around her so suddenly it took her by surprise. The feel of his hard body against hers. His spicy scent engulfing her. 'Don't ever do that again,' he said. 'You had me worried.'

She felt a lump grow in her throat. 'I'm sorry,' she said.

The way he looked at her with concern was unnerving. One moment he was reprimanding her, the next he was worried about her, holding her. She thought perhaps she preferred his disapproval. That was far safer than this kindness. Stefan seeming to care was a danger to her.

He leaned back and brought his hand up to cup her cheek, his thumb smoothing over the blossoming bruise she knew was there. 'Back in Denmark, I could have killed that man for what he did.'

She shook her head. 'You can't kill everyone who tries to hurt me. Besides, I think you gave him enough of a fright,' she said.

Stefan had shown immense courage. In the past day she'd been back in his company, he'd demonstrated he was a capable leader of his men and an extraordinary fighter.

'And yet I still think he got off lighter than me.' He grimaced. And she realised he'd also shown compassion to his opponents, twice, as he had to her.

'How deep is it?' she asked, carefully stepping away from him, looking down at the patch of blood spreading over his tunic. 'Can you make it back to the palace?'

He gave a curt nod. 'I can make it.'

# Chapter Seven

They made it back to his lodgings with Ædwen supporting him as he walked, his arm draped heavily over her shoulder. But Stefan was still shaking with rage that that man had dared lay his hands on her.

When he'd got back to his room and found her gone, it had thrown him. He'd dropped the kirtle and pinafore Maccus's wife had given him and he'd sprinted down the corridor, through the cloisters and back into the courtyard. He'd thought the worst, thinking, somehow, her father's men had got to her. That she'd run from him. He'd checked the church first, but she wasn't there. He knew she couldn't have gone far, but he also knew how busy the streets were in the capital and his chest had pounded in alarm.

He'd asked the soldiers on duty if they'd seen a woman dressed in a blue bridal tunic, thinking she would be easy to spot, and his hope had soared when they'd said they had seen her, going between the stalls asking questions. And he'd been livid that she'd decided to leave him of her own accord. What was she up to?

Then he'd caught a glimpse of her golden hair, heard a scuffle as he'd passed the passageway and his heart had lurched. The moment he'd seen that man's hands on her, he'd seen red. He would never have forgiven himself if something had happened to her. And he had never been so relieved to be back in his room.

Ædwen helped him down on to the bench and she quickly reached for a barrel of ale, pouring him a cup and offering it to him.

'I'm sure you could do with some of that, too,' he said and she poured one for herself as well.

He downed his in one swig.

'Ædwen, I need you to fetch a needle. Some thread. From over there. In the trunk.'

Dutifully, she did as she was told, rushing off, kneeling down to open the wooden box, throwing things out of it in a hurry to find the things he had asked for. He was aware he was losing a lot of blood and they needed to suture the wound fast.

She came back and placed the items on the table before him.

'Good,' he said, nodding. 'Now I need you to stitch me up.'

'What? No!' she gasped, stepping back from him, aghast, her face paling. 'I can't. I need to go and get someone. Call for help.'

He gripped her wrist. 'No, Ædwen, I don't want my men to know. Nor the King.'

She shook her head.

'You've done it before,' he said.

'That was a long while ago. That was different. I didn't know you…'

'I thought we were strangers now?' he said, his eyebrow raised. 'Come on, you can do this. I know you can.'

He poured himself another tankard of ale and shrugged off his mail coat. Then he began to peel off his tunic, easing it away from the sticky wound, grimacing. She reached forward and helped him, lifting it up and off him. Once it was gone, she swallowed, staring down at his body again, her eyes meeting his, her face flaming.

'It's not like you haven't seen it all before, Ædwen.'

'Also a long while ago,' she whispered.

She took a deep breath and sank down on to her knees before him, to get a closer look at the damage.

'This is all my fault,' she said.

'So make it better,' he said, giving her a brief smile and inclining his head towards the needle.

She nodded and, after downing her own drink, she set to work, cleaning the blood off with a cloth and some alcohol, causing him to wince.

'Sorry,' she said. 'Why don't you want them to know you've been injured?'

He shrugged, causing a searing pain to ripple across his stomach. 'No need,' he gritted out.

Her brow furrowed and she picked up the needle, her hands trembling.

'Ædwen, take a breath,' he said, covering her hand with his.

She nodded.

He focused on her beautiful face as she drew his skin together. He knew she was being as gentle as she could be, but each stitch smarted. If it had been anyone else, he might have lashed out, said a few choice words, but he found it helped to focus on her nearness, the floral scent of wildflowers in her hair.

Last night, when she had fallen asleep on the table in

the alehouse, she had looked so beautiful it had made him ache. And he'd wanted to hold her, to draw her closer, so he could breathe in her scent. For someone who had protested she didn't want to be there, that she felt on edge around him, she'd fallen asleep pretty quickly. She must have been exhausted.

He'd wrapped his arm around her shoulder and gently pulled her backwards, into his chest. He'd taken the chance to study her freely, learning the lines of her face again, her eyelashes resting against her cheeks, her perfect rosebud lips. She fascinated him. It had felt good to have her back in his arms…and that kiss! Damn.

He could still feel her tongue moving against his. It had pleased him more than it should that she'd responded so eagerly. Yet he hated that he still wanted someone who had kept so much from him, who had witnessed the murder of his family and pretended it hadn't happened. He was furious with himself that he'd acted on his desires with someone who was just as capable of betraying him as… No! He would not think about *her*. That was all in the past. Before Ædwen. Another lifetime ago.

How had he allowed himself to be deceived by two women? It would never happen again.

'Tell me about Maccus,' she said now, and he knew she was trying to distract him from what she was doing.

'Do I have to?' he jested.

'He seems nice.'

'He's a good man. We've gone into battle with each other a few times. He has my back.'

'And you his,' she stated. 'He obviously looks up to you. Is he also from Denmark?'

'Yes, although he came over when he was much younger than me. He showed me round when I got here.'

'And he doesn't mind you climbing the ranks, rising above him?'

'If he does, he's never said.'

'What brought him here?'

'The same as everyone else. A better life. They decided it was better to try their luck across the sea.'

'Quite a risk to cross the sea.'

'Especially when you don't know what's waiting for you,' he said, the pain making him irritable. But he instantly regretted his snide comment when she pressed her lips together and ceased their conversation.

When she finally finished the last stitch, she sat back on her knees in obvious relief and looked up at him. 'All done.'

'Thank you.'

She dropped the needle into a bowl and wiped off her hands, before fetching a blanket and draping it over his shoulders. 'You should keep warm. The shock could set in.'

Their fingers brushed as he took it from her. 'I'll be all right now.'

He noticed she was staring at his wrist again. His new ink. He could tell it fascinated her.

'It's a sun,' she said. 'I wondered. In the alehouse. I wondered if it was a sun or fire...'

'Speaking of which, I'll light one,' he said, standing up, keen to change the subject. He didn't want to talk about his new ink and what it meant to him, why he'd got it. He wasn't ready to talk about it yet. She was still a mystery to him...he was still trying to work her out.

He knew he couldn't trust her and today hadn't helped matters. Had she been trying to escape him? Yet she confounded him at every turn. Why had she shown mercy to Lord Werian and that man out there so much kindness, after he'd attacked her? Why had she forgiven him and given him her ring?

'Shouldn't you rest your wound? It's probably not a good idea to move about too much,' she said and he was aware she was following him with her eyes as he walked across the room. He shrugged off the blanket as he crouched down, carefully, so as not to rupture his stitches, and he began to light the hearth.

'I'm fine, Ædwen. Better now.' He rubbed the flint-stones together and got them to spark, lighting the kindling.

'Why did you give that man your ring?' Had it been a gift from her betrothed?

She shrugged one slender shoulder. 'It wasn't important to me. And it doesn't seem like I'll be needing it now. But he did.'

Interesting... 'By the way, I got you a tunic and kirtle to wear tonight,' he said, nodding in the direction of the garments he'd thrown down in haste earlier.

Her lips parted on a gasp. 'Surely we're not still going?'

'Why wouldn't we?' he said darkly.

'Because I just got attacked... You nearly got killed!' she said, standing up, putting her hands on her hips.

'Did you hope my wound would get you out of it? Unfortunately not. It's just a scratch. Nothing a good meal and another tankard of ale can't fix.'

She gave him a defiant look. 'It's hardly a scratch.'

'Why don't you want to go?' he said, standing, too.

She raised her outstretched palms. 'I don't know. I don't know anyone. And I've never met the King. Or Queen. What if I'm not liked?'

And there it was, her vulnerability, hitting him in the chest again.

He came back towards her. 'When have you ever not been liked?' he said.

'*You* don't like me.'

He raised one perfect eyebrow at her, his hand coming up to smooth over her cheek. 'No, I don't think *like* is the right word to use here at all.'

Her pulse flickered in her throat. Was he causing that reaction?

And then he removed his fingers from her skin.

'Here,' he said, reaching inside a pocket in his breeches to pull out the armband and gold chain he'd taken from the brute outside. 'Shall I put this back on?' he said, nodding to the necklace.

'Please,' she said.

She turned around and gathered up her hair, moving it out of the way, giving him access to her long, slender neck. He wanted to bend his head and kiss her on her pale expanse of skin, trail his tongue over the curve of her shoulder. Instead, he placed the chain around her neck and deftly did up the clasp, smoothing the metal links down over her skin. She shivered.

'You said it was your mother's?'

'Yes,' she said, turning round to face him, toying with the little gold cross pendant.

'It's the only thing I have of hers, to remind me of her. My father got rid of everything else.'

He nodded. 'And you still don't know why she left?'

Ædwen had told him, when they were younger, about her mother leaving one day, when she was nine, and never returning. The woman had never even said goodbye. He wondered now at how the loss of her mother at such a young age had impacted her. He'd known it had hurt her, deeply. She'd wanted to understand. She had blamed herself, thinking she'd done something wrong. And she'd blamed her father, too.

'No. I still don't know. As I've got older, I wonder if she'd just had enough. Of him. Of me.'

'I'm sure it had nothing to do with you, Ædwen.'

'If I had been a boy…maybe that would have ended her suffering at my father's hands.'

'I'm glad you're not.' He smiled. 'You never told me much about her. What was she like?'

'Young. Beautiful. I remember her smile. Her touch. Her tucking my hair behind my ears. But more than that, I remember how she made me feel. Safe. Loved. But I was too young to really know her as a person…she was just my mother. Always there. Until she wasn't.'

He stared down at her, wondering if she knew how ironic her words were. He felt for her, about her situation, but it didn't justify her own behaviour. She was criticising her mother for leaving her, when she herself was the queen of abandonment. For she had done exactly the same as her mother, hadn't she? She had given up her child.

He reached out and took the little cross pendant between his fingers. Her eyes widened and he felt her breathing halt. 'This was one of the first things I saw that day on the beach when you leaned over me,' he said. It had been glinting in the sun breaking through the clouds. He had often wondered if it was a sign.

He abruptly turned away from her, breaking the moment, reaching for his tunic, taking it over to soak in a bucket of water. 'Why don't you try the garments on Kendra has given you? Up there,' he said, gesturing to the stairs and the platform above.

'But—'

'Ædwen,' he warned. 'It's that or stay here, cooped up with me all night.'

She thought about that for a moment, then blew out a frustrated sigh. Resigned, she gathered up the items Maccus's wife had lent her and reluctantly began to climb the stairs.

He wondered what had her so worried. And was that why she ran? Or was it something more? Something she wasn't telling him. *Again.* She was definitely hiding something. She would never usually tell him that he was right. He was shocked she'd said the words outside in the street, and almost felt she'd uttered it to stop him asking her more questions. Yet, when he'd given her the chance to leave, she had stayed to help him. That was something, at least.

He reached in a trunk and pulled out a fresh tunic and tugged it on, trying to avoid it grazing his wound. Damn, it was sore. But he'd better put on a brave face tonight. He didn't need the King knowing he wasn't on form.

When Ædwen came back down moments later, he was waiting for her. His eyes raked over her, admiringly.

'It's a beautiful colour. It was very kind of Maccus's wife to lend it to me. Will it do?' Ædwen said, turning from left to right, smoothing her hands over the silk, biting her lip.

His mouth dried. The fabric fitted as if it was made for her. She looked stunning. Perfect. Apart from that graze to her cheek. 'I asked for blue. To match your eyes,' he said. 'You look beautiful, Ædwen.' Temptation itself.

He looked down at her. 'But there's something not quite right,' he said, crossing the distance towards her, tugging her hand out of her mouth.

'Oh, yes, my wimple. I forgot,' she said.

He grinned. 'I was going to say a smile, but I'm pleased to see you're learning fast.'

# *Chapter Eight*

Stefan led her along the winding corridors, deeper into the palace, to a pair of enormous wooden doors. Hearing the rumble of noise behind them, she guessed they led into King Canute's grand hall. Ædwen's heart was pounding and butterflies fluttered in her stomach.

'Ready?' Stefan asked. He looked relaxed and rakishly good-looking. For once he wasn't wearing his armour. He was dressed in a dark tunic that clung to his perfectly sculpted body and looked every bit the hero who had saved her today.

He slipped his hand into hers, taking her by surprise. But for once, she didn't struggle, or extract herself. Instead, her fingers curled instinctively around his. Right now, she was glad of his support—even welcomed the burning heat shooting up her arm. It was a distraction from all that lay ahead of them behind these doors.

She nodded, biting her lip. She had never thought she'd get to meet the King. If only her father could see her now—he'd be furious and, rebelliously, the thought pleased her a little. But would she be made to feel welcome here, or had her father made her Canute's enemy?

The doors swung open and the view of the hall in all its

glory was displayed before her. She had never seen anything like it. There were two thrones at the top of the grand room, on a platform, where the King and Queen were sitting, receiving their guests, and all around them there were long, overflowing banqueting tables full of meats and fruits, people vying for space on the benches. Hunting trophies and tapestries were hanging on the walls and she had truly never seen such a magnificent room, full to the brim of people chatting, coming together to eat, the noise deafening. This was the beating heart of Wintancaester.

Stefan squeezed her fingers, encouraging her to move forward, and she brought her other hand up to her lips.

'Stop fidgeting,' he whispered and she dropped it, instantly.

She wondered how he could walk so well, so tall, not giving anything away about the pain he must be suffering from his wound. Had he always been this good at hiding his feelings?

Ædwen was still berating herself at having put him—and herself—in that situation earlier. It was all her fault he'd been hurt and she felt like such a fool.

Stefan had offered her the chance to leave, said she could go. But in that instant she'd known she had to stay and help him. Yet every moment longer she stayed here, every conversation, every touch, she felt he was getting closer to finding out about Ellan. Talking about her mother had opened up old wounds and she felt as if everything was bubbling up to the surface, wanting to be set free. She wasn't sure how much longer she could keep the truth hidden from him, or even if she wanted to. Perhaps if she told him, he might be angry, but surely eventually that would pass, and he might be able to help. A man of his power and responsibility would know things. Know people. Would he be able to find their daughter? Would he want to?

'Your Majesties,' Stefan said, approaching the King and his wife. 'Allow me to introduce my wife, Lady Ædwen.'

'Lady Ædwen! So you're the reason Lord Stefan has been neglecting his duties,' King Canute said with a wink. 'Welcome.'

He rose out of his throne, coming down the few steps to greet them. He was an enormous man, she realised—remarkably tall and strong. He had a hooked nose and an impressive beard, yet he was fair and handsome. He looked like a man who might be able to unite a country of Christians and pagans.

'Thank you,' Ædwen said, giving a little curtsy, her knees trembling.

'I trust you had a pleasant journey?'

'As well as could be expected.' Pleasant was not the word she'd use to describe being held tightly in Stefan's arms, between his legs. Oppressive would be a better description. Intense. Sensual... And again she wondered how he made her forget all that had gone before, how he had let her down and instead made her yearn for things, want things, things she knew she shouldn't desire from him. She could feel his nearness even now. His heat. His gaze, watching her.

'Not too much excitement?' the King asked, his eyes crinkling as he looked at Stefan.

'Just the right amount,' Stefan said and they both smiled.

Stefan looked so assured, yet she felt anything but.

'When he sets his sights on something, this man always makes it happen,' Canute said, clasping Stefan on the shoulder, and there was a fondness there, she could tell. 'It is good to have you back.'

'Good grief, he's only been gone a day!' Queen Emma interjected, rolling her eyes, curling her hand round her husband's arm as she stepped forward to welcome Ædwen herself.

'Lady Ædwen, we are very happy to have you here. Lord Stefan has told us much about you.'

Had he? She glanced questioningly up into his face. What had he said? His eyes glittered down at her. She opened her mouth to say something, but the Queen beat her to it.

'Once you are settled, I hope you will join me for a walk around the palace gardens. On the morrow, perhaps?' Queen Emma said.

Ædwen was stunned. She had heard stories of Queen Emma and had always admired the most powerful woman in the country from afar. Twice Queen, she had heard of her beauty and could now understand why two kings had wanted to marry her. She was extremely elegant, her hair severely parted in the centre of her head and looped into an intricate bun at the back. She never dreamed she'd get to meet her. And now the woman was inviting her for a stroll?

'I should like that very much, Your Majesty. Thank you.'

Yet how could she be making arrangements, acting as if nothing was wrong, when her child was lost to her? For a fleeting moment, she wondered if she could ask the Queen for help. As a mother herself, perhaps Emma would understand her heartache…but she would have to tread carefully. She could tell the Queen was loyal to her husband and to Stefan.

'And how are things in Eastbury, Lady Ædwen?' King Canute said, his all-knowing gaze assessing her. 'I trust your father is well?'

She swallowed. 'He is—'

'Stable,' Stefan interrupted. 'For now, Your Majesty.'

Ædwen's face burned. She was ashamed of her father and suddenly, she needed the King and his wife to know it. 'Your Majesty, whatever it is my father has done, or is about to do, I wish you to know I want no part in it. That I do not share his wishes, or intent.'

Stefan swung to look at her, as if he was surprised by her protest of her innocence.

'Lord Stefan has made us well aware of that, Lady Ædwen. You have nothing to fear.'

He had? Her gaze collided with his again and she felt a lump grow in her throat. She was touched by his support of her, before he'd even come to Eastbury to fetch her. But she didn't understand it. She had thought they were enemies. She had thought he loathed her. But perhaps he didn't despise her quite as much as she thought...

'We would not have granted him permission to bring you here otherwise, Lady Ædwen,' Queen Emma said. 'Now, please, take your seats. Eat. You must be hungry after your long ride.'

Stefan took her elbow and led her to a seat near the platform. Seated according to rank and skill, Canute must think very highly of Stefan indeed to place him in such a position.

She lowered herself on to the bench and watched as Stefan did the same, gingerly, tucking his long, muscular legs under the table, and she wondered if his wound was smarting. His thigh pressed against hers under the table, but she didn't move away. She couldn't. There was no place to go. The bench was crammed full of people.

'Are you all right?' she asked him discreetly.

'Fine,' he lied. 'Now was that so bad?'

She shook her head. He had got her through it. But she had questions…questions she would need to ask him later. What exactly was her father planning? And why had Stefan stood up for her? Was it merely so the King would accept her being here? And she wondered again what it was Stefan wanted with her, after all this time.

A serving girl came over to pour them some ale and the young woman blushed as Stefan thanked her. 'Can I get you anything else, Lord?' she asked.

'No, thank you,' he replied. She knew he had drawn the attention of most of the women in the room, and she could feel the responsive simmering of jealousy in her stomach. Had he lain with any of them? No, she didn't want to think about it. She felt sickened at the thought.

'Does she love him, do you think?' she said, leaning in to speak to him, ridiculously wanting to bring his attention back to her.

'Who?'

'Queen Emma and Canute.'

Stefan looked up at the royal couple, talking between themselves on the platform. 'Why do you ask?'

'Well, it must be a political marriage. I just wonder if she had a choice.' After all, Canute had taken the country in violent conquest. Had his conquest of his bride been just as brutal?

'I believe she did have a choice. But I imagine she married him in part to save her children,' he said.

*Yes*, Ædwen thought. Almost definitely. For she could relate to that. A mother would do anything for her children.

'Yet I believe there is genuine affection in the relationship,' Stefan said, staring down at her, his eyes dipping to her mouth, and her breath caught.

'I agree… The way she looks at him and he her…'

She had always been fascinated about Queen Emma's relationship with a Dane, thinking they had that in common… It was unusual in these times for such a thing to come about, when there was so much hostility between the two peoples.

Looking up, she saw the men from their journey slowly begin to enter the room, some alone and some with their wives, and they descended on their table, squeezing in, pushing her even closer towards Stefan.

'Sorry,' she muttered, the side of her body pressed against his.

'Don't be,' he replied.

Ædwen spotted Maccus and was glad to see someone she knew. Someone else to talk to. She saw a woman who must be his wife, right behind him, but then her blood ran cold, for she saw she was carrying a tiny bundle in her arms.

Ædwen's pulse hammered, as she glanced round, looking for a way to escape. But there was no mercy. The enthusiastic woman was already upon her, beaming down at her.

'Lady Ædwen, it's so nice to meet you,' the woman gushed, rushing forward, forcing Ædwen to twist around on the bench. 'I'm Kendra, Maccus's wife. The tunic and kirtle look good on you. I'm so pleased.'

Ædwen nodded, trying to find her voice. 'Thank you very much for letting me borrow them,' she said tightly, unable to focus on anything but the child in the woman's arms. She needed to get a look at her to see… to check… 'It was very good of you. I am grateful for your kindness.'

'Not at all. It's the least I could do. Especially for Lord Stefan's wife. He has been so good to us. I must admit, I've been so excited. I just had to meet the woman who had tamed him. I could scarcely believe it when Maccus said he was wed,' Kendra said.

Tamed him? 'And…and who is this?' Ædwen asked, her voice strained, gesturing to the child, her heart pounding.

'This is our daughter, Clover,' Maccus said, pride radiating from his face as he put his arm round his wife's shoulder. 'She's but two weeks old.'

Two weeks…

A mixture of relief and disappointment washed over her.

But she should be glad it wasn't Ellan… This was *their* child.

Why was it that everywhere she went, there were pregnant women, or women with babes in their arms, or children playing? Even seals breeding on the beach… Stark reminders of all that she had lost.

'Congratulations. She's beautiful,' she managed to say, taking a quick glance at the baby, her chest tight with pain.

'Would you like to hold her?' the woman asked.

And it slayed her. 'No. No, it's all right,' she said, turning her body round on the bench, her back to them.

She knew she was being impolite, but it was instinct, a way to protect herself from more hurt. 'I'm about to eat. I'm starving actually. From the journey. Perhaps another day?'

Stefan sent her a look, but she avoided his gaze.

'If you're sure, my Lady,' the woman said from behind her. 'Congratulations again on your marriage.' Ædwen watched Kendra and Maccus take their seats, sharing a glance between them, clearly wounded by her rudeness.

Ædwen's eyes collided with Stefan's.

'You didn't need to be so rude, they were only being friendly,' he said, chastising her. 'Why didn't you want to hold the baby?'

'Does a woman have to want to hold a baby?' she bit back.

'I guess not...' he said, his eyes narrowing on her. But she hadn't missed the censure on his face, as if he was judging her. He obviously thought she was callous. As if she didn't have a maternal bone in her body...

They began to help themselves to the food, but Ædwen had lost her appetite. She felt terrible that Stefan thought she had been discourteous to his friends, after they had been so kind to her, letting her borrow the garments she was wearing. She felt wretched. Yet holding their precious child would have been too much for her to bear.

She tried to cast it off as she sat through the rest of the feast, picking at her chicken, listening to the banter among the men, admiring the Queen from afar, fascinated by the interactions between her and King Canute, and all the time excruciatingly aware of Stefan's solid thigh pressing against hers, his arm brushing her skin each time he reached for his ale.

How could she be so aware of him?

'I thought you were starving,' Stefan said, turning to speak to her a while later. 'And yet you've barely touched a thing. Again.'

Did he have to notice everything about her?

'It must be all the excitement of the day. I think I'm just tired.'

'Do you want to be a parent one day, Lady Ædwen?' Kendra asked her from across the table, obviously deciding to give her another chance, to try to engage her in conversation again, as the serving maids began clearing the bowls away. 'Perhaps it won't be too long before you and Lord Stefan have a child of you own?'

Ædwen felt herself blanch. Kendra might as well have rammed a knife into her chest. Twisting it.

She was so aware of Stefan and everyone else on the table looking at her, as she tried to control the emotions flickering across her face.

She already was a parent! And that parental love had kicked in the moment she'd found out she was with child. Her child might have been removed from her care but she was still a mother. And she had been a good one, up until the day Ellan had been taken. There was no difference between her and Kendra, or her and the Queen. She loved her child just as fiercely. She still thought about Ellan every waking moment, tracking her would-be milestones, constantly. It was just the woman sitting before her was lucky enough to have her baby in her arms.

'Yes, don't wait too long,' Maccus added, winking. 'Then our children might be able to play together.'

It was too much. The conversation moved on, but Ædwen stood silently, needing to extract herself from the table. Stefan's hand came around her wrist, tight. 'Where are you going?' he said.

She looked down at him, his hand searing her skin, and she felt desperate. 'I…I just need some air.'

Her eyes pleaded with him. *Please. Let me go…*

She needed to get out of here, fast, before she crumpled in grief.

He released her, frowning, and she managed to make it out of the hall, half walking, half stumbling. Then she was running, hurling herself down the corridor, wanting to get far away from them all. She didn't want them to see her cry. She didn't want them to know what had happened, how she had failed.

She reached the door to Stefan's lodgings and was relieved to find it unlocked. She pushed it open, slipping inside, before slumping down on to the floor, devastated, letting the tears finally fall.

Would the pain ever get any less? Or was this something she would have to live with and endure for ever? She sobbed inelegantly, releasing some of the heartache. But moments later, the heavy door was thrown open and she gasped, her head shooting up to see Stefan in the doorway. He looked down at her, his gaze locked on hers. She drew her knees up to her chin, wrapping her arms around them, afraid.

'What's wrong?' he asked, his hand still on the doorknob.

'I'm just tired,' she said, defensive. 'Maybe too much ale…'

He closed the door and then he surprised her, by sighing and dropping down to the floor to sit beside her, wincing at his wound as he did so. He rested his head back against the wall and stretched out his legs. They sat there in silence for a long moment and she was grateful he wasn't demanding she talk to him, or that she must return with him to the hall. Instead, he'd just come to sit by her, offering her that small kindness.

She was clutching the scrap of muslin for comfort. She brought it up to her nose and breathed in, in the hope of catching Ellan's scent. She wasn't even sure if the milky smell of her daughter was still there, or if she just imagined it, but it brought her great comfort. It was the only trace of her she had left.

'What is this?' Stefan said, turning towards her, reaching out to close his hand over the material, bringing it down, so he could look into her face.

'Nothing.'

His eyes narrowed on her.

'Really? Don't you think it's time you told me what's troubling you? Why you acted so peculiar out there?'

'I...' She shook her head.

She knew he deserved to know the truth—she knew it was wrong that she hadn't told him he was a father. How could he begin to understand what she was going through when she hadn't explained? But would he hear her out? Would he listen and sit here long enough, as she told him she couldn't stop thinking about her daughter, that ever since she'd been parted from her, she'd felt as if her whole life was in disarray? That she felt she couldn't breathe without her? The way she hadn't been able to breathe when he had left her...

If she told him now, it would have consequences.

She couldn't be sure how he'd react or what he would do…and what good would it do? She didn't even know where Ellan was.

Yet there was the small glimmer of a hope that he might help her, if he could ever forgive her for keeping the truth from him.

Ædwen looked heavenwards, as if seeking strength from above. What did she have to lose? Things couldn't get much worse…

'Stefan, I have something to tell you…' she began.

He took a deep breath and nodded. 'All right.'

'I haven't told you until now because I wasn't sure how you would react. I guess I've been afraid…'

'Go on,' he said. He drew his own knees up, resting his arms over the top of them. 'I'm listening.'

'When you left the monastery, not long afterwards, I discovered I was with child.' There. She'd confessed it. Well, the start of it. She bit her lip. She couldn't meet his gaze. She was fearful of what she'd see there, so she just stared ahead, out into the room.

There was a pause as she gave him a moment to let her words sink in. She had expected him to gasp or flinch, to stare at her, incredulous, horrified, but he didn't. Instead, he just sat there, an unnatural stillness about him.

'Why didn't you come to me, find me?' he asked finally.

She frowned. 'Things ended so badly between us. And I didn't know where you'd gone. I thought you might even have returned to Denmark. And you'd said you didn't want me. I didn't think you'd want a child—'

'And neither did you?' he said coldly.

She shook her head. 'I was shocked, at first. Frightened. But I did want her…right from the outset. As my stomach began to grow, it was the first joy I'd felt in a long while.'

His brow furrowed. 'So what happened?' he said, turning to look at her, judgement clouding his blue eyes. 'You had the baby and then gave up my child?'

'What? No!' she said, reeling, her back coming up against the wall. She was shocked by the force of the distrust in his eyes.

'She was taken from me!' she blurted.

'What?' he said, his voice like ice.

She lowered her knees and turned her body towards him, facing him fully now. 'I eventually plucked up the courage to tell my father about her. I'd kept it from him, throughout most of my pregnancy. But I knew he would eventually find out. So I gathered up the courage and told him, and he was furious. Even more so than I thought he'd be. I told him all about you, what had happened between us, and he said I was a disgrace.

'He left me in the monastery, and I thought that was it, that I wouldn't see him again. That I'd lost both my parents and I'd have to make my own way in life, and I was prepared to do so. He'd only asked that I keep it a secret, to protect our family's honour. So I did. I gave birth and everything was all right. I was coping… I loved her so much,' she said. 'But then one night, not long afterwards, she was taken, while I slept. I woke in the morning and found her crib empty.'

Saying it out loud was even worse than she'd imagined and a fresh wave of pain lanced her. Relentless tears rolled down her cheeks. 'At first, I thought perhaps the nuns had taken her to look after her while I slept—that she'd been crying and I hadn't heard her. But when I went to find her, no one had seen her and I began to feel frantic, panicked. I knew something was terribly wrong. I should have anticipated my father would do something.'

'Your father?' he asked, as if he was trying to work out some kind of problem.

'Sister Edith requested that I went to see her. My father was there... Seeing him, I just knew. He said he had removed her from my care—that he had found another family who wanted a child and that they were going to raise her.' A little sob rose up and escaped, and she swiped at her fresh tears with the muslin. 'He said that it was my punishment for laying with a pagan and bringing disgrace upon the family.' She had heard wailing in the monastery and then realised it was her, howling in grief.

Stefan shook his head and she wondered what he was thinking. To discover he was a father...it must be a shock. And then to find out that he had been denied the chance to meet his child... He must be devastated, as was she. But she couldn't stop now. She had to get this out. Tell him everything. He needed to know.

'My father said the only way I would see her again was if I agreed to marry Lord Werian. That if I did, he would arrange for me to see her...'

Stefan cursed softly, pushing a hand through his hair.

She wrung her hands as she tried to explain. 'I realised, what I wanted didn't matter. My will was not my own. I just knew I had to do whatever it took to see her again, to try to get her back.'

His eyes narrowed on her. 'Do you really think your father would have let you see her if you'd married Lord

Werian? That he would have kept his word? That he had the power to arrange that?'

Her brow furrowed. 'I don't know.' She shrugged. 'But I was desperate. I had to try. And then you were there. You came to the wedding. You stopped it from taking place...and that's when I knew...' she shook her head sadly '...that's when I knew I would never see her again.'

He dragged his hands over his face, as if he now understood her torment. Her tears on the hillside just yesterday. 'That's why you were so upset,' he said. 'Not because you wanted to marry Lord Werian...'

'Of course not!' she gasped. 'I was doing what I had to do.' She waved the muslin in front of her. 'I carry this with me at all times,' she said, a little sob escaping her lips. 'It was hers. The only thing I have left of her. Her name was Ellan.'

She wiped her hands over her face, trying to pull herself together.

'I'm sorry I walked out of the feast, Stefan,' she said, her voice cracking. 'Your men and Kendra, they are so kind. I behaved badly. But seeing her and Maccus with their daughter, them asking me to hold her, questioning if I wanted to be a mother one day...it was all too much. It hurts. So badly. Sometimes I feel as though I'm drowning with grief. I can't breathe. I know I'm a terrible person for failing to protect our child. I know you'll never be able to forgive me. And I know that, because I can't forgive myself,' she said and her shoulders began to shake with repressed sobs.

He didn't reach for her. He didn't touch her. Instead, he unfurled himself off the floor, standing so abruptly, it shocked her. The warmth of his thigh pressed against hers suddenly disappeared and she looked up to see where he was going, what he was doing. He paced over to the door and she saw him glance back at her over his shoulder, conflicted, his face grave, then he walked out of the room, leaving her there, stranded with her sorrow.

He despised her, she thought. That much was clear. More so than ever. He couldn't bring himself to say anything to her, or even bear to be in the same room as her. He would never be able to forgive her. And she felt as if she had lost them both all over again.

But this time, she had told him the truth. Everything. And he'd abandoned her anyway. Stunned, a chill trickling through her blood, she stared after him, bereft. She had no one…she was all alone. She felt as if God, along with Stefan and her mother, had forsaken her.

She slumped to the floor, her cheek pressed against the cold stone. She wasn't sure how long had passed—a moment? An entire night?—when suddenly Stefan was back, walking towards her, through the door, a bundle in his arms.

Her throat closed in shock.

No, not a bundle. A child!

Her heart trembled.

*Their child?*

She scrambled to her feet so fast, her head swam. She held still in expectation and hope as he lowered his arms, presenting the baby to her.

She hesitated before moving closer, reaching out tentatively to move the muslin away from the child's face and looked down in euphoric disbelief. It was her daughter! Ellan… Her tears fell faster. She was overwhelmed with joy and relief.

'How…?' she sobbed.

'Sister Margaret found me,' Stefan said, his voice thick with emotion. 'She said she'd been tasked with finding a new family for your baby. She said she couldn't go into details, but you couldn't look after her. And I wasn't to tell anyone she'd come to see me.

'I'm sure you can imagine how I felt, finding out I was a father—that I had a child I never knew existed. It was the first I knew of any pregnancy, any baby. I was furious with you before. And then, to discover this… It was the second thing you'd kept from me. And then to learn that you were giving up my child…'

Ædwen shook her head fiercely. 'I would never,' she said.

He nodded, letting her know he knew that now. That he believed her, about this at least.

She looked down at Ellan again. 'Can I…can I hold her?' she whispered.

He gave a sharp nod and passed the child over without hesitation, their bodies brushing as he placed Ellan in her arms. She drew her daughter close to her chest, staring down at her in wonder. Warmth and love radiated through her whole body, joyful tears streaming down her face.

'I can't believe it,' she gasped. 'She was here, with you, all this time?'

He nodded. 'When I told the King I had found out I was a father, that I had a child, he brought me inside the palace. He arranged for some help from the nuns in the convent here. I couldn't have done it without them.'

'She's grown,' she said, smiling through her tears. 'She's beautiful.'

'She's perfect,' he agreed, his lips curling upwards.

And then he inclined his head towards her. 'She looks just like you.'

Ædwen walked over to the bench and sank down on to the furs, mesmerised by the bundle in her arms.

'I'll go. Leave you two to get reacquainted,' Stefan said, backing away out of the room.

'No, please don't,' she said, looking up at him and then back at their child. She gave her head another little shake. 'I have so many questions… I can't think straight. I don't know where to start.'

'We have plenty of time for that, Ædwen,' he said.

She bit her lip. She couldn't wait. She wanted to know it all. Every detail. Now. 'When did she come to live with you? How long have you had her?'

He closed the door again and slowly made his way back over towards her, coming down on the bench beside her. 'About a month ago. Maybe a bit longer.'

She nodded, more tears falling, splattering on to the blankets that were swaddling her baby. She sniffed, trying to stop their descent, not wanting to wake her.

'How has she been? And you…?'

He stretched his arm out behind her on the table, leaning back. 'It was a shock at first. I didn't have a clue what I was doing.' He grimaced. 'And she cried. A lot. But we coped.'

'How did you feed her?' It had been one of her biggest worries—how her baby would be fed. Not only had it been a cruelty to her, first suffering the pain of her full and swollen breasts, her milk overflowing, but then when it had dried up, it was almost too much to bear.

'Cow's milk… She wasn't happy at first, but she's used to it now.'

Ædwen nodded. She was glad he hadn't used a nurse maid. 'Why didn't you tell me—that you knew about her? That you *had* her, when you first saw me again?' she said.

He raked his hand through his hair, sitting forward on the seat again. 'I regret that now. Now I know what you were going through. But you have to see… I didn't realise you cared. I had so many questions. I needed to see how you felt about her first. I thought you'd given her up. That you didn't want to be in her life. I wanted to know why…to understand… I had to know your feelings about her before I told you.'

'So…was this all some kind of test?' she asked, looking up at him.

'Of course not!' he said. 'I didn't know she'd been taken from you, Ædwen. If I had, I would have told you she was safe. That she was with me. Sooner. I would have ended your suffering and put you out of your misery.'

Seeing his daughter in her mother's arms for the first time stirred Stefan's emotions. His heart swelled.

As he'd listened to Ædwen tell him about their daughter, he couldn't believe what he was hearing. That she was innocent. That she had been a devoted mother after all and her father had cruelly arranged the removal of her child, without her consent. He felt like such a brute.

Now he knew about Ellan being taken from her, he felt awful. So certain was he of her guilt, he hadn't even given her the benefit of the doubt. Had he become that cynical? To think he could have intervened and ended her pain before now. But, unable to forgive and forget, he'd thought the worst of her.

He should have known this was all Lord Manvil's doing. Was there no end to this man's malice? Yet Stefan had been so quick to blame Ædwen, so swift to judge and see fault in her because he'd been wounded by her before.

When he and Ædwen had tentatively embarked on a romantic relationship the previous winter, she had suggested leaving, getting far beyond her father's reach. Perhaps she'd always known what he was capable of, that she'd feared he'd do something like this. She had told him Lord Manvil wouldn't allow her to marry a Dane. She had told him no one must know about them and there had been a part of him that had thought she might be ashamed of him.

But Stefan had wanted to do things right. Yet he'd never been given the chance. When he'd finally seen the man in person, all his memories had returned in an instant and he'd been horrified to discover it was her father who had slaughtered his family. He'd found out about Ædwen's deceit…all of which had impacted how he'd handled this situation now.

But hearing her story, listening to her open up to him, feeling her loss and hurt, he had known he couldn't keep her child from her a moment longer. He'd had to tell her. Immediately. To end her suffering. And seeing them together now, Ædwen holding their daughter, he knew that she loved Ellan, because once she had looked at him that way.

Ædwen was transfixed, unable to contain her smile, her tear-washed eyes wide and glowing.

'I'm sorry you had to go through that, Ædwen,' he said. 'I don't know how you coped with her being taken.'

But even though she had been the victim here, it didn't change what she had done before. And it didn't change the fact that she still hadn't come to him, found him and told him the truth about their child.

He couldn't abide secrets, any withholding of information. He knew it stemmed from the sickening discoveries in his past, from being let down so badly.

It's why he knew he must resist his desire for her now. Why he must keep his invisible armour in place.

'I didn't. I felt as if every day was another day of heartache I had to endure. The future was bleak. At first I couldn't even bring myself to get out of bed. I had no motivation to get up. I had no interest in activities, conversation or mealtimes—or even prayer. I felt alone and I guess I retreated inside myself.'

He had left her alone to deal with her pregnancy and all that entailed. To cope with the shame he knew now he must have brought upon her, the nuns believing she was having a child out of wedlock—or to a pagan. He wasn't sure which was seen as worse. He hadn't known about the child back then, but still, he felt like such a beast.

'And I hated my father. The anger began to set in. But I needed that. It fuelled me to keep going.'

He couldn't believe Lord Manvil had put her through such pain. To think that man had taken his father from him and tried to take his daughter, too. Stefan's own anger stirred.

'So was he lying?' she gasped now, realisation dawning. 'If I'd married Lord Werian, he wouldn't have arranged for me to see her? He couldn't have, because she was with you. Did he even know where Sister Margaret had placed her?' she said in a disbelieving voice.

'I don't think he could have, for I'm sure he wouldn't have allowed her to live under my protection. Unless he didn't care. I will be for ever grateful to Sister Margaret for taking the initiative and tracking me down.'

Ædwen responded with a slow nod. 'She left around the time Ellan was taken… She had helped me greatly in those early days, after the birth. I didn't know where or why she had left… I was distracted by my grief.'

'She resides here in the monastery now. She is still in Ellan's life. She has been a huge support to us.'

'I must speak with her on the morrow,' she said. And then she shook her head. 'Stefan, that's why I left your room today…why I foolishly went out of the palace. I had determined I was going to find her. That I'd start by asking questions, finding the local orphanage, or any families who had recently come to the city with a child.'

'I had thought you were running away from me,' he said wryly. 'I wish you had just told me.'

She shrugged. 'I was afraid to. I wasn't sure how you'd react. I'm so sorry you got hurt by that man today because of me.'

'It will heal. And you? The birth…was it…?'

She knew what he was asking. 'Painful, yes. But also wonderful.'

Guilt floored him. He should have been there.

'Thank you, Stefan,' she said suddenly. And she leaned over and kissed him. It was a soft, gentle kiss on the cheek and so spontaneous, it startled him. 'Thank you for taking her in. For looking after her.'

He felt a lump grow in his throat. 'She *is* my child. What else was I going to do?' he said. 'Besides, she's incredible.'

She looked back down at her. 'She is. I can't believe she's here,' she said. 'That I'm really holding her. Did you...what did you call her?'

'Sister Margaret said you'd named her Ellan...and I kept her name. I liked it.'

'Thank you,' she said, blinking fresh tears out of her eyes.

She leaned down and planted a soft kiss on Ellan's forehead, breathing in her milky scent. And then she righted herself, drawing in a breath. 'So...what happens now?' she asked. 'I guess the sooner we make arrangements as to how we should proceed, the better.'

His brow furrowed. 'What do you mean?'

'I mean...where do we go from here? I want to take care of her. I love her. And I'm her mother,' she said, determined. 'I know you care for her, too, and that you'll want to see her as often as possible...'

His frown deepened.

'So, what are you thinking will happen between us now? We will need to come up with a plan.'

He shook his head, rising off the bench, pacing away from her, before coming back, his hands on his hips. 'Nothing has changed. You will both stay here with me in Wintancaester. You'll be her mother, Ædwen. And you'll be my wife!'

She looked up at him, stunned. 'No!' she gasped, shaking her head.

'No?' he asked, staring down at her, his brow pulling together.

'I mean, yes, of course I want to be her mother. Am her mother,' she stuttered. 'But I can't stay here, with you—'

'Why not?' His voice was deadly. 'Where else are you going to go? You have no coin, no home.'

'I don't know. I'll manage… I am grateful to you for—'

'Grateful?' he repeated, disbelievingly, taking a step towards her.

'Yes. For looking after her, while I couldn't. But I can't be your wife, Stefan.'

'You already are!' he exploded, incensed, raising his hands up in despair.

'I realise now that you brought me here for Ellan. To get answers. And so that she has a mother… But surely you can't mean for us to carry on this ridiculous pretence of us being married?'

He blew out a breath, raking a hand through his hair. 'How exactly is it a pretence? We said our vows…'

An old fury took up place in his stomach. Had she ever meant the words she'd said to him before? Had she ever taken their union as seriously as he had? He wondered now if she had ever thought he was good enough for her?

What was it with women committing to him and then changing their minds? Well, he'd had enough.

She shook her head. 'We were young and naive. Maybe we meant the words we said back then, but now? I don't want to be your wife, Stefan. You don't even like me,' she said. 'Why would you want to still be married to me? To continue acting as though we mean something to each other when we don't? It wouldn't be a real marriage. Not without love.'

He gave a grim twist to his mouth. 'If I hadn't taken you to bed, you would never have got with child. Ellan is my responsibility. So are you, whether we like it or not.'

She recoiled and he knew he'd hurt her, calling her a responsibility, a duty. But then she had hurt him, too, proclaiming that she didn't want to be his wife!

It took him back to a moment years before, when he was in Denmark…a moment of great humiliation and rejection…and he knew he needed to take control of this situation, fast.

Out in the hall earlier, he'd been proud to have her on his arm, to introduce her as his wife. He'd noticed the admiring glances she aroused from the men and women in the hall and, although he didn't want the men looking at her too hard, he knew why their gaze was turned. Her beauty surpassed all others. He had never met an equal. He still wanted her. And there were worse things to base a marriage on than desire.

'This marriage makes you respectable. And Ellan legitimate,' he added. 'You were prepared to be married to Lord Werian for your daughter. How is this any different?'

Apart from the fact there was an unfinished, undeniable attraction between them.

'Where I come from, marriage is a sacred union between us and the gods. We don't take our vows lightly and I will honour that union—you must, too. We will make the best of it. For Ellan,' he said, grimacing. 'Because that is what a marriage is, Ædwen. A choice. And once you have made it, you stick with it. For better, for worse, you make it work.'

# Chapter Nine

Ædwen looked down at her daughter and forced her fears about staying here with Stefan out of her mind. She would think about that later. Right now, she wanted to enjoy being with her child again.

She carried her precious bundle up the stairs and settled her down on the bed. She lay beside her, studying her tiny features, her rosebud mouth and cherub cheeks, and her perfect little fingers. She couldn't believe she was here, that they were back together, and her joy was immense.

To think Ellan had been safe with her father, all this time. There was nowhere she would rather Ellan had been. She could tell Stefan had taken good care of her—her skin was glowing and she had grown. She was heavier than she remembered and was sleeping contentedly.

Stefan had surrounded himself with good people, she thought. Despite what had happened out in the lanes earlier today, she had liked everyone she'd met here in Wintancaester so far. The King and Queen were people to look up to, to aspire to. She liked Maccus and Kendra and she would make sure she made amends to them for her earlier behaviour. And the fact Sister Margaret was here, too…that was perfect. She would have to search her out, first thing on the morrow, and thank her. She wanted to hear everything. All that the sister could tell her.

But could she and Ellan stay here?

She wondered if her own mother had once cuddled up to her and looked at her in wonderment like this. Had she felt pure elation at having such a perfect thing in her life? No, she must never have loved her, for how could she and do what she did?

She had felt the loss of her mother even more acutely when she'd had Ellan as she had known she could never leave her child, not like that woman had left her. And she had wondered, often, what she had done to contribute to her mother's rejection of her.

She knew her parents had suffered an unhappy marriage, for Ædwen had felt the effects of it every day as she'd grown up, longing to escape their constant battles. She had carried the burden of it and she didn't want Ellan to witness that same hostility between her and Stefan.

Did Stefan just want a wife to make their family legitimate? He had spoken as if she and Ellan were a duty. As if it was something he would have to endure. But she didn't want him to be with her because he felt he had to be—to make amends for planting a seed in her body, getting her with child. She had heard the resignation in his voice, the reluctance about their future, and it had felt as though someone was reaching into her chest and squeezing her heart. He had looked as if he was accepting their marriage as punishment and she knew he would end up hating her. Begrudging her. They would fight all the time and she couldn't bring Ellan up in such a marriage. One like her parents'.

No, it was far better to leave now than for her and Ellan to face his almost certain desertion of them later on.

Yes, he'd told her he wanted her back in his bed, to make her his again. There was no way she could live with him in his lodgings like this and be able to ignore this burning attraction they felt for each other. But to think a marriage could work because they found pleasure in each other's bodies would be a mistake. Because what would happen when that desire had been sated? Would there be anything left? No, a marriage had to be based on love. Acceptance. Trust. And she wasn't sure they had any of those things.

He did not love her and she felt sure he would soon grow tired of them. He would leave when things got tough. And she couldn't let him do that to her again.

She felt flawed in some way, as if she was unworthy of love. Her mother had left, her father had never cared for her—she couldn't believe he had sent his own grandchild away, not even caring where she had been placed—and Stefan had abandoned her all too easily, unwilling to hear her out, rejecting her for her deceit. Yet his betrayal had been far worse than hers had ever been. If he hadn't have left her, none of this heartache would ever have come to pass. He had broken his promise. He had let her down. She must never forget it.

She could not risk a future with him. If they kept their union going simply for the sake of their child, she knew it would be a mistake. They would make Ellan, and themselves, miserable. Choosing to be alone was better than chancing rejection and the even greater hurt it would cause. She could not risk her heart again. She didn't think it would survive a second time.

Ædwen knew she would have to talk to him and make him see reason.

She was so tired, she tried to sleep. But every time her eyes drifted closed she snapped them back open, worried Ellan wouldn't be there when she woke up.

And where was Stefan? He had gone back to the hall a while ago, saying he would give her and Ellan time alone, but the dark hours were dragging by and she was starting to feel frustrated. Surely he should be back by now? Was he not exhausted? Who was he enjoying the company of? And why did she care?

She had seen the way the women in the hall had looked at him earlier, their eyes raking over his handsome face, his muscular body, and ridiculously, she'd wanted to place her hand on his arm, staking a claim on him. The fierce possessiveness that had risen up inside her shocked her.

Was he with another woman now? No, she could not bear to think about it. She flipped over on to her back, frustrated, and stared up at the roof. But he was the father of her child. She was lying in his bed. Didn't she have a right to feel a little bit proprietary?

Finally, after what felt like an age, Ædwen heard the sound of familiar footsteps coming down the corridor, the heavy door being pushed open. There was a moment and then Stefan came charging up the stairs. She raised her head off the bed, startled, and their eyes met across the candlelit room.

His hand came across his chest in a gesture of utter

relief. 'I thought… I thought you might have gone,' he said, his dark gaze holding hers.

'In the middle of the night? And not said goodbye? No.' She frowned, propping herself up on her elbows. 'I learned my lesson earlier today.'

He nodded, sighing, gripping the wooden handrail, trying to regain his composure. 'Good.' He raked a hand through his hair, glancing over at Ellan.

He didn't trust her, she realised.

He had been hateful back in Eastbury, the day he had left her. He had been quick to doubt her, condemning her, saying unforgivable things, and she wondered what had happened in his life to make him assume the worst in people. She knew what had happened when he'd arrived on these shores had been atrocious, but she had a feeling there was something more. Something that had happened even before that. Something he hadn't told her.

'Sorry. I didn't mean to wake you,' he said, retreating.

'You didn't. I couldn't sleep.' And then before she could stop herself. 'Where have you been? Who…?'

His brow furrowed. 'With the King.'

'Just the King?' She hated herself for asking, but she couldn't seem to help it. She'd been lying here in the darkness, her jealousy simmering, her imagination spiralling, getting the better of her.

He raised an eyebrow at her. 'What do you care?'

She shrugged her shoulder. 'I don't. You're a free man.' She shrugged.

His eyes narrowed on her. 'But I'm not. Am I?'

Her stomach flipped, but she ignored his question. She certainly didn't believe he had stayed true to their marriage vows all this while they'd been apart.

'What's the matter, Ædwen?' he whispered, keeping his voice low so as not to wake Ellan.

She sat up fully in the bed. His bed. His scent on the furs surrounded her. 'I don't know. It's just it's my first night here, in a strange place, and you left me here all alone.'

'I thought that's what you wanted…' Then his mouth curled upwards into that wicked grin. He put his hand up on the wall and leaned in. 'Don't tell me you missed me?'

'No!' But she wasn't prepared to stay here if he was going to spend every night out in the company of other people. Other women. But why was she even thinking like this? After all, she'd already decided she was leaving…hadn't she?

'Get up. Come downstairs.'

'I'm tired,' she protested.

He cocked an eyebrow. 'You don't look all that sleepy to me. Come on. We need to talk.'

She sighed heavily. She checked Ellan once more and then swung herself off the bed.

He made his way down the stairs and she tentatively followed him, back into the living space.

The candle on the table was still burning and he looked so male and virile, so formidable, his dark frame moving around in the soft light, as he poured them both a drink. She stood frozen, watching him from the bottom of the steps, rubbing her hands over her arms. Once again, she wondered how he thought the two of them could live together like this. Just being so close to him, cooped up in here, did things to her body. It made her yearn for things she knew she shouldn't want from him.

'Here,' he said, handing her a cup.

'Thank you,' she said, taking it from him and raising it to her mouth, wetting her lips.

Once, this had been all she'd wanted. To live with Stefan, to be with him all the time. That's why she had said her vows to him so readily. Why she had bedded and then wedded him so fast. She had been completely in love with him. Now, he was the father of her child and she knew everything he had said to her about them being together, for Ellan's sake, and for her reputation, made sense.

But she couldn't do it…she couldn't stay here knowing he didn't care. He had made it sound as if it was a sacrifice he was prepared to make for her and his child. A sacrifice of his own happiness. And it would be too painful seeing him having to put up with her, reluctantly. And eventually, when times got tough, he would leave. That's what people always did.

He had left her before. Broken her. And she wasn't sure she'd ever got over it.

'Stefan,' she said, stepping towards him. 'So much has happened between us. Maybe too much to forgive. There is so much mistrust between us. You can't really think that this is for the best, me living here with you, like a couple.'

He pinched the bridge of his nose before dropping his hand and looking down at her.

'Ædwen, we *are* a couple,' he said, exasperated. 'When are you going to stop trying to deny it? You chose to marry me and I you. We made our choice.'

She had thought he had values, but when he'd left her, walked away, he'd proved he did not. Now he wanted her back? To try again? She couldn't comprehend it.

He took a step towards her. 'And I will not have a second failed marriage!'

She reeled. Her throat closed in shock. 'What?' she managed to whisper.

He had been her first. Her only lover. She hadn't been naive enough to think he'd never been with another woman before her. He had certainly acted, moved, with experience. But she had never pried, never asked to know the details. She had just hoped that anyone before her hadn't meant as much to him. This was the first time she was hearing about this. About another woman in his life who had obviously been important.

He sighed and sank down on to the bench. For a moment, he put his head in his hands and then dragged his fingers over his face, before sitting up again to face her. He looked tired. Shattered, in fact. 'I was married once before. A long time ago.'

'You were?' She couldn't believe it. How did she not know this? Why had he never mentioned it before? Surely he should have? This was huge... It made her wonder what else he was keeping from her. But then, she had kept things from him, too.

'Who was she?'

He shrugged his shoulder, as if she barely mattered. Yet Ædwen knew he wouldn't have entered into a union lightly... This faceless, nameless woman must have meant a lot to him, as she thought she had, once.

'Her name was Dania. She was the daughter of a neighbouring tribe leader in Denmark. We were promised to each other when we were children, to maintain a peaceful relationship between our clans as we moved around from place to place. Fortunately, we got along, grew up liking each other.'

'What happened?' Her words sounded strange. Ædwen felt as if someone had wrapped a hand around her neck and was gently squeezing. She had thought she was the only woman he had ever cared for and she suddenly felt jealous of a stranger, a person she didn't even know. Dania.

'I thought we were happy. But I came home from a fishing trip one day and found her in our bed with another,' he said, detached, his voice devoid of emotion. 'A close friend of mine. He was like a brother to me.'

She raked in a breath. He sounded so cold, looked expressionless, but she knew that must have hurt. The betrayal must have cut deep.

'I'm so—'

'I vowed I would never put myself in that position again,' he said, cutting her off, as if he didn't want to hear her words of pity.

And yet he had. With her. This went some way to explaining why he'd judged her so quickly. Why he'd been so quick to blame her at the first sign of trouble. And now he wore his distrust like armour, because without it, he was unguarded; vulnerable. Now she understood his reluctance to rely on anyone else.

'Did you...separate?'

'Yes. Our marriage was over. In Denmark, pagans are allowed to divorce, if it is what both people wish, unlike here in England. And I could not forgive her for her deceit.'

She could understand that, yet it sounded as if he somehow felt he was to blame.

'She said it was a mistake. She begged for forgiveness, but I withheld it from her. I told her to leave, that she should go and be with him. And eventually, she agreed to go. Unfortunately, things didn't end well for them...'

She drew in a breath.

'What happened?'

'Never mind what happened,' he bit out, raising his head to look at her. 'I am older now. Wiser. I won't make the same mistakes again. I know that when you enter into a marriage you make it work, you fight for it, no matter what... So that is what we are going to do, Ædwen. Especially as you and I now have a child to think about. We must deal with the consequences of our actions.'

'So what are you asking? You want me to pretend we are in love in front of others?'

He clenched his jaw. 'You're good at making someone believe something is real when it isn't. It shouldn't be so hard for you.'

She inhaled sharply, ignoring his hurtful comment.

'And then what? Here, in your home, we live like strangers, tiptoeing around each other?' She realised she was gripping the cup so hard between her fingers, she was worried it might break, so she set it down on the table.

'No. I am not suggesting that at all,' he said, stalking over to her. 'I am proposing we are married in every sense of the word. All the time.'

'You mean...?' Her cheeks flared. 'You mean you want me to be a wife who comes to your bed?' she said, crossing her arms over her chest. 'Despite everything...'

'Is there another kind of wife?'

'But why?' she said, hating that she sounded panicked. That she was letting him get to her.

'You expect us to live like this and not sleep together?' he asked, running a hand around the back of his neck. 'I'm struggling to not to take you in my arms again and kiss you, even now.'

Her heart pounded in her chest. 'But—'

He silenced her by coming towards her and placing a finger over her lips. 'Tell me, would it be such a hardship? You seemed to enjoy it before, Ædwen.'

She swallowed and his eyes glittered down at her, challenging her, daring her to deny it. Her insides were melting just looking at him and he wasn't even touching her properly. Yet. Just undressing her with those blue, expressive eyes.

Finally, he lowered his finger so she could answer. She tipped her chin up. 'That was a long time ago. I don't know you. Not any more.'

'But you want to.' He reached for her hand, drawing it up to his chest, and held her there. She instinctively flattened her palm against the solid heat. 'And you will. Living under the same roof will make it hard for you not to know me. And you'll come to my bed because you won't be able to stay away. And you'll enjoy it. I promise.'

His total assuredness, his certainty of her pleasure, made her ache between her legs. She felt her knees tremble slightly, her body heat and she wondered at the power he had over her. How his words and his touch could make her forget everything that had gone before, and all her worries for the future.

'This is madness,' she said, her voice barely a whisper.

'It would be madness not to give each other the satisfaction we both require. You can try to resist me if you like. I shall wait till you're ready... Hell, I've waited a long time already.'

'I can't imagine you've been celibate all this time we've been apart,' she said, suddenly indignant, removing her hand from his chest. What was it Kendra said earlier—something about her taming him?

He gripped her elbow, holding her fast. 'Actually, I have,' he said. 'There has been no one else. I told you I take my wedding vows seriously. I haven't lain with another woman since you.'

It was staggering. 'No one?' she asked, stunned, and a traitorous elation shifted through her. 'I don't believe you,' she whispered.

'It's the truth,' he said, sliding his arm around her back and pulling her up against him. His words and actions shocked her and delighted her at the same time. His face was so close she could see the golden flecks in his eyes. He hadn't taken another woman to bed in the fifteen months they'd been apart? Why?

'I assume you haven't been with anyone either?'

'Of course not!'

'Then that settles it,' he said.

Her pulse was beating so hard in her chest and her thighs were trembling. She knew she had to fight this. Him. Because his desire was only temporary and, once it was satisfied, where would that leave them? She knew she had to protect herself, her heart... But when he looked at her like this...

As if to torment her, he pressed her closer, eradicating any distance between them, so she could feel all the hard ridges of his body and it made her insides quiver.

'What are you doing?' she said, her panic rising, yet

her hand was trapped between them, flattened against his chest again and she curled her fingers into him. She gripped his tunic and she could feel his heart beating beneath.

'Don't worry. I'm not about to seduce you right now. Unless you want me to,' he said. 'I'm just going to kiss you goodnight.' His other hand came up to hold her jaw, his thumb stroking the corner of her mouth.

The tension in the room was so thick, and he smelt so good, like leather and spice.

'Stefan...' she breathed.

She was aware she hadn't said no, the tips of her nipples painfully hard as they brushed against his chest. He leaned in gently, his hand drawing her head closer. His lips pressed against hers, softly, carefully, and her eyelids fluttered shut. She could feel her pulse pounding in her chest, her throat, as she sank against him, unable to do anything else but give in, and her mouth was just as compliant, opening up to him, all too easily. Still holding her jaw, he slid his tongue inside, exploring her mouth, tasting her fully, setting her body alight.

Chest to chest, thigh to thigh, the kiss went on and on, every stroke of his tongue making her hot with need. Suddenly, she wanted him to put his hands on her. All over her. The thought of him touching some other woman out there in the hall had been unbearable, because, she realised, she wanted him for herself.

But all too soon, he pulled away, reluctantly, his half-closed eyes staring down at her. He had a lot more control than she did.

'I hope you're not still going to deny that you want

me?' he breathed, his lips curling upwards into that devastating smirk.

She could hear the arrogance in his voice and she felt exposed. Weak that she had just succumbed to him so easily. Again. Yet she still wanted more. She wanted to get closer. Her face burned and she pushed at his chest, backing away from him, before running up the stairs, unsteady on her feet.

'Goodnight, Ædwen,' he called after her, watching her go.

She stopped halfway up, turning back round to face him. 'Do you…do you want your bed back?' she asked, trying to sound normal, trying to pretend that scorching kiss hadn't just happened. That it hadn't affected her.

'No. You take it,' he said.

'Where are you going to sleep?' she asked.

'Down here, on the furs. For now.'

*For now.*

'As I said, I will wait for you to come to me, Ædwen. When you're ready.'

Stefan shrugged off his tunic and took the furs from the bench, laying them down by the dwindling fire. He wondered if Ædwen was asleep. All was quiet and he strained to listen for her or Ellan's breathing upstairs, but he couldn't hear a sound. He was a fool to have kissed her, he thought, as now he couldn't think about anything else but the feel of her in his arms, her soft body pressed against his, her lips moving against his mouth. He'd promised he wouldn't rush her, said he'd wait until she was ready, so with the restraint he'd cultivated these past fifteen months, he'd pulled away, denying himself the satisfaction he so desperately craved.

But damn, how was he ever going to get to sleep now?

Ædwen had seemed shocked when he'd admitted there had been no other woman since her. Yes, there had been times when he'd wanted a woman, yet no one had compared to her, none had been beautiful enough, or interesting enough to tempt him to break his vows— and he'd often thought perhaps that had that been his comeuppance, for leaving her.

When he woke up in Eastbury in that bed in the monastery, his imagination, his memories…everything was muddled. Ædwen was the only thing that he knew for sure in his life and he had pinned all his happiness, his future, his dreams on her.

That's why he was so thrown when he saw her with her father.

All his memories had come back and he had been blinded by rage—that she was the daughter of the man who had slaughtered his kin. He had turned his back on her, furious with her for deceiving him and appalled with himself for being so gullible, for allowing himself to be betrayed by a woman for the second time.

When he left her, his life was in turmoil. He'd lost everything. He was all alone—with no home, no food, only the clothes on his back. He had been starving, for days, weeks on end. He'd slept under the stars each night, freezing to death.

He'd vowed never to forgive Ædwen or her father and to one day seek vengeance for his family's deaths. For losing his entire family all at once.

His anger ran deep. He blamed her for a lot of it.

He had sought out his own kind in England and Canute's crusade helped to rid him of some of his rage. He'd taken his anger and pain out on every opponent he'd met on the battlefield.

All these months, his resentment towards her had allowed him to keep his distance. Learning that she'd kept his child from him had been the final blow, like an angry boot stamping on burning embers, extinguishing the flame that had burned bright between them for good. But in just one day, she had obliterated all that he'd believed to be true about abandoning Ellan. She had never given up on her. Instead, she hadn't stopped fighting to get her back, doing all she could. She had even been willing to sacrifice her own future happiness to find her, by agreeing to marry Lord Werian. It was admirable, although maddening. Ædwen was a stronger woman than he'd given her credit for.

He couldn't believe Lord Manvil would treat her like property. Marry her off to a man against her will in return for an army. Thank goodness he'd made it to the church and prevented the wedding from taking place, rescuing her.

Would her father come for her? he wondered. Canute had asked him that very question this evening and he'd given his answer. Yes, he was certain he would and he thought they should prepare for an imminent attack.

He turned over, on to his side, staring at the dancing flames of the fire. He kept going over the events of the past few days. As Canute's chief commander, he was responsible for keeping the King and his throne safe. That included the people of Wintancaester and, of course, his wife. His child.

Had bringing Ædwen here put everyone in danger?

It had taken months for the King to secure peace in these lands. The last thing he wanted was to start up a war. And this wasn't a battleground, it was a city. There were families and homes to protect.

Had he been selfish? Was his judgement off—all because of Ædwen?

Yet Canute had reassured him they'd known the battle was coming anyway. It was only a matter of time. That's why Lord Manvil had wanted more soldiers. Stefan going to Eastbury and taking Ædwen had just speeded things up.

Thoughts of Lord Manvil readying his army stirred his anger. Part of him longed to fight him, to take revenge at last. But that man was also Ædwen's father. Ellan's grandfather. It had taken all his restraint not to challenge him in the church. To rein in his hatred. If he fought him now, how would Ædwen feel about that?

Stefan couldn't be sure he'd made one good decision since he'd seen her again in that church. He couldn't fathom why he'd thought any of this was a good idea, as he lay in the darkness, his body tense, his groin hard with need. This was torture…being so close to her and not being able to have her. Yet what was the alternative? She was his wife. This was where she belonged.

But could he trust her?

He would never be able to forget what her father had done. Even though she hadn't been responsible for running that blade through his father's chest, for knocking down his brothers, she had kept it from him. What else was she capable of?

He couldn't believe he'd told her about Dania. The

woman who had fallen short in her role as a wife, affecting his security and trust. He never usually spoke of her to anyone. He was ashamed of that period of his life. He'd agonised over what he might have done to contribute to Dania's rejection.

When he'd slowly begun to recover in the monastery, memories had returned of his upbringing, his family and Dania, and despite deciding never to get close to anyone again, he had fallen for Ædwen. He had known he hadn't felt true love until then. With Dania he had felt familiarity, what was expected of him…but not this insane desire or need to possess someone completely. And for a while, Ædwen had even made him forget that if you let someone in, they'll end up hurting you.

But of course, eventually, she had.

Did all women lie? It was a fact he had come to believe. So if they were to be husband and wife again now, he would need to keep his distance, his control, so he wouldn't be dishonoured again.

Yet he knew that the only way he could rid himself of this burning need that was stirring up his blood was to claim her again. When?

He heard footsteps on the stairs and felt his whole body tighten.

'Stefan?'

He lifted his head towards the sound of Ædwen's voice in the darkness. 'What is it?' he said, his voice hoarse.

'Is this where Ellan usually sleeps?' she asked.

'No…she usually sleeps in her crib.'

'Where is that?' she asked and he knew, without even

seeing her, she was frowning. That there was a little crease between her brows.

'I had it moved out of here before I came to Eastbury.' He hadn't wanted her to see it. He hadn't been sure if he could trust her. 'I'll have it brought back in in the morning.'

'Thank you.'

There was a creak on the stairs. She'd turned to go. 'Stefan?'

'Yes.' He heard the strain in his voice. He was still hoping she'd take the remaining steps down and come to him.

'Do you still believe my father will send his men here, after me?'

'Yes. I don't think he will let this lie.' There was a pause and then he softened. 'But you're safe here, Ædwen. And Ellan. I'll make sure of it.' Even though the weight of that responsibility lay heavy on his shoulders. 'No harm will come to either of you. I promise.'

Yet despite knowing Ædwen and Ellan were both under his roof, in his bed, secure, Stefan barely slept. It was as if his body was coiled like a tight spring, responding to Ædwen's nearness, tensing every time he heard a movement.

When he finally heard Ellan wake, gurgling away upstairs, he quietly climbed the steps. Ædwen was still fast asleep, her hair splayed out across the furs, her lips slightly parted, and he lifted his daughter up and away carefully so as not to disturb her mother.

He fed her and dressed her as usual, ready for Sister Margaret to collect her, and kissed her goodbye on the forehead. He had just closed the door and gone over to the basin to clean his wound, when Ædwen came tearing down the steps. He glanced over his shoulder. She looked aghast.

'Ellan!' she wailed, looking all around them, wide-eyed with fear.

'Is safe,' he said, dropping the cloth and walking towards her. 'Sister Margaret fetched her just now.'

Her shoulders sagged and her hand came across her heart, as his had last night, when he'd realised she hadn't left him. 'I thought… I thought the worst. That she'd been taken again…'

'I didn't mean to worry you.' Damn, he should have pre-warned her. He should have known she would have been upset to wake and find her gone.

She drew in a few breaths, calming herself, but frowned. 'Sister Margaret? Why?'

'Sister Margaret usually looks after Ellan for me during the day, while I'm on duty.'

She shook her head. 'But I'm here now. I can look after her.'

'It's good to keep to the routine.'

She stamped her foot on the ground, suddenly angry, taking him by surprise. 'Do I get any say in this? What about what I want? I'm her mother, Stefan, and I've only just got her back.'

He crossed his arms over his bare chest. 'And I'm her father and have been her sole carer this past month. And the Queen has requested an audience with you on a walk this morning, or have you forgotten? Ellan will be fine with Sister Margaret for a short while. You can fetch her when you're finished with the Queen. Besides, she's used to the woman. What's the problem?' he asked.

She gripped the wooden rail at the bottom of the stairs. 'I don't appreciate you making decisions about my daughter without me.'

He cocked an eyebrow at her. 'And if I hadn't done that, where would that leave us now?'

She swallowed, her body sagging, and he could see her cave. 'I'm scared something will happen to her. That she'll be taken from me again,' she whispered.

He held her gaze. 'I told you. I'm not going to let anything happen to her. Or to you.' He moved closer towards her. 'Did you get *any* sleep?' he asked, studying her features. She looked exhausted, her blue eyes puffy and her skin sallow, her hair beautifully tousled.

'Not much. I was afraid to close my eyes. I kept checking on her and...' She shook her head. 'Am I going crazy?'

He tipped his head to one side and grinned. 'Maybe a little.'

'I can't lose her again,' she said, adamant.

'You won't.'

She lifted her head to look up into his eyes. 'What if you decide to take her from me?'

He reared back slightly, offended. 'You think I would withhold her from you?' His brow furrowed. 'I would never do that, Ædwen.'

There was still so much distrust between them. He wondered, if this hadn't happened, if Ellan hadn't been taken from her, would Ædwen ever have told him about his daughter if he hadn't come to Eastbury and stopped the wedding? Would he ever have seen Ædwen again?

Yet frustratingly, despite everything, the past wasn't hindering his attraction to her now.

Suddenly, the air in the room became heavier. He became excruciatingly aware that they were alone, that she wasn't wearing her pinafore, just her tunic, her hardened nipples showing through the material... His body reacted with force. And by the way she was backing up the stairs, her huge eyes widening, roaming over his bare chest, he knew she felt it, too.

'Stefan,' she whispered in submission.

In two strides he was up the stairs, taking her in his arms at the top, his lips coming down on hers in frantic urgency, the pent-up frustration of lying awake all night, thinking about doing this, about kissing her, touching her again, making his movements fiercer than they perhaps should have been.

His hands came up into her hair, holding her head, tipping it back as his tongue pressed between her parting lips, and she moaned into his mouth in desperate, eager response, spurring him on. His own body ignited and he knew he couldn't be further from being in control. He didn't want to feel this way. And yet he couldn't stop.

He pulled away slightly to run the tip of his tongue along her jaw, the column of her throat, scorching her skin with his kisses, her knees buckling as he held her up, her eyelids half closed, as his lips trailed over her shoulders and down, where her tunic was loose at the collar.

And then his mouth was back on hers, his tongue plundering her lips once more, as she gripped on to his shoulders, helpless against his onslaught. He trailed his hand up her side, to curve over her breast, and he caressed her gently, stroking her through her tunic, the peak hardening, making her shiver. He delighted in the weight and feel of her before squeezing her too-soft flesh and she groaned.

He wanted her. Badly. It had been too long. 'Too many clothes,' he ground out, against her mouth. And with a savage fervour even he couldn't contain, his hands skated down over her hips and gripped the material of her tunic, raising it, rucking it up over her thighs, as he pushed his knee between her parted legs, gently lowering her down on to the bed, coming over her, his hard shaft nudging into her stomach.

Could she tell how much he wanted her? The need to touch her became desperate. He wanted to put his hands on her, everywhere. He wanted to be inside her, taking ownership of her body again.

Things were happening fast. She writhed beneath him, his naked chest pinning her down, her tunic bunched around her waist as his splayed fingers roamed up her bare thighs, seeking out her intimate places. Her breath stilled in anticipation of his touch before his hand slid between her legs, his thumb gently skimming over her tiny nub, and she gasped, before he pushed his finger deep inside her, and to his elation and surprise, she came apart—instantly—crying out into his shoulder in wonder and ecstasy.

His forehead against hers, he stared down at her, as he watched her fight for composure, struggling to get her heart rate back to normal. And it allowed him to claw back some of his own control, too.

'That was fast.' He grinned.

Her hand still on his shoulder, she looked up at him, uncertain, her cheeks flushed.

She bit her lip. 'It's been a while.'

He moved to lie beside her, retrieving his hand from between her thighs and using it to tuck her hair behind her ear.

Her gaze flicked over his chest, his ink…and she gripped his wrist. She turned it over in her hand, studying the new design.

'It is definitely a sun,' she said.

He had a feeling she'd been wanting to ask him about the design since she'd seen it in the alehouse. Why did she have to know everything about him? Still.

'Yes,' he said, taking her hand in his, entwining their fingers. 'The name Ellan…it means sun ray, doesn't it?'

She looked at him, startled, and he held her gaze. 'Yes. Is that why you got it?'

'Yes.'

She shook her head in wonder. 'You're a devoted father, Stefan.'

'How did you choose the name?' he asked.

'Because looking at her was like looking at this shining, beautiful thing. It seemed to suit her.'

'It does.' He nodded, then he pressed a kiss to her palm before lifting away from her, pulling her tunic back down her thighs, covering her up and coming off the bed. He took her hand again and tugged her up so she was sitting on the edge of the bed. 'I'd better get dressed. I have to go and meet the King…and you, you have a walk with Queen Emma.'

'I don't know what I will talk with her about.'

'Just be…honest.'

'I always am.' And then she looked at him, biting her lip. 'What about…? Don't you need…want…?' She frowned, blushing again.

He grinned. 'I want to possess you again, so badly, it's all I can think about, Ædwen. But I am prepared to wait till we have more time. Till I can have you properly. No distractions. Right now, I have to meet with Canute and my men.' He took her chin in his fingers and tipped her face up towards him. 'Come to my bed tonight.'

She inclined her head. 'You're very persistent,' she whispered.

'Actually, I'm very patient.'

## Chapter Ten

Standing waiting in the palace gardens, Ædwen had butterflies in her stomach. Would Queen Emma find her interesting company? She had lived such a sheltered life. She tried to think of some subjects they could talk about, to ease the conversation, but the biggest adventure she'd had in her life was Stefan. Even now.

She knew she had to be careful. Over the long two winters that they had spent apart, she'd kept reliving what had happened between them, going over and over it, wondering what she could have done differently, why he'd behaved how he did. Last night, the things he'd told her went some way to explaining his mistrust of her. Of women.

She knew he had fetched her from Eastbury for one reason alone—for her to be a mother to Ellan—and that even though he might desire her, once he had got what he wanted from her, he might leave her again, so she knew she should push him away before he had the chance to do so.

Yet she had somehow managed to end up in his arms again, in his embrace this morning, letting him touch her, intimately. And it had felt so incredible, to have his hands on her again, inside her, as he kissed her, she had come apart in mere moments. Knowing it would be wrong to take her pleasure and deny him his own satisfaction, she had tried to touch him in return, but he had a lot more control than she. Now he had told her to come to him tonight. How could she refuse, when she had already taken pleasure from him? She owed him…

Her stomach flared at the thought of falling into his arms again…in trepidation—and excitement. Could she really go through with it? There was a battle raging within her. She knew she should be protecting herself from further rejection and more disappointment; she needed to keep him at arm's bay. Yet when he was near, her body rebelled, not wanting that at all, wanting to draw him closer, to seek satisfaction in his arms, to take whatever he was offering her.

'My Lady Ædwen, it is a delight to see you again.'

Ædwen glanced up to see Queen Emma approaching. She looked refined, graceful—and formidable—in a high-necked cloak, her hair immaculately fixed. She noticed the Queen wasn't wearing a wimple, unlike herself. She would challenge Stefan on that one later.

'And you, Your Majesty.'

'You seemed lost in thought. I trust you are well today? You look far better than last night, if you don't mind me saying so. You have a bit of colour back in your cheeks.'

'Thank you, Your Majesty.'

'Let us walk this way. It is a little more secluded through here,' the Queen said, leading her through an arch in a hedgerow to a private orchard and vegetable garden, where they began to stroll through the trees. The guards hung back a little in the protected space, allowing them some privacy. 'I couldn't help but notice you left the feast early last night.'

'Yes, I'm sorry about that. I wasn't feeling myself, but I am much better today.'

'I'm very glad to hear it.'

The Queen began to point out some of her favourite winter blooms and Ædwen showed an interest in them, not having seen some of them before on the coast in Eastbury.

'I trust you are finding the palace accommodations comfortable and you have everything you need?'

'Yes, thank you, Your Majesty.'

The woman seemed to peer closer. 'And I am sure you are pleased to be reunited with your husband? He is a good man.'

Ædwen blushed and glanced away. Was there no escape from him? He seemed to be consuming her every waking thought. And now her conversations. She wasn't sure how she should respond, or what Stefan had told the King and Queen about their relationship, or lack of. Was she meant to make believe that they were in love? Or should she pretend that he meant nothing to her?

'Being reunited with my child, Ellan, is an absolute joy. And I'd like to say thank you for helping Lord Stefan and my daughter. I believe you have been very good to them both.'

The Queen stopped on the path. 'Oh, I am so pleased he told you,' she said, clasping her hands together. 'We weren't sure of the situation. We knew Stefan was leaving for Eastbury to fetch you, but none of us could be sure about your relationship with your child. He asked us to remain silent on the matter… I believe he had told only me and the King about it.'

Ædwen quickly relayed the situation to the Queen, about what her father had done, feeling she could confide in her, and Emma looked horrified. She placed a hand on her arm. 'Lady Ædwen, how awful. I know what torment it is to be separated from your child. My own three children from my first marriage have been sent across the sea, back to the French court in Normandy. Two beloved boys and one girl.'

Ædwen's heart went out to her. 'I am so sorry, Your Majesty. That must be a great suffering indeed.'

'It is a deep hurt. I miss them terribly.' She turned to look at Ædwen. 'I understand my husband's wishes. My children are a threat to his throne and not of his blood. And at least this way I know they are safe.' She continued to walk and Ædwen kept pace with her. 'Actually, I would like you to be one of the first people to know… I am with child again. Canute's child.'

Ædwen gasped. 'That is such happy news, Your Majesty. For you both and for the country. Congratulations.'

'Thank you. And I am hoping I shall have a friend in you, Lady Ædwen, to get me through these next few months.'

'I should like that, Your Majesty. Very much,' Ædwen said, smiling. 'Is the King pleased? He must be.'

'Oh, very. But he is eager for it to be a boy…'

'That is a lot of pressure. I guess I'm lucky I didn't have that,' Ædwen said, thinking what strain the Queen must be under to produce a male heir.

'If your child had been a boy, perhaps your father might not have been so cruel and might have allowed you to keep him?' the Queen suggested.

Ædwen pulled a face. 'Probably not. The child would still have been a half-Dane, whether it was a boy or girl.'

'There is nothing wrong with being a Dane. Your father is extremely short-sighted. Did you know my great-grandfather was the Northman warrior Rollo, the founder of Normandy?'

'I didn't, Your Majesty.' That would certainly explain a lot about Emma and her warrior-like stance.

'Go on. You may ask me the question I know you're burning to ask,' the Queen said to her, knowingly.

Ædwen's cheeks heated. 'I don't know what you mean, Your Majesty.'

'You want to know if I love him. Canute. Or if I married him to save my children's lives.'

'It is none of my concern, Your Majesty,' Ædwen said, shaking her head fiercely. 'Your decisions are your own and I would never judge you for them.'

'I know that. That's why I like you. And why I think we shall get on very well, Lady Ædwen. I should like a friend I can confide in. And one who isn't afraid to share their thoughts with me.' She moved a branch out of the way of the path and held it aloft so Ædwen could pass through.

'Thank you.'

'At first, I respected him. Canute. His battle tactics, his power and ruthlessness. He was a worthy foe. And then I was afraid for my children, unsure what he might do. But when I realised he wasn't cruel, when he kissed me, well...'

Ædwen smiled. She thought about the way Stefan had kissed her this morning. Fiercely. So passionately, it had taken her breath away. Her cheeks heated at the memory.

'Looking at your face, I'd say you know exactly what I mean.' The Queen smiled. 'I can tell you married for love, Lady Ædwen. And whatever troubles you and Lord Stefan had, I hope they are behind you. The truth is, I love my husband. Will you have more children, Lady Ædwen?'

She had never thought it possible…never thought a man would ever want her again. Had never thought she'd be with a man again. And now Stefan had told her to come to him tonight… Her treacherous heart leapt again in anticipation. Yet how could she even contemplate it? They couldn't risk bringing another child into this world when things were so uncertain between them. She couldn't believe she hadn't even thought about the consequences until now. She was such a fool. She would have to talk to Stefan, make him see reason, before things went too far again.

'I have only just got Ellan back. I would like to enjoy her for a while.'

The Queen's gaze flicked over her. 'And enjoy your husband, too, no doubt. Lord Stefan is a favourite of the King's, you know. And mine. Loyal and a formidable fighter. We are lucky to have him. As are you.'

Ædwen swallowed, her throat feeling thick with emotion.

'Did you know my husband was already married?' Queen Emma said. 'Before me?'

Ædwen looked up at her.

'To Ælfgifu, a noblewoman who was born here, in England. He put her aside for me, allowed to do so because it was a pagan marriage.'

Ædwen felt the flicker of alarm go off somewhere in

her body. Stefan had told her he had been married before. That they had been able to separate by their laws.

'She now lives in Denmark. And I am sure she must despise me,' the Queen continued.

'I am sure she understands the politics of the situation. That Canute needed to unite England. She doesn't need to know he couldn't help falling in love with you,' Ædwen said.

Queen Emma smiled at her. 'Thank you, Lady Ædwen. I needed to hear that.'

Ædwen was pleased she had reassured the Queen— she had known she would like the woman, she just hadn't realised how much. And yet, unwittingly, in return, Queen Emma's words had unsettled her deeply.

As she made her way to the monastery to fetch Ellan, her thoughts swirled like a hazy snowstorm in her mind. So the King had been allowed to put his first wife aside because it had been a pagan marriage, not recognised under Christianity.

Doubt exploded in her chest.

If Canute renounced one wife for another...if he had abandoned his first wife for a second, allowed to do so as his marriage had been a pagan one, what did that mean for her and Stefan? Theirs had not been a Christian marriage. They had merely whispered their vows to one another, binding their hands together...was it even a marriage at all?

Stefan knew all of this. He knew the King had disposed of his first wife. Stefan must know he could easily do the same if he tired of her. Despite his adamance that their union was legally binding, she knew now it didn't offer her the security that she would need to stay, or legitimacy for her child. She felt her old fears of abandonment resurging—the need to protect herself. She must not allow herself to fall for him again.

She tried to push her dark thoughts away as she headed into the monastery. She found Sister Margaret and Ellan, and let out the breath she'd been holding. Would she always feel this relief upon being reunited with her daughter, grateful to have her back? In a way, it made her feel strong enough to cope with anything else. Even Stefan...

Ædwen was pleased to see the kindly nun again. They embraced and the woman kept dabbing her eyes with a cloth. She was tearful, overjoyed that Ædwen had been reunited with Stefan and Ellan, but also repentant that she had kept the truth from her.

'I'm sorry I couldn't tell you. I was so afraid. Afraid of what Lord Manvil would do if he found out I'd lied, if he found out where I'd placed her...but I did not give up hope that you would be reunited with Lord Stefan and your daughter, Lady Ædwen.'

'It's all right, Sister Margaret. It is not your fault. And you did a wonderful deed, bringing her here to Stefan. I only wish to thank you for keeping Ellan safe,' Ædwen said, gripping the woman's hands tightly.

'Well, I just couldn't do what you father was asking me to do. I couldn't separate Ellan from you for ever. I hoped that Lord Stefan would find you. And I'm so pleased that he did. He is a wonderful man.'

People kept telling her that. She had thought so herself once and was in trouble of thinking so again. Yet he had proved she couldn't rely on him. Why should anything be different now? She mustn't put her trust in him, or pin her hopes on him. She must not let herself care for him again because it was at that moment, when you'd given someone your heart, that they dropped you, leaving you to wallow in misery.

She had felt the distance he'd put between them so acutely when he'd walked out of her life. She had spent days aimlessly walking the halls, regretting her choices, wondering where he was and if he'd ever come back to her. Sister Margaret had likened her symptoms to those of the local drunks, who were being forced to go without ale. It was like giving up a habit, suddenly and brutally. It had been agony. She never wanted to put herself through that again... And this time, she had so much more to lose if things went wrong.

No. She had to protect herself. She had to protect her child.

When Stefan arrived back at his rooms later that day, Ellan was screaming. He had spent the morning patrolling the walls, doubling up the men on each watchpoint and making sure they'd increased both the production of weapons and the training of his soldiers. And yet he hadn't been able to focus. His thoughts kept returning to Ædwen and he had decided to quickly check in on her.

A slight prickle of unease passed through him as he wondered if he was surreptitiously keeping track of her, needing to know what she was up to, as he still viewed her with distrust. Would he always feel as if he was looking for signs of deceit, trying to uncover lies she might have told, believing there must be more?

Yet the scene was not what he'd been expecting. Ædwen looked fraught, patting Ellan's back, swinging her in her arms, trying to settle her, but the ferocious crying continued.

He unclasped his belt, dropping his sword down into a basket, and came towards her.

'Everything all right?'

'Does it look all right?' she snapped, her hair dishevelled, her face flushed. 'She's been like this all afternoon, since I got back. She just won't stop crying. I've been through the list in my head. She's not too warm, or cold. I've offered her milk...and changed her. I've rocked her, walked her up and down the corridor and out in the cloisters. I've tried everything,' she said, desperate. 'I don't know what to do. I'm worried something is wrong with her.'

'Here,' he said. 'Let me take her. You look exhausted.'

'No, I'm fine,' she said, not wanting to admit defeat. She was far too stubborn and proud.

But when he reached for Ellan, she finally relented and allowed him to take their daughter into his arms. In an instant, the crying stopped. Peace descended on the room. Ellan gurgled and, moments later, she was fast asleep.

Ædwen looked up at him, forlorn, as he cradled their child. 'She wanted you,' she said in disbelief. 'That's what all this was about. She wanted you, not me.'

'I'm just more familiar right now.' He shrugged.

'But she was inconsolable.'

'She gets like that sometimes.'

She wrung her hands. 'Have I been away for too long?'

It had felt like aeons. 'Of course not,' Stefan said. 'Look, if I can do this, then you definitely can.'

He headed over to her crib on the far side of the room

and lowered Ellan into it. When he came back, he sat beside Ædwen on the bench. 'She'll get used to you again,' he said. 'It'll just take a while.'

He pulled her against his shoulder, running his hand up and down her arm, attempting to soothe her. But she bristled, her body stiffening, and she pulled away from him.

'Did you have a good day apart from this?' he said, frowning.

'Yes.'

'Queen Emma…?'

'All good.'

He could sense something was wrong. Something she wasn't telling him. Her answers were short and to the point. She was good at keeping things in, but he'd already told her he wouldn't stand for that. Not here. Not again.

'What's the matter?'

'Nothing,' she said, getting up and making herself busy, clearing the table.

'*My* day has been non-stop,' he said, trying to get her talking. 'We're looking to build up the fortifications of the city. We walked round the entire outskirts of the boundary, checking for weaknesses.'

She stopped what she was doing. 'Why? Does it have anything to do with my father?' she asked.

'It's just a precaution.' He shrugged. 'Your father has been a threat for a while.'

She nodded, letting that sink in.

'Hungry?' he asked. 'We could go out to the market and pick some things up.'

She frowned. 'What about Ellan?'

'It's a good job Sister Margaret adores her.' He grinned.

'No,' she said, shaking her head. 'You go. I'll stay and watch her.'

She glanced over into the crib, checking on Ellan again perhaps for the fourth time in so many moments. She was being obsessively concerned.

He frowned. 'No, we go together or not at all.'

'We don't have to spend every moment together, Stefan,' she bit, moving to walk past him.

He gripped her arm. 'Is everything all right?' he asked. 'You don't seem yourself.'

'I'm fine.'

What had got her so upset? Not Ellan crying? No, he felt sure it was something else.

'Well, if you're not going, I'll stay with you,' he said, smoothing his thumb across her wrist, offering her a dangerous, wicked smile. 'All alone again.'

Her eyes flared; her lips parted. She tugged her hand from his grasp, as if he'd burned her.

'Or we could take her with us...' he offered as an alternative.

She nodded, her face suddenly relaxing, relieved, appeased by his suggestion. 'Yes, let's do that.'

And it was good to get out. The sun was shining, despite the winter bite, and today the market was a different experience. With Ellan strapped to his chest, fast asleep, they strolled along the bustling streets, browsing the best stalls he could recommend.

They used some of his coin to buy wool and flax, which Ædwen said she could weave into clothing, but he insisted on exchanging some of his armbands to buy her an imported blue silk pinafore and a plain dark tunic of her own, so she didn't have to keep wearing Kendra's garments. She tried to stop him, saying she felt guilty about him spending his hard-earned coin, but he insisted. He proudly handed over the silver for the item and enjoyed presenting the clothes to her.

'Thank you,' she whispered, running her hands over the silk.

Next, they stopped by a few food stalls and Stefan spoke to the vendors, telling them Ædwen was new to Wintancaester, convincing them to let her try some of their produce, and they were only too pleased to indulge the King's chief commander.

When he'd arrived here last winter, he'd become reliant only on himself. It was hard, navigating a new place, new people, and he knew he stood out. A pagan among Saxons. He was different and they'd treated him as such. It was a relief to find Canute and other Danes. He'd been determined to make his old life across the ocean, and the one he'd made with Ædwen in Eastbury, a long-distant memory.

Now he'd made a name for himself and commanded respect among all the people. He was no longer an outsider. Everything had changed. Everything except his desire for this woman at his side.

He picked up a cube of cheese and offered it to her now. 'Try this,' he said and she leaned in, taking the morsel from his fingers and popping it hesitantly between her lips.

'Mmm...crumbly,' she said, smiling through the mouthful.

'Now this,' he said, passing her a cup of wine.

She took a sip and swallowed it down, offering him the cup to take some, too. 'Your turn.'

'Bit early for me, I'm still on duty.' He grinned. He was enjoying himself. He hadn't had this much fun in a long time.

'Now you've got to have this,' he said, taking her hand and pulling her with him to the next vendor.

'What is it?'

'Lemon pastry. A local delicacy.' He picked up a slice and held it up to her mouth and she shyly took a bite, licking the crumbs off her lips.

Her eyes widened.

'Sweet and sour. That's amazing and far too good to share with you,' she said, trying to take it from him, and he laughed. He was glad she'd got her smile back.

He was enjoying spending time with her, getting to know her anew. But it disturbed him that he was starting to like her again, so quickly. Had he ever stopped? While he wanted her in his bed again, he had vowed to himself that he would not lower his defences and give up his heart. He must remember how she had deceived him last time and he would not be fooled again.

But then he thought of this evening and his heart leapt in anticipation. He had told her to come to him and, if she did, he knew he wouldn't be able to deny himself. A thrill of excitement rushed through him and heat pooled in his groin.

'You know, I think that's the most I've seen you eat all week,' he said, raising his thumb to brush a crumb from her lips.

She swallowed. 'Well, you have to admit this sugary

lemon thing is better than that woman's pottage in the alehouse,' she said.

He frowned, thinking back to that evening. 'That must have been hard for you, seeing that woman with child, what with the trauma you were suffering. Now I understand your reaction. But in that moment, I was cross with you, wondering why your face was like one of my wooden carvings.'

'There were reminders everywhere I went...'

She came up to Ellan in his arms and stroked a finger down her cheek, then looked up at him. 'Now we've been reunited, I just want to be a good mother,' she said. He was struck by her openness and honesty. Her vulnerability. And that he believed her, about this at least.

'Come on. Let's head back. Canute will be wondering where I am and I think it's going to rain.'

She looked up at the dark clouds and nodded in response.

But as they made their way back to the palace, she seemed distracted, glancing about, looking for something, or someone.

'Everything all right?' he asked.

He peered closer. Her face had turned ashen.

'I thought I saw...' She frowned, then shook her head. She looked all about them one more time. 'No, it's nothing. I must be imagining things.'

'Saw who?' he asked, stopping in the street, just as the clouds burst and the rain began to pelt down on them, soaking them to the bone.

'It's just... I thought I saw my mother.'

# Chapter Eleven

'Are you sure it was her?' Stefan asked, as he handed her a tankard of ale.

They had dropped Ellan off with Sister Margaret, Stefan telling her that was the evening routine until he was finished at the King's feast each night. This time, Ædwen hadn't dared argue. She would go along with it if Ellan was happy. She had learned her lesson about breaking the routine. And she trusted Sister Margaret, wholeheartedly. She was still apprehensive as Stefan led her away, but she knew it was just nerves. Normal feelings for when a mother left her child. Nothing sinister was going to happen.

'No.' She took the cup, her hands trembling.

It had certainly looked like her mother. For a moment, the flash of blonde hair and side profile of her face had stirred something within her. But it was impossible, wasn't it? But then she had thought she might find her daughter here—was it so far-fetched to imagine her mother might live here in the city, too? But what were the chances?

So much had happened these past few days. Her world had been turned upside down. The ruined wedding seemed like an age away and thank goodness it hadn't come to pass. She couldn't believe she had almost gone through with it. Her life would have been over.

Instead, she had come on a journey here with Stefan, imprisoned in his arms. She thought back to that skirmish at the alehouse…and that kiss. She'd met the King, become friends with the Queen and was overjoyed to have been reunited with her child again.

She was afraid to admit to herself that she liked being here. She liked Wintancaester. She liked the people. And she liked being with Stefan. More than she should. She was enjoying spending time with him again. Out there at the market, it had been almost as if they were a real family. But she mustn't do that. She mustn't forget he had brought her here because of Ellan. Because he'd felt he had to.

And now, she thought she'd seen her mother again. It had rocked her.

Images of the final night she'd seen her crept into her head. Her mother had tucked her into bed, kissing her goodnight on her forehead. It was the last time she'd gone to sleep content, feeling safe, until she'd met Stefan. When she'd woken, her father had announced over their morning meal that her mother had gone. That he didn't know where she was, but she wouldn't be coming back, so the quicker she got used to it, the better. He had been so cold, so matter of fact, uncaring that her heart had been breaking.

She didn't want to believe what he was telling her and she felt he was most certainly to blame. It was one of the only times Ædwen had dared to raise her voice at him, shouting that she didn't believe him before pushing away her food and bolting from the room. She had locked herself away for days, wallowing in her misery, unable to comprehend that her mother had abandoned her. Why hadn't she taken her with her?

Seeing that woman in the market, who looked so much like her mother, had reminded her of those traumatic days and, teamed with learning from the Queen about the ease with which hers and Stefan's marriage could be dissolved, it heightened Ædwen's fears. Because he could leave her, too. *Again.* So easily…

'Would you like me to ask around, to find out if anyone is aware of her living here?' Stefan asked, his hands on his hips, peering down at her.

She shook her head. 'No. I'm guessing even if she is here, she doesn't want to be found. That she wouldn't want to see me.'

And it hurt.

'That's how I felt about you,' she blurted, unable to help herself, her emotions getting the better of her. 'I thought that you should know about the baby, but I didn't think you'd want me to find you, after you left.' She took a deep breath. 'But I never stopped thinking of my mother. And I never stopped thinking of you, Stefan.'

He stared down at her, perhaps shocked by her sudden announcement. His mouth pressed together in a hard line. 'I imagine it was difficult not to with my child growing inside you,' he said.

They still hadn't spoken of what had happened that day. They hadn't properly discussed what hurt it had caused them both and she thought it was time they did.

'Stefan, there's things we haven't spoken about… about what happened back in Eastbury.'

He visibly tensed beside her and drew a hand over his beard. 'Ædwen, I don't want to discuss it,' he warned. 'It should stay in the past, where it belongs. I don't see the point in bringing up old wounds.'

'But we must!' she said, her hands outspread. 'If we never talk about them, how can they ever heal? There are things I want to explain,' she said. 'Things I want you to know.'

'Another day maybe,' he said and picked up her fingers, studying them. 'You've stopped biting your nails. They've grown in the past two days,' he observed.

She knew he was changing the subject, trying to distract her. Then, to her surprise, he plucked a little silver band from his tunic and pushed it down on to her finger. Her wedding ring finger.

'I got it at the market, while you were browsing the silk and wools. I thought that we should make it official,' Stefan said. 'It looks strange, us continuing to tell people you're my wife when you're not wearing a ring.'

Her breath hitched and she twirled the trinket on her finger, studying it warily. 'It's beautiful,' she said. 'And you're right—we really ought to keep up appearances. We must make it look like a genuine marriage,' she said cynically.

His eyes narrowed on her. 'That *is* what it is,' he said.

She wished it was, she realised now. He was her first love. Her only love. The father of her child. This was what she had always wanted—yet she had heard the resigned tone of his voice again. As if he thought that this was just the right thing to do. She felt her heart crumble…because she wanted him to say they must marry because he couldn't live without her. That he loved her. That he always had.

The ring only made her want to talk about the past even more.

'Stefan,' she pressed, 'I know what it is like to lose a parent. I miss my mother desperately. I know the grief you must feel at having lost your father, your brothers… and I'm so sorry.'

His whole body seemed to clench and his hands bunched into fists at his sides.

'I'm sorry I didn't tell you about my father being the one who—'

He pulled away from her, almost violently. 'I told you, I don't want to discuss it. I do not want to talk about your father, Ædwen. And I do not want to talk about that day.'

'But we have to,' she said, standing to meet him. 'You know we do. Because until we talk about it, you're always going to hold it against me. You're never going to trust me. You won't ever forgive me, like you couldn't forgive Dania.'

Instantly, she knew she'd said the wrong thing.

His features froze, his eyes blazed.

Yet she couldn't seem to stop. 'But don't you see it is hard for me to trust you also?'

He stepped towards her, glowering at her. He was so close. 'What?'

'I want to. I want to believe you won't leave me again. Abandon me. Like you did before, like my mother, when I needed you most.'

'That's what you think I did?'

'Yes. You didn't even hear me out. You just left.'

'And do you think that it was easy for me? Leaving you and coming here?' he said, his voice vibrating with rage.

'I don't know, you tell me.'

'It wasn't. Trauma extends far beyond the brutality of battle, Ædwen. Do you not think I didn't wonder, every day, why I had survived and my family hadn't? Did you not think I felt the emptiness of their loss in every single breath I took?'

She had never seen him so angry. He was furious, but then so was she.

'And then I lost you, too. I discovered you'd deceived me—'

'You judged me so quickly. You didn't give me a chance to explain. I think you owe me that, Stefan.'

His blistering blue gaze stared down at her, his features hard. 'Do I?' he said, his hands on his hips. 'Why? We both know what happened…why talk about it further, go over it again? It's not going to change anything. It's not going to change the fact you lied to me.'

But he was wrong. It might change everything. Why was he being so stubborn? He wouldn't hear her out back then and he was refusing to do so now, too. Suddenly, she felt incensed with him and this whole situation.

'Did you know the King was married before?' she said, her eyes burning up at him.

His brow furrowed, as if unsure of her change in conversation. 'Of course.'

'I think the Queen is worried Ælfgifu, his first wife, will come back and try to claim her throne.'

'I'm sure Canute won't allow that,' he said.

'I'm just trying to get my head round it, though,' she said, her eyes flaring. 'If it's acceptable for Canute to put aside his first wife, as they had a pagan handfasting ceremony…'

Realisation dawned; she saw it in his eyes.

'Well, I was just thinking, if that is the case, our marriage must also have no binding power, no validity, either… This ring won't change that. And you know it,' she said, pointing a finger into his chest, jabbing him with it. 'You knew ours wasn't a legitimate marriage, didn't you? And so did my father. He was right. Yet you stormed into the church the other day with your soldiers, declaring it real, saying you were there by order of the King, giving my father no choice but to let you take me.'

A muscle flickered in his jaw and he stepped towards her.

'I'm getting tired of this. Why are you still arguing whether we are husband and wife or not? As far I see it, we've said our vows and, whether it was under the eyes of my gods or yours, we meant them at the time.'

*At the time.*

She tilted her chin up towards him. 'You might see it that way. But no one else will ever see it as a real marriage, will they?' she said.

'So would you rather I hadn't turned up? Would you rather I'd let you go ahead with your *proper* Christian wedding to Lord Werian, let him take you to his bed and for you to never find out I had Ellan?'

'No!'

'Exactly,' he said. 'It's not as if you wanted to marry Lord Werian. So what is the problem?'

'The problem is you lied to me. You brought me here anyway, despite our union not being seen as valid. To live in sin.'

'Is that so bad?' He smirked darkly. 'You seemed to enjoy it this morning.'

But she was having none of it. She placed her hands on her hips. 'If Ælfgifu can be cast aside when a better offer came along for Canute, what's stopping you from doing the same? What's stopping me from doing that to you?' she said.

Any trace of a smile wiped off his face. 'So that's what you want, is it? Where this is heading. For our marriage not to be valid, so you can escape me, leave me and take Ellan with you?'

'I'm sure you'd be relieved to be released from your duty.'

She turned her back on him and went to walk away.

But his rage was palpable.

He reached out and gripped her wrist, swinging her back round, and hauled her to him, bringing her right up against him.

'What if I told you I don't want you to leave? That I don't want to be released from my duty? Because I want you, need you, desperately. And despite everything you're saying, I know you want me, too.'

She pushed at his chest, fighting him, trying to turn away from him, still angry, but he tugged her back into his body, his arms capturing her waist, tightly, so she couldn't escape, and he crushed her mouth with his. The moment his lips met hers, all reasonable thought fled, and nothing else mattered any more. She relented, succumbing to his touch. Her whole body softened, sagging against him, her tongue meeting his in his mouth, greedily exploring him, deeply. All she could think was that she wanted this. His mouth on hers. His hands on her body. He was right, she wanted him.

When he pulled away, they were both gasping for breath.

'Admit it. I need to hear you say it,' he whispered. 'Or I'll walk away, leave you in peace, right now.'

She knew she couldn't deny it any longer and she relented. 'Yes, I want you,' she admitted, a torrent of longing tearing through her blood. 'There, are you happy now?'

He smiled slowly. 'Now was that so hard?'

But to her despair, he took a step back. She had told him she'd wanted him to get closer, not further away.

He ran his hand down her arm, taking her hand in his, a smile playing at the corner of his lips as he tugged her with him towards the door. 'Come with me. I want to show you something,' he said.

'Now?' she asked.

He grinned. 'Yes.'

He gripped her fingers tightly and pulled her down the corridor, and she wondered where he was taking her. She told herself not to be disappointed that he hadn't continued kissing her. That he hadn't picked her up and carried her upstairs to his bed. That this was for the best.

'Where are we going?' she asked.

'You'll see.'

He led her down some winding steps, to rooms underneath the far side of the palace. The grey stone floors soon turned into colourful mosaics and marble statues of past kings decorated the corridor. Then the corridor opened out on to a huge green pool of steaming water. There was a beautiful domed roof, and she gasped at the incredible sight.

'A gift from the Romans,' Stefan said. 'Another perk of living in the palace. These are the King and Queen's private baths. The water is heated by natural springs.'

'It's incredible,' she said. The steaming water looked so inviting, a brilliant glimmering green.

'I thought you might want to bathe before the feast tonight.'

At home in Eastbury, she was used to bathing in the sea, or the river. Very rarely, on special occasions when she was little, her mother would organise for her to have a bath in a barrel filled with steaming water. This was something else.

'But are we allowed?' she asked, looking around at the grand arches and colonnades that led off into other areas.

'Yes, I asked for permission.'

'The King really likes you, doesn't he?'

'I'm a likeable man,' he said, winking. 'You can have the place to yourself for a while,' he said, releasing her hand. 'You deserve this, Ædwen. Take some time to relax.'

But she gripped his fingers tight. 'No. Don't leave. Stay,' she said, looking up at him.

'Ædwen...'

'Don't leave me down here on my own,' she said. 'Please.'

He nodded, relenting, and then he gave her the courtesy of turning round. 'Get undressed. Let me know when you're in, beneath the water,' he said. 'That first step down feels amazing.'

She fumbled with the brooches of her pinafore, her fingers trembling. She wasn't sure why. Was it because she was taking her clothes off when he was so close by? Then she quickly dropped the garment to the floor, while pulling off the tunic beneath. She lay it down on a stone bench, being especially careful as it was Kendra's, not her own.

Stefan still had his back to her as she stepped down into the pool and sank beneath the water. It felt glorious, just as he'd said, and so good to wash away the dirt and grime from the past few days. She dipped her head beneath the water and rose up, feeling amazing.

She waded over to the side of the pool and put her arms on the side, looking up at him. 'Aren't you coming in?'

He turned around and looked down at her, stroking the back of his neck. 'Do you want me to?'

'You can stay over that side, can't you?' she said, raising her eyebrow.

His eyes narrowed on her. 'If I take my clothes off and get in there with you, that won't happen.'

She swallowed.

He put his hand to the base of his tunic and hauled it off, keeping his heated gaze on her. He discarded the tunic on the floor. She felt like this was another test and she was going to fail.

And then he put his hand to the waistband of his breeches. 'Are *you* going to turn around?' he asked. 'Or do you want to watch?'

She gasped, shocked she was still staring up at him, mesmerised, taking in his magnificent body. She turned around immediately.

He chuckled softly, then she heard him wading through the water, him coming up close behind her. Too close.

She swallowed. 'I thought you were going to stay over there.'

'That was never going to happen and you knew it,' he said.

He pressed his body up against her back and she gasped. He brought his hands up round her front, to cup her breasts, and drew her up against him. She tipped her head back as he kneaded her flesh. She could feel him, pressed up against her buttocks, and she was shocked at the sudden intimacy. How easily he'd got her naked in his arms. How fast things were spiralling. And she tried to fight for some kind of restraint.

But she had told him she wanted him. There was no going back from that.

His mouth came down on her shoulder, pressing soft kisses to her neck, her jaw, the tops of her swollen breasts, and every touch of his lips sent a spiral of heat down between her legs. She moaned softly, then turned her head, so he could claim her mouth again. She loved the feel of his firm lips on hers, his tongue inside her mouth, seeking, plundering. The kiss went on and on and she brought up her hands to hold the back of his head, while his hands stole down to hold her hips firmly, his fingers splaying out across her stomach.

When he eventually tore his lips from hers, his voice was hoarse. 'What was the word you used earlier? Obligation…?' he asked. His hand stole down and curved over her mound, her damp curls, and her legs parted willingly under the water, allowing him to push his finger deep inside her. She whimpered. 'Do you think this an obligation, Ædwen? Or purely for pleasure?' he teased her.

But as if he knew she couldn't take much of that sweet torture, perhaps worried this would all be over too fast, he began to move her hips, twisting her.

'Turn around. Let me see you,' he said, his voice rasped.

Was he struggling, the way she was, to retain control?

Bravely, she turned fully in his arms, the glistening water waist-deep, and she stepped away, letting him look at her. She felt the colour climb in her cheeks, but she forced herself to keep her hands down by her sides. His hungry gaze raked over her. She was suddenly acutely aware that her body had changed. That her breasts were bigger, but softer, not as firm as they once were. And her stomach... Would he be disappointed?

'You're even more beautiful than I remember,' he said. 'Stunning.'

And she drank him in, too. She stepped towards him. She brushed her fingers over the smooth skin that covered the hard muscles of his chest, trailing over the dark, swirling ink markings she had traced before.

One of them, she remembered, he'd called Laguz— the rune of water, travel and love. She recalled him saying he loved the possibilities the ocean offered, as he'd believed it had brought him to her.

Her eyes fell upon his wound. 'Is it all right?' she asked. 'In the water?'

'It's fine. You did a good job.'

As they faced each other, chest to chest, her breathing was rapid, her breasts rising and falling.

'Come here,' he said.

She took another step towards him.

'Closer, Ædwen.'

And when she pressed herself up against him, his arm came around her waist, holding her tight, dragging her right up against his body. She could feel him, right there, his hard, silky shaft against her thigh, the water lapping against them, engulfing them both. He pushed his knee between her legs, binding her to him, and kissed her again, fiercely.

She couldn't believe she was naked in his arms again. She had allowed him to touch her again so easily. But then, she had never been able to resist him.

He picked her up, walking her back to the steps, and he lay her down on them, so she was half out of the water. He came over her, kissing her, his mouth roaming down to steal over her chest, lathering her wet breasts, licking and kissing and sucking the peaks to glorious, aching life. He made every part of her body come alive and she wanted him to touch her again, where he'd touched her this morning.

His head stole lower, his mouth planting hot kisses over her stomach, and she cringed at the little silvery lines there, from when she was carrying Ellan and her skin was stretched to the limit. She brought her hands up, trying to cover herself up, the water lapping at her thighs, but he gripped her wrists, pressing them down either side of her on the steps. His tongue trailed over her hips, over her little birthmark he'd been fascinated by all those many months ago, then he went lower and her whole body tensed in anticipation.

Surely he wasn't going to...?

He was!

Her thighs parted spontaneously and his mouth hovered over her wet curls and the intimate places below.

She scrambled up on to her elbows, trying to back away from him and the exquisite intimacy, the indecency, but he held her thighs fast.

'Let's see if we can make it last a little longer this time,' he said, his blue gaze staring up at her through the steam rising off the water.

Her pulse leapt wildly and all she could do was surrender. She tipped her head back and let him dip his head and kiss her, explicitly, where she'd never been kissed before. It was a gentle kiss, the lick of his tongue curling around her sensitive flesh, and she cried out in wonder. It was so unexpected.

She never knew that it could feel so good. Was it even allowed? He had never done this to her before. But she knew, now he had, she never wanted him to stop.

His lips opened wider to taste her and her face burned with the tenderness of it, his tongue swirling over and around her, his soft strokes driving her wild. The pleasure was blinding, building, bubbling over. She couldn't believe the sensations he was creating. She couldn't believe she was letting him do this. Kiss her. Like this. There.

His hands came beneath her to hold her buttocks, lifting her up to him, pressing her closer, his beard grazing her skin, his tongue becoming more insistent, intensifying the sensations. She gasped at the thrill that rushed through her body and she cried out, the pleasure of her climax suddenly torn from her lips, reverberating around the chamber. He came up and over her, holding her by the waist, until the spasms stopped rocking through her body.

He pulled her body down, deeper, dragging her totally

beneath the surface, and he kissed her on the mouth underneath the water. When they came up, breathless, he laughed and it was infectious. She laughed, too, without restraint, pushing the water out of her eyes. He pulled her back into his arms, kissing her nose, her lips…and she knew…she must touch him back. It was only fair.

Her hand stole down between them, to take hold of him, wrapping around him. But he rested his forehead against hers and stalled her fingers.

'Not here,' he whispered. 'I told you when we do this, I want all of you. I won't settle for less. Tonight…'

# Chapter Twelve

Stefan and the King were late for the feast. They had been busy meeting with the ealdormen of the neighbouring burghs, trying to rally support should Lord Manvil's army attack. There had been rumours that his force was on the move and all the settlements between Wintancaester and Eastbury had been warned.

Stefan thought about Ædwen. He struggled to reconcile how such an evil man, a man who had killed his family, had produced such a beautiful daughter. A woman he struggled to keep his hands off, despite knowing what blood she had flowing through her veins.

He had been livid with her earlier, after the market, when she had questioned their marriage again and when she had threatened to leave him. His anger had transmuted into desire and he had wanted to lift her skirts, wrap her legs around his waist and thrust into her. Hard. He had wanted to claim her again, at long last, and show her he was her husband. That she belonged to him. And that she would never be able to escape him.

He couldn't understand why she kept fighting him on it. Why was she trying to find fault with everything?

Why was she trying to get away from him—like Dania—when he had never wanted another woman other than her?

But he knew if she was going to leave him, he couldn't let her go without having her first. Tonight.

When they entered the hall, he saw her, sat at the table they'd been seated at last night, surrounded by his men. Dressed in the new garments he had bought her, she looked stunning. And he wished he had chosen something less striking, for the soldiers were all fawning over her, leaning in to speak to her, and she laughed shyly at something one of them said.

Jealousy seared through him.

All evening, he hadn't been able to stop thinking about her rising out of the water, like some goddess, her swollen breasts and hardened peaks tempting him to touch her, everywhere. When he'd come up behind her in the water, she'd come alive under his exploring fingers. She'd pressed herself against him as if to prove she wanted him and writhed against him as if she needed satisfaction... And he'd wanted to give it to her. He'd never wanted anything so much.

When he'd seen her sprawled naked beneath him on the steps, the water lapping at her thighs, he had known he wanted to taste her with his tongue. It had been intimate, a private moment between them, and he had never wanted it to end. But now he wanted to take her body with his own. He couldn't wait much longer.

As he stalked towards her, her eyes rose to meet him and her cheeks flushed.

The men caught the look between them and instantly moved back, making room for him, knowing she was his.

'You're not wearing your wimple,' he bit out, as he lowered himself down beside her.

'No, I'm following the fashions of the Queen.'

'But how will people know you're taken?'

'Luckily, I have your ring.' She smiled sweetly.

The atmosphere in the room was different tonight. The voices more shrill, as if they were all aware an army was looming, heading their way. He felt tense, or was that just because he knew that tonight he and Ædwen had a date with destiny?

'How long do you think we have, before the army from Eastbury arrives?' one of his men asked, from the other side of the table.

He felt Ædwen tense beside him.

'We think they'll be here within the week.'

She swung to look at him. As if she had no idea. He wasn't surprised. He had tried to keep it from her, knowing she would worry, knowing she would feel responsible.

But she had to know this would have happened whether he'd come to fetch her or not. This was who her father was.

She barely spoke to him for the rest of the meal, until the King and Queen retired and the men and women began to leave the room. Finally, during a quiet moment, she turned on him, her tone accusatory. 'Why didn't you warn me?' she said. 'Why didn't you tell me my father was on his way?'

'Because I didn't want you to worry.'

'You accuse me of keeping secrets from you, but then

you do the same! When will they be here? And what does he want?'

'To kill me, I expect,' he said wryly. 'And to claim you back. But his greater goal has always been the crown. To rid the English throne of a Danish king.'

'Surely he's not that ambitious?'

'Do you not know him at all?' he accused.

'No, obviously I don't,' she said, standing suddenly and going to leave the table.

He stood to meet her, gripping her arm. 'Going somewhere?' he asked.

She swallowed. 'Yes, I want to go to bed,' she said, dragging a hand over her face.

'Is that an invite?' He smirked.

And she looked up at him, wary.

He relented, deciding to go easy on her. 'Tired?' he asked and she nodded.

He wondered if she was afraid. After all, this shimmering thing between them was pretty terrifying. It was a big step to take, to sate themselves in each other's bodies, after the hurt they'd both suffered at each other's hands before. Hell, she'd broken him. Completely destroyed him. Could he really survive her a second time?

Yet what choice did they have? This burning need only had one cure.

He took her hand in his. 'Come on, let's get you back,' he said.

They walked in silence through the palace, his fingers wrapped around hers, and when they reached the corridor that led back to his rooms, he stalled.

'Shall I go and fetch Ellan?' he asked. He was giving

her time. Time to make her decision. He told himself if she said yes, he would just have to be patient.

But when she slowly shook her head, drawing her lip between her teeth, his heart began to clamour.

He didn't recall unlocking the door, or ushering her inside his room. He was only aware of the door closing, shutting the rest of the world out, and in one swift movement he swung her round, backing her up against the door, his tongue stealing its way inside her mouth again, and she groaned. It was a powerful, lingering kiss, and one that conveyed their desire. What they both knew was going to happen. What they needed from each other. Every moment seemed to have led to this.

Ædwen's head tipped back and Stefan took the opportunity to move his mouth down the column of her throat, leaving a hot trail of kisses across her skin and over her collarbone.

She pulled away slightly, her eyes bright, her cheeks flushed, and for a heart-stopping moment he thought she was going to stall him.

But instead, she reached for him, placing her hand on his chest. 'How do I take this off?' she said, running her hands over the thick material of his mail coat.

His pulse started up again at double the pace. Lust licked his groin. She wanted this, just as much as him. He took a step away from her and put his hand to his top button, undoing it and the next, peeling the chainmail off him and discarding it on the floor.

She came back towards him, tugging at his tunic, pulling it out of his breeches and up, over his head. Bare-chested, he caught her against him again, trapping her hands between them, and her fingers spread out across his skin, as she looked at him in wonder. His lips came back to hers, finding the trail he'd left before. She arched her throat and his tongue swirled over the top swells of her breasts.

'You're wearing too many clothes, Ædwen. I need to see you. To kiss you. Everywhere,' he said, his voice hoarse. And his trembling hands came down to loosen the brooches at the base of her pinafore straps, letting them fall, the material pooling at her feet. It was so beautiful, it was a shame to take it off, yet he knew the real treasure lay beneath. Gripping her tunic, sliding it up over her thighs, her waist, he lifted her arms up above her head and pulled it off, then it was gone.

Naked before him, she shivered and he took a step back, looking at her in heated admiration.

'Stefan,' she whimpered, pressing her thighs together.

'What? I'm allowed to look at you. You're my wife.'

His one hand came up to cup her breast and he loved the feel of her soft, silky skin, the weight of her in his hand, as he gently caressed her in his palm. He dipped his mouth to suckle her rosy tip and she held his head, combing her fingers through his hair, wanting more. His other hand ruthlessly, wickedly, roamed down, threading through her intimate curls, curving over her, his fingers trembling in urgency as he lightly grazed her moist, secret places.

Her knees buckled, her body quivered and he knew she couldn't take much of that sweet torture.

'Stefan... I don't think I can stand,' she whispered. 'Please...'

Worried this would all be over too fast, he removed his hand from between her legs and scooped her up, into his arms, and she gave a little yelp as he made his way towards the stairs. When he got to the top, he lowered her down on to the bed and came over her naked body. His heart thumped wildly in his chest. It was finally going to happen, he was finally going to have her. She was back in his bed, beneath him.

He had waited so long for this that, now the moment was here, it felt huge.

'You want this? You want me?' he asked. He needed to be sure.

'Yes,' she whispered, staring up at him.

It was the only word he'd wanted to hear.

Wrapping one arm around her waist, he lifted her, dragging her upwards on the furs, as he came down on top of her.

She looked up at him, into his eyes, as she reached for the waistband of his breeches. With fumbling fingers, she loosened the tie, the material coming away, and his breath caught at the anticipation of her touch.

'Your wound,' she said. 'Am I hurting you?'

'It's so far from my mind right now. Ædwen, touch me.'

She slipped her fingers beneath his breeches to take hold of him, gripping him in her palm, and he groaned, resting his forehead against hers.

He kicked off the material, and carefully lowered himself to the side of her, taking her jaw in his hand and bringing her face to his, kissing her, passionately.

His fingers trailed over her body, exploring her, over her thrusting swollen breasts, circling the pebble-hard peaks, which were darker now than they had been before. They were a beautiful plum colour and they looked good enough to eat. He lowered his head to take one in his mouth, tugging it between his teeth, testing, teasing her, dragging his tongue playfully around the tip, and she writhed beneath him.

His palms flattened over her stomach, and down, parting her thighs again, and he touched her with precision, finding her soaking, rolling her little nub beneath his fingers, and she whimpered, spreading her legs wider, letting him push his fingers inside her. He loved that she grew wetter with desire for him.

Her head tipped back on the furs and, by the sounds of her soft sighs, he knew she was close. And so was he. He'd overestimated his control and he wasn't even inside her yet.

She squeezed him harder in her hand, moving her fingers up and down the length of him, and he wasn't sure how much more of it he could take.

'Ædwen, stop,' he said, in whispered torment. 'You've made me wait too long for fulfilment. If you carry on, this will be over before I've even got started. And there's so much I want to do to you...'

He reared over her body, moving his knees between her thighs, pushing her legs wide apart, and she looked up at him, wrapping her hands around his neck, bringing him down towards her.

'I want to take you every which way. And I want to make you sore, so you know where I've been. I want you to feel branded by my touch. And I want you begging for more...'

He brought his hand down between their bodies, taking his shaft in his hand, tilting himself towards her, gliding it along her crease, opening her up to him. He was straining against her entrance. And he felt hot, feverish. He could feel her heartbeat thudding against his chest, or was that his? And all he could think was he was about to take possession of her again. At last.

With an intensity Ædwen wasn't expecting, Stefan entered her, piercing her flesh with one smooth thrust, and she cried out in pleasure at the breach, burying her head in his shoulder. He felt huge, even better than she remembered.

He captured her hands in his, holding them above her head, forcing her to look at him, as he stared down at her.

'Are you all right?'

'Yes,' she said. 'You feel good. I'd forgotten how good.'

She could not hold back. Not now. He must not know she was afraid. It would make her vulnerable.

'Forgotten? Then I'd better make this a night you'll never forget.' He grinned.

He thrust again, deeper, penetrating her body fully with his. Her head tipped back and he bent his mouth to her neck, covering her skin in open-mouthed kisses.

She writhed beneath him, bringing her legs up to wrap around his hips, allowing him to sink deeper, and he groaned against her throat. Their bodies pressed against each other, slick with sweat. He surged inside her, seeking, needing greater satisfaction, all that she could give.

Her arms came up to his shoulders, clinging on for support. Her breath quickened against his neck, her fingers clinging on to him for dear life, and he began to move faster, harder. He was in so deep it was as if they were joined, like one.

As he stormed her, over and over again, she screamed in feverish, panting pleasure, thrashing about wildly beneath him. She felt a swell of emotion bloom within and, as his mouth came down on hers, kissing her fiercely on the lips, their tongues meshing, her powerful climax took over. Shudders of contentment racked her body and, as he pulled out of her, he roared out his own intense release.

Ædwen lay there, underneath him, trying to get her breathing back to normal. Her thoughts were splintered. It had been incredible. Passionate. All she could have wished for and more. Yet…he had pulled out at the last moment.

He had said he would not take her until he could have the whole of her. And she had surrendered her whole self, uninhibited. But despite his anger, his urgent need, he had been more controlled. Careful.

Did that mean he hadn't lost enough of himself to come apart inside her? And ridiculously, she felt a lump grow in her throat.

In the moment, she hadn't even thought of the consequences of their actions. Again. She had just wanted… and she would have let him do anything to her. But he had remembered. He had been cautious.

But wasn't that a good thing? She should be glad that one of them had been sensible enough to think about the repercussions of their lovemaking. They certainly weren't in a position to have another child. They weren't even sure of each other.

So why then did it bother her? Was it because like so many other things, they hadn't discussed it first? Or because she felt as if he'd held a part of himself back, when she'd given him everything?

She didn't know how long they lay like that, neither of them moving, before finally he shifted, rolling off her on to his side and turning to face her. Through her own half-closed eyes, she could see him watching her from underneath his lashes, his large, possessive hand cradling her breast. It felt like real intimacy, but was it?

Was he as shaken as she was by the intensity of what had just happened?

'Are you all right?' he asked finally, his voice gravelly and warm.

She nodded, tears threatening. She didn't know what was the matter with her. She felt overwhelmed. By him? With her feelings?

How had she let this happen? She had told herself she would not allow herself to be seduced by him again. She had been determined to protect herself. Yet who was she fooling? She had been ecstatic the instant he had walked into that church, back into her life.

*Be honest*, a little voice inside her head mocked her. *You wanted this to happen from the start.*

And perhaps that was true.

But lying here, in his arms now, she wondered if it was really possible for them both to move past what had happened before. She wasn't sure, especially if he refused to even talk about it.

She went to sit up, to get away, but he gripped her hand, fast, tussling with her, pinning her back down on the bed, clamping her hands down above her head.

'Don't even think about leaving. Not after what we just did.'

'Stefan…'

'What?'

She relented and he loosened his grip on her a little.

'Where do you want to go? I told you… I want you every which way. I haven't finished with you yet.'

Their eyes connected, blue on blue.

And his mouth met her lips, his legs entwining with hers, his body coming over her again, and when he lifted his head, her breathing was unsteady once more.

'What's wrong?' he asked.

'Nothing,' she said, shaking her head on the furs, her mouth pressed together.

'Then why are you so eager to get away from me?'

'I'm not.'

'Good. Because just as soon as I get my breath back, we're going to do that again. And again. And again,' he said, kissing her on her lips, her jaw. 'Does that sound all right to you?'

He dipped his head to the curve of her neck and his mouth went in hot pursuit of her breasts, kissing over her chest, and she moaned as he lathered her nipples with his tongue, until they were swollen peaks once more. He looked up at her, smiling.

'Did you enjoy it, Ædwen?'

She knew he was fishing, perhaps needing some kind of praise, to know he had pleased her, as she hadn't said anything about his performance, but she suddenly felt the need to protect herself. To act as if he hadn't just rocked her world. 'Did *you*?'

He grinned. 'It's never been better. It was perfect, in fact.'

That appeased her a little. Only, how could it have

been that good if they hadn't made it together, right at the end?

'You didn't finish properly,' she blurted, not meaning it to sound as accusatory as it came out, but unable to keep it in.

His brow furrowed. 'Believe me, I did,' he said.

'Not inside me.'

He lifted himself away from her a little. 'That would have been reckless.'

She knew he was right, so why had it upset her so much? She turned her face to the side, looking away from him. Was it because he'd made that decision without telling her? That he hadn't surrendered wholeheartedly to her, as she had to him. And she wondered... did it have something to do with the fact he still didn't trust her?

He pulled away, sitting up on his knees.

'I thought it was for the best... I thought you'd agree,' he said.

She shrugged, not meeting his eye, suddenly feeling exposed, lying there naked, him looking down at her. He seemed so at ease, his magnificent, powerful body on show for her to look at.

'I do. It just...it felt cold.'

'Cold?' he asked, incredulous. 'What we just did felt cold?'

She couldn't help but smile at that. 'No...'

'I was going to say...it doesn't get much hotter than that, Ædwen.'

Ædwen's face was beautifully flushed and he gripped her hand, pulling her upwards so she sat in front of him, and Stefan raised his hand, his knuckles grazing over her cheek. Then he leaned in and kissed her, tenderly.

It had been amazing, being inside her again. She was everything he'd ever wanted.

He wondered at the hold she had over him. He'd felt it from that very first day on the beach. He had always wanted to be near her, close to her, inside her—and it was so much easier to give into it than to fight it.

It had been so intense, he'd felt as if he was soaring, his pleasure immense. He'd had to fight for control at the end. Her body had shuddered with pleasure, and she'd cried out against his shoulder, the same wonderment in her eyes that he knew was shining out of his own, yet he couldn't believe that she'd called him cold! Had he ruined it, hurt her, by pulling out at the end? That hadn't been his intention.

He just didn't think she'd thank him if he got her with child again.

He'd just have to make it up to her the next time. Because there would be a next time. He intended to make love to her again now. And all night long.

He kissed her intimately, caressing her tongue with his own, before he lifted her up by her bottom, as if she didn't weigh a thing, and as she wrapped her legs around his waist, he lowered her down on to his newly straining shaft, easing inside her again, her intimate muscles clenching around him.

'Oh,' she gasped.

She sank further down on top of him, taking him in to the hilt, and he groaned, resting his forehead against hers.

'Open your eyes,' he whispered.

And as he began to make love to her again, sliding deeply in and out of her, their eyes stayed connected. He couldn't get over how well they fit together, as if she were made for him. His mouth clung to hers, their ragged breaths mingled, but he was determined to take this time with her, setting a torturously slow, unhurried pace, wanting to savour every long, deliberate stroke and make it last.

His fingers held her buttocks tight, so there was no escape from his erotic onslaught, and he watched her eyes dilate as she threw her head back and cried out helplessly as her climax took over. His own orgasm came thick and fast, and felt explosive, as he erupted on to the creamy skin of her thigh.

He gently lifted her off him and leaned back against the wall, pulling her with him, so her head was resting on his shoulder, her hand on his chest, and he caressed the soft skin on her arm. It took a while for his body to stop trembling, his heart pounding beneath her fingers.

'Still cold?' he asked.

'Not so much… I was prepared that time,' she said, her hands tracing the lines of ink on his body.

When she'd got her breath back, she looked up at him. 'Stefan, why didn't you take another woman while we were apart?' she asked. 'You must have had needs…'

He shifted beneath her, coming down the bed a little.

'I told you. I take my vows seriously…' Then he relented. 'I wasn't able to think of another woman like that. Like you.'

And he never would. He hadn't wanted anyone but her. Even though they'd parted ways, even though it had ended badly. In spite of it all…

'Today has been a good day,' he said. 'Did you enjoy it?' he probed again.

'Yes,' she said shyly.

'Which was your favourite part?'

'I think it would have to be the lemon pastry.' She smiled, teasing him, and he laughed.

But all of a sudden there was the noise of men bellowing down the corridor, a commotion, coming closer, and Stefan's whole body tensed.

Like lightning, he was up, out of her arms and pulling on his clothes.

'What is it?' Ædwen gasped, her eyes wide.

'I don't know. Something's happening. I'll be needed. I want you to stay here. Stay inside. Lock the door behind me. Do you understand?'

But his heart pounded in his chest. Ellan…

# Chapter Thirteen

'They're coming, my lord. A great army. They've been spotted not far from here. We raced back to tell you as fast as we could.'

Still fastening his chainmail, Stefan had opened the door to find soldiers on the step, come to relay their urgent message.

'You're certain? They're heading this way?'

'Yes, my lord.'

Ædwen secured her final brooch behind him, her fingers trembling with fear.

'How many are there?' she heard him ask.

'Two hundred. Maybe three. They'll be upon us by daybreak.'

Stefan cursed and reached for his sword, just as she appeared at his side. 'Is it a force from Eastbury?' she asked. 'Is it my father?'

The men glanced between themselves, before looking at Stefan and then her. 'We believe so, my lady.'

She shivered as she realised the danger they were all in. She knew all too well what her father's men were capable of.

Was this all because of her?

Stefan grabbed his shield. 'Man the walls. Prepare for attack,' he said with no hesitation and she watched in admiration as the men immediately began to fall out, to follow his command.

'Stefan,' she said, placing a hand on his arm. 'I could ride out. I could speak with my father.' She couldn't bring danger to the door of the people who had welcomed her here. She had to do something.

'No,' he said. 'We cannot risk him or his men seeing you, or finding Ellan here. We don't know what he's prepared to do.'

'But you can't put other people at risk because of me.'

'That is for me and for the King to decide.'

Anger roared in her stomach. If this fight was about her, surely she should have a say in it?

He stepped through the door and she followed him.

'I told you to stay here,' he said.

'I can help…' she protested. 'I know how to wield a sword.'

'No!' he said, turning back to face her, swiping a hand over his face. 'I do not want you fighting. I wouldn't be able to focus.'

'And I need to get Ellan at least…' she said.

He growled and they both went through the door, slamming the wood behind them.

His long, powerful legs strode out and she tried to keep up with him. Soldiers were running ahead of them, out into the cloisters, to the courtyard, following his orders. And people were rushing along the corridors in panic, trying to get back to their homes, to get their children and animals inside.

Surely the people would want to hand her over, rather

than put their families in danger? This wasn't their fight. Yet Stefan had implied her father had been planning this for a while. Had what had happened in the church the other day only escalated things? Was Lord Werian with him?

She shuddered. She did not want to be forced home with her father to marry someone of his choosing, especially not now she had been with Stefan again. And there was no way she could be parted from her child. She would rather die. But could she really ask Stefan, and the people of Wintancaester to put themselves at risk for her?

At the end of the corridor, Stefan turned to go towards the King's hall and she went the other way, towards the monastery. But not before he pulled her back, taking her chin in his hand and kissing her briefly on the lips. 'Be careful,' he said.

Ædwen had sped towards the monastery, bursting inside, asking the nuns where Sister Margaret was. And when her eyes fell upon her, her blood ran cold. For Sister Margaret was talking to a woman and Ædwen knew, instantly, who it was.

It was the woman she had seen in the market.

Her mother. She was alive.

'Hello, Ædwen,' the woman said, rising to her feet, wary.

Ædwen reeled, momentarily forgetting all else, the danger they were in. Her mother was here, coming towards her. The woman she had missed for so many years. She had always hoped she would return. And now here she was, looking down at her, offering her a tentative smile.

Ædwen glanced up at Sister Margaret, throwing her a questioning look, then back at her mother, unable to believe it. Was she dreaming?

'What are you doing here?' she managed to say finally.

'I live here now. In Wintancaester.'

A lump grew in Ædwen's throat.

She hadn't died. She hadn't been killed. She had been alive all this while, but she had not come to find her.

She looked different to how Ædwen remembered her. She was older, of course, and had more lines around her eyes and her lips. Her eyes were a more jaded blue and her hair was lighter, a blondish white. But her face was still the same.

Emotion swelled up inside her. Joy. Hurt. Confusion. This was the woman she'd longed for as a child. The woman she'd wanted when she'd fallen over and hurt herself. The woman she'd needed when Stefan had left and her heart had been broken. And the woman she'd needed when she'd discovered she was with child.

The woman who had abandoned her.

Where had she been?

Why had she left?

Why hadn't she returned?

'Where have you been?' Ædwen said.

'I've always been around,' her mother said, stepping towards her. 'I was never far away, keeping an eye on you from afar. Despite what you might think, I was always watching over you, needing to know you were safe.'

What good had that been to her?

'But...why?' Ædwen said, her brow crumpling into a

hurt frown, needing answers, to understand. 'Why did you leave me?'

'I shall go,' Sister Margaret said, holding Ellan in her arms.

'No, stay,' Ædwen commanded and the woman faltered before sitting back down.

'I have much to tell you. Much to explain,' her mother said.

Ædwen shook her head. How could anything she had to say make a difference? How could her words make the hurt disappear? What she had done was unforgivable. Unthinkable.

Is that how Stefan felt about her?

She glanced at her child in Sister Margaret's arms and suddenly felt the need to hold her, to keep her close. She took her precious bundle from the nun's arms and drew her towards her chest.

'Your father and I, it was an arranged marriage. An unhappy marriage. He never cared much for me, or I him,' her mother said, wringing her hands. 'You, Ædwen, were the only good thing to come of it. And I loved you, desperately. I cherished you above everything else. Apart from you, my life was so bleak. So desperate. Until I met a man. A Danish man. And we started an affair.'

Ædwen glanced at Sister Margaret. A Danish man? A man like Stefan?

'I got carried away with it, totally caught up with him. I'm sure you know how that feels…'

Her mother glanced down at Ellan, then back at her.

'I became pregnant with his child. Your father and I had been trying for a son for many winters, after we'd had you, and we had given up hope. Then I met this man and got with child… It was a boy. And your father could never forgive me for it.'

Ædwen could imagine. Perhaps that was one of the reasons why he was so anti-Dane and didn't want a Danish king to rule here.

'Your father made me choose. A new life with this man and my son, or to stay with him and you. It was a tragic decision.' She shook her head sadly. 'I knew if I stayed your father could never love my son. And he despised me. I knew the impact our arguments were already having on you. So I made the choice to leave. But it broke my heart to do so, Ædwen.'

The woman stepped towards her.

'I couldn't bring myself to say goodbye. I know that was selfish of me. But I thought it would be easier for both of us if I just disappeared. I had my son and we moved here, to Wintancaester, but I couldn't get over leaving you behind. When I could, I would ride out to Eastbury and watch you playing on the beach, or reading in the monastery gardens, to check you were being well looked after.

'I never gave up hope that we might be reunited one day. And when I saw you here in the streets of Wintancaester today, with a Dane, I couldn't believe it. I thought you must finally be free of your father. I wondered if it was at last possible for me to see you again… So here I am.'

Ædwen shook her head, unable to comprehend all that the woman was telling her. 'Why didn't you make yourself known to me?' she said bitterly. 'I thought you were lost to me, for ever.'

'I was afraid.' She shrugged. 'I so wanted to know you again. But I thought you might despise me, for abandoning you as a child. For being a terrible mother. And because I'd made a promise to your father. So I stayed away. I know you may not be able to forgive me, or even want to see or talk to me, but I had to come here. I had to try.'

She couldn't believe that just a few days ago, she had left Eastbury, not realising her child, her husband and her mother lived in the city. It was overwhelming.

'I don't know what to say,' Ædwen said. 'It's a lot to take in.'

'I know. I'm so sorry.'

'Does that mean I have a brother I need to meet, too?' Ædwen said, drying her tears.

'Yes,' her mother said. 'His name's Ethelred. He works in the palace.'

'Ethelred?' she gasped. 'I think I know him! The King's messenger?'

'Yes.'

This was all so surreal.

'I started to think about you a lot more when I had Ellan. How you could leave me...'

'She's beautiful,' her mother said, inclining her head towards the baby. 'I can't believe I'm an *ealdormōdor*. She is half-Dane?'

'Yes.' Ædwen nodded.

She wasn't sure she could forgive her. She wasn't sure what to say. She wasn't sure she could deal with this right now. And then she remembered, why she had come. 'Father's coming,' Ædwen blurted. 'He's bringing a great army. I fear I have put the people in danger.'

Her mother cursed. 'You're the excuse he has been

waiting for to attack. He can't abide a Dane being on the throne. This was always going to happen regardless of you and the King's man.'

Ædwen handed Ellan back over to Sister Margaret.

'Nevertheless…you need to stay inside the monastery. Stay hidden. I must help Stefan. The people… Take care of her for me, until I come back,' she said to the holy woman.

And the nun nodded. 'Be careful.'

Ædwen looked back at her mother, deciding what she must do. 'If I have had a part in it, I must help stop it,' she breathed. 'And you, Mother, you will help me.'

Stefan and Canute were going over their plan to defend the city, leaning over the model of Wintancaester out in the courtyard, finalising their plans, their most skilled men surrounding them. They were all dressed in their armour, holding torches. Canute had directed the generals to ready the various sections of the armies, to warn the people to stay inside their homes and not to panic. Stefan knew the walls were strong. They would protect them for a while, but he was aware they might have to take the fight beyond the boundaries, to keep the people safe.

He had known this would happen. He had known Lord Manvil would come. Canute had been preparing for him to lay siege to the city for some time, but Stefan was under no illusion that him wounding the man's pride in Eastbury the other day, taking his daughter from him, would have aggravated the tension. But he had thought it might take him longer. Perhaps he had underestimated the man's need for revenge.

He didn't want to be responsible for bringing blood-shed upon the people and guilt assailed him. While the enemy had been approaching, he'd been busy seducing Ædwen, taking her to bed, rather than preparing to defend their city. He'd been distracted. He should have done more.

Yet would he take back the things they'd done together earlier? No. It had been everything he'd wanted and more. All he'd dreamed of. She had felt so good, moving beneath him, on top of him.

Yet now he had to prepare to face down her father, the man who had killed his family.

'I shall lead the infantry out of the gates, on to the battlefield,' he said now. 'We need to keep the fight away from the city.'

'You should stay with the King. Command the forces from within the walls,' Maccus said.

Stefan shook his head. 'No. This is my fight.'

The King stepped forward and placed his hand on Maccus's shoulder. 'Stefan is the best fighter there is. We need him out in the field. We need him leading the men. Just like his father.'

Stefan's body went stock-still and he swung to look at his King. What had he said?

'You knew my father?' he asked, incredulous.

The King gave a sharp nod. 'Yes. I knew him. It's why I gave you a chance, when you came to me. Why I championed you. I knew what you would be capable of. I knew I could rely on you on a day like today.'

Stefan's brow furrowed. He couldn't believe it. 'Why have you never mentioned this before?' His throat felt tight. It was a struggle to get the words out.

The King shrugged. 'I wanted you to be your own man. And you are. Besides, I know you took his death hard. That can sometimes have an impact on a man.'

'How did you know him?' Stefan pressed.

The men seemed to crowd closer.

'Perhaps we should talk about this later, over an ale,' Canute said.

Stefan shook his head. 'No. Now.'

An expectant hush reverberated around the courtyard at the way Stefan spoke to the King, but Canute showed no sign of surprise and let it lie.

'He was one of the first of my people to come over here, to England. To pave my way to the throne. East-bury has always been a place of strategic importance. We knew if we took it, it would make it easier for more of us to come over.' Now it was the King's turn to frown. 'I thought he told you. That you knew that's why you were here... He commanded the respect of his men, just like you do. Which is why I'm glad I have you at my side now, to finish what he started!'

Stefan's whole world tilted. He felt sick. He had thought they'd come here in peace, not to attack. He had professed his people's innocence to Ædwen time and time again. But he'd believed a grave untruth.

'So my father came here not to find land, not to farm, but to raid and conquer? *You* sent him?'

'Land to farm was always the end goal, Stefan. But he knew we had many battles on our hands before that could happen.'

Stefan's head hurt and he raised his hand to run over the scar on his forehead. Discovering his father's true intentions for their voyage to England was overwhelming.

He had put his sons' lives in danger. And Stefan wondered how he hadn't seen it, been aware of it, realised it. Suddenly, he felt his judgement couldn't be trusted.

As if everything he thought he knew was a lie.

Had everyone in his life deceived him? Could he not even trust those he held in the highest regard? First Dania and now his father. Even Canute had withheld the truth from him, to a point. And Ædwen, he had this insatiable need for her, he always had, but he was still hurt and angry over her decision to lie to him about his family and her father's role in their deaths, making him unwilling to trust her and give her his heart again.

Suddenly he felt resistant to his resurging feelings towards her. He was disgusted at his weakness that he had managed to forget her lies and deception of that day so easily. That he'd just had sex with her.

He had been weak and he felt angry with everyone.

At that moment, Ædwen came rushing into the courtyard.


Ædwen's father had reached them sooner than they'd thought. Outside, nothing could have prepared her for the sight. Hundreds of people were running into the courtyard, coming into the palace off the streets. They looked frightened: mothers sheltering their children, fathers standing side by side with the soldiers lining up in the square. Ædwen realised they were under attack. That the enemy must be here. She and her mother called to them to take shelter, directing them inside the monastery. It was all so unreal, like a bad dream.

She looked around for Stefan, wondering where he could be. She just wanted to be back in his arms, making love with him, to pretend none of this was happening. She wanted him to be safe.

Finally, she spotted him, the King at his side, rallying the men, and her heart almost stopped beating. Surely they weren't going to ride outside the gates? Surely they weren't going to charge on the enemy? She couldn't lose him. Not now. She couldn't believe that it had come to this. That her love for a man had brought about so much hate. That her father was laying siege to the King's palace. She hoped that Canute and Emma, and the people of Wintancaester, would one day forgive her.

She had thought about slipping away, without Stefan knowing, to find her father and try to reason with him. But she was too late. And she knew Stefan might never forgive her if she went without his permission and she didn't want to do anything to ruin his trust. Not after how far they'd come.

She had the desperate need to tell Stefan about meeting her mother, even though she knew it wasn't the right time. The revelation was huge. She had not been expecting to ever see her again, let alone have the woman announce she wanted to be a part of her life. That she always had. She wanted to know what Stefan thought about it. His opinion meant a lot.

Her mother leaving her had affected her whole life and her relationships with others. It had made her distrustful, sparking her fears of abandonment. Her return and desire to be in Ædwen's life was astounding. It rocked the very foundations of her beliefs.

If her mother could return and reveal she had never stopped loving her, that she wanted a second chance, could the same be true of her relationship with Stefan?

Could it be possible that he might care for her again, too? Reconciling with her mother had given her courage. Perhaps, if she was brave enough to admit her feelings for Stefan, would he stay with her, always? Because she realised now, she had never stopped loving him.

She hadn't seen Stefan since they'd left his room. Since he'd made love to her again. But despite the imminent danger they were in, her thoughts kept returning to the way he had moved inside her, his blue gaze fixed on hers as he pleasured her again and again.

If these few days had taught her anything, it was that she didn't want to live in the past. That's where all the mistakes and heartache belonged. She wanted a future. She wanted a future with Stefan.

Rushing across the courtyard, she heard him giving orders to his men. She took a deep breath, digging deep for her courage. The conversation with her mother had helped her resolve a lot of her fears. She had realised how much Stefan meant to her and she had to tell him. Now. Before he went into battle. She was ready.

'Stefan…' she said, as she approached.

He turned and their eyes collided across the open space. But his intense blue gaze was ice-cold and full of…what?

Her heart lodged somewhere in her throat. Her blood froze. Was something wrong?

Goose pimples prickled along her arm.

'Stefan, I need to talk to you.'

'Not now,' he barked.

He averted his gaze. It was almost as if he couldn't bear to look at her. As if he was closed off from her.

Pain lanced her heart, wounding her. It was not the

greeting she'd been expecting, especially after the way he'd touched her earlier. After the intimate things they had done. It was as if it was a different man staring back at her. A stranger.

She wavered.

Was he behaving like this because his men were here? Because he had to focus on the fight that lay ahead? Was she just a distraction he didn't need?

But she couldn't bear it if something were to happen to him, if he were to get hurt, and she hadn't told him how she felt. 'It's important,' she pressed.

'So is this fight. In case you hadn't noticed, your father has brought an army to our door. We're at war.'

Her heart lurched. Was he simply worried about the battle and the safety of his people? Although his voice sounded full of…blame. Disgust.

'Stefan, please don't do this. Please don't fight him. Let me talk to him.'

'There's nothing to talk about, Ædwen.'

Did he mean them or him and her father?

Her father was coming for him again…was it stirring up his anger from the past? It was possible, as he was looking at her with a kind of disdain. As if he felt bad about what they'd done, as if he regretted it.

Yes, that was it, she thought, the realisation stealing her breath away. He regretted making love to her.

He had taken what he'd wanted from her and now, after sating his desire, it was as if he was done.

Hurt ripped through her. She had known this might happen. Always thought it was a risk. She knew she should have said no to him. Yet she hadn't been able to resist him. She was even about to profess her love for him. She took a step back.

'I thought you were going to find Ellan. I thought you were going to look after her,' he bit out.

'I did. I am…' she said, frowning.

'Good. After all, we are honouring our commitment, this marriage, just for her sake, yes?'

It was the final blow. She felt ill, her legs weak. She had hoped it was about love.

He slammed down his helmet and swung himself up on to his horse. Were those the last words he would ever say to her? Was this the last time she would ever see him?

# Chapter Fourteen

Outside the city gates, in the middle of the blackest night, Stefan heard the enemy approaching before he saw them. The ground rumbled and shook beneath his feet, Lord Manvil's army roaring and stamping a ferocious battle cry, and his men began to jostle with each other as he told them to stand their ground, nerves getting the better of them. Then, in the distance, he finally caught the alarming sight of soldiers approaching, their fire spears appearing on the horizon.

His men had been right. By the time dawn broke, they would be upon them. Wintancaester would be under siege, unless he and his men took them down first. Unless they intercepted them.

So it was here the battle would take place.

Back in the city, people had taken to their farmsteads, locking themselves inside, and he prayed to his gods that he would be able to keep them safe. That Lord Manvil wouldn't get through him and breach the walls.

His body was vibrating with shock and anger.

Images of Ædwen came into his head and he tried to push them aside, but it was no good. They were there to stay.

Was she?

Could he rely on her?

He wondered what he had stopped her saying to him. His thoughts were nothing less than anarchy.

Her father, Lord Manvil, was once again preparing to attack. The man would try to kill him, just as he had his family. And yet…if Stefan's own father had been successful in his crusade, if he'd razed Eastbury to the ground, it might have been Ædwen lying lifeless on the beach that day instead.

It was an abominable thought.

*'I'm glad I have you at my side now, to finish what he started!'* the King had said.

But could he do it?

He realised now his father was guilty of the crime he'd blamed Ædwen and her father for all this time and it made him sick to his stomach. The Danes might not have got to wreak their savagery upon the Saxons that day, but the intent had been to do so.

He had never thought his people would do the things Ædwen had accused them of. He had known the Danes had come here, devastating Saxon lands, but not his own tribe. Not his family. But he had got it so wrong. His father had come here to attack. To ravage and rampage. And that blood ran through his veins.

He picked up a spear and lit the tip and, with all the strength he could muster, threw it across the battle site, taking his frustration out on the fire and wood.

Why hadn't his father told him of his plans? If only he could go back and ask him. There was so much left unsaid…there were things he wanted to know. To ask. To say himself and to have explained. Now he realised how much the regret of things left unsaid could hurt…

*'For helvede med dig,'* he cursed. Damn.

There was so much he should have said to Ædwen. But after what Canute had told him about his father, he'd been reeling from the reminder that he couldn't trust even those he held most dear. He had taken his anger and fear out on her and now he was going into battle, not having reconciled with her. Did he want to?

He might lose. He might die. But if he won, if he killed Lord Manvil, wouldn't that make him just as bad as his father?

But there was nothing for it now. He would have to fight. Things were too far gone.

Stefan readied his men. He shouted his orders, encouraging them to make a stand, inspiring them to stir up their courage.


Finally, when the first crack of dawn broke and he saw Lord Manvil's men racing towards them, he commanded his men to charge and threw himself into the fray.

He kept fighting, cutting down the enemy, taking down one man, then the next, dispatching them in fury. It was bloody and brutal. He just knew he had to keep the city safe. His wife. His child. His King. And the people. He could not fail.

Lord Manvil had raised the fyrds, amassing a great army, and the fight raged on and on, both sides relentless. There were fires breaking out all over the place, everything in disarray. Just like Stefan's thoughts and feelings. He was in turmoil.


Some time later, he saw Lord Manvil fighting a few feet away and Stefan continued to dispose of men as he tried to reach the Saxon brute. But for the first time, Stefan realised Lord Manvil had actually had a right to defend himself and his settlement that day in Eastbury, like he and Canute had a right to defend themselves today. Lord Manvil had known an enemy was coming to their shores, to kill and to destroy, and he had made sure that didn't happen. And Stefan couldn't blame him. Wouldn't anyone have done the same?

Today, had Lord Manvil come here because he felt his enemy, a heathen, had stolen his daughter and his honour? After all, if Ellan had been taken by his foe, Stefan knew he wouldn't let it be. He would go after her. He would fight. He would do everything in his power to get her back. Even wage a war against the King. Yet… he would never treat Ellan the way Lord Manvil had treated Ædwen.

Suddenly, an arrow struck his faithful steed and the horse tumbled, casting him off his back and on to the ground. His shoulder burned. Crawling over to the animal, he pulled the arrow from its leg and the steed curled itself back upwards. Stefan breathed out a sigh of relief. 'Go!' he told his faithful companion and was relieved when the horse cantered off back towards the city gates.

Seeing his chance to attack him while he was down, Lord Manvil approached, looming over him, a ferocious look on his face, but Stefan knew the older man was no match for his skill.

He leapt to his feet and the Saxon lord began to circle him, swinging his blade. Stefan's father's sword clashed against it. It was all a blur of raining blows, blades swinging, both of them grunting as they heaved their heavy weapons, all while arrows were pelting down around them, then the heavens opened and real rain began to descend.

He had wondered how he'd feel coming face to face with the man who had killed his family, but seeing him now, he realised they were both to blame. If Lord Manvil hadn't struck first, his father would surely have taken the advantage. And he couldn't bear to think of what that might have meant for the people in Eastbury. For Ædwen.

Had his father had to die to keep her safe?

Lord Manvil was a skilled fighter and his blows were persistent, but Stefan was stronger and, as both men began to tire, Stefan began to overpower him, knocking him backwards. The man lost his footing and fell. He scrambled backwards on the ground, trying to get away, to reach his lost weapon, looking aghast, but Stefan bore down on him, kicking his sword away, pointing his own blade at his chest.

The man's eyes narrowed on him, realising all was lost. As Stefan peered down at him, he saw he had blue eyes, like Ædwen's eyes.

'Go on. Take your vengeance,' Lord Manvil said. 'You've waited a long time for this. We both have. But my God has decided that I deserve death. Perhaps if I'd listened to my daughter that day you came to our shores...'

Stefan stalled his sword. 'What?'

'Ædwen. When we saw your ships coming. She was desperate for me to show mercy to you that day. She could never stomach any bloodshed. But I was angry, hated your kind, for my own personal reasons. I will never see what my wife, or my daughter, see in your type.'

Stefan's heart lurched. Had Ædwen really tried to stop it? Had she been looking out for him, even before he'd reached this isle? His *Hamingia*.

His thoughts returned to how she had wanted to talk about the past and he'd refused. He hadn't wanted to hear it. Her betrayal still hurt too much.

He had been so angry, so shocked to see her standing there with her father that day, so overwhelmed by all the memories that had come flooding back all at once, that he had never given her chance to explain. Not then, or now. He'd been so blinded by rage, wanting vengeance, he'd never stopped to see the impact him leaving had had on her. Her own pain.

She had shocked him when she'd accused him of abandoning her, like her mother.

Like he'd abandoned Dania?

But deep down, he'd known she was right.

He had known it must have been hard for her, him leaving her, her having a child on her own, and she had suffered greatly when her father had taken Ellan away. Now he realised she was right to blame him for that. Because if he'd been there, none of it would have happened. He rubbed his chest with his hand.

Could they forgive each other for all that had passed?

She had known what her father had done, but she hadn't wielded the blade. She'd tried to stop it, in fact. She'd rescued him. Saved him. Yes, she had withheld information, but was it possible she had only acted out of care for him? He'd allowed Dania's past betrayal, and his grief, to make him assume the worst and he'd pushed Ædwen away to protect himself.

But he didn't want to push her away any longer. He

had let his fear of getting hurt rule him for too long. It was time to let it go. Because he loved her...

He loved Ædwen.

*Helvete!* He loved her. He wanted to shout it across the battlefield. From the tops of the ramparts. He wanted to whisper the words into her ear as he was showing her just how deeply he felt about her...

'Let us put an end to this, once and for all,' he said, making his decision, turning his focus back on the man beneath his boot, and Lord Manvil braced himself for death. He stared down at Ædwen's father, knowing vengeance was his, but he didn't want it. Not any more.

Stefan threw his sword down and stretched out his hand.

Ædwen had been right. He knew now, if they were to have any kind of future together, they had to deal with the past. Starting right now.

Stefan no longer wanted revenge and it felt strange to release his anger. His pain. He'd wanted to take his rage out on the man he felt had ruined his life for so long, but now, he just felt a deep sense of regret, for all the wasted months.

He knew he had to stop this war, between Saxons and Danes, for the sake of his child. For the sake of his future with the woman he loved.

'I do not wish for your death, Lord Manvil. There has been enough bloodshed between our people already. And we are both to blame.'

The man looked stunned, shocked. It was as if he was unable to reconcile the man standing before him with his idea of who he thought the men from the North were, as if Stefan's actions completely toppled his own prejudices of what he'd always thought of the so-called heathens. He'd thought that they were all barbarians, come to destroy their homes and their lives, taking their women. But this man…this man was merciful.

'I do not want to live with hatred in my heart any more. And neither should you,' Stefan said. 'I believe the love I have for your daughter, and your granddaughter, is enough to overcome any animosity we have for each other. Now stand your men down. Let us put this behind us and forgive each other. Let us be friends and live out our days in peace.'

Lord Manvil hesitated for a moment, before reaching out, and meeting Stefan's hand. He gave a sharp nod of his head and Stefan tugged him upwards, bringing the man to his feet.

'You have been given a second chance, Lord Manvil, and I will make sure the King is lenient with you. But perhaps you could be lenient with him also and listen to what he has to say?'

And with a grim twist to his mouth, the man nodded and ordered his men to put down their weapons. All around them, the fighting slowed, then stopped, and Stefan released a breath he hadn't realised he'd been holding. It was over.

His wife and his daughter were safe.

'You really love my daughter?'

'Yes. And your country. Is that so hard to believe? All this fighting is unnecessary, when deep down, we all want the same things.'

But all of a sudden, he heard screams coming from behind him. He turned and looked up at the skyline of the city. The roof of the monastery was engulfed in violent flames, with beams from the roof beginning to come crashing down on to the ground below. And then he saw Sister Margret shouting for him, calling his name, from the top of the ramparts. His gaze shot to her arms and he was relieved to see she was holding Ellan.

But what about Ædwen? Where was she?

And then he realised. He already knew where she was. She was helping the people. He had seen her in the courtyard earlier, encouraging people to take shelter inside.

Please…no.

'Ædwen's in there,' he whispered. Ædwen was in the burning building.

The Saxon lord looked horrified. 'Go!' he said.

In his own way, the man loved her, Stefan realised, his thoughts a blur as he raced towards the monastery. Perhaps some people just had a greater capacity to love than others.

He loved his wife with all his heart and every breath he took. That was why his hurt had been so great, because his love had been so immense.

Stefan was running, sprinting through the gates, along the narrow lanes where devastated market stalls now lay scattered in his wake, people tending to the wounded in the passageway where he'd rescued Ædwen from that brute just the other day. Where Ædwen had taught him to show compassion. He raced through the courtyard, his heart pounding in his chest. It was carnage and this was all his fault.

He had told her to stay inside…and now was she trapped? In trouble?

'Lady Ædwen? Have you seen her?' he asked a group

of people coming out of the monastery. He was frantic, his breath coming in short bursts.

'In there,' one woman said, choking on smoke. 'She was trying to get the people out.'

Of course she was. She was so selfless. He couldn't believe he had once thought she was dishonourable. She was the kindest, noblest person he knew.

If anything happened to her, he would never be able to forgive himself. He wouldn't be able to bear it, yet now he questioned if he even deserved her.

Had he ever?

She had saved his life that day on the beach, when his family would have taken hers.

He'd asked her to put her trust in him, promising to keep her and Ellan safe. And now look what had happened.

Would she still want him now?

And he realised that he wanted to be the man who was worthy of her. He would spend the rest of his life trying to be, if she would just make it through today...

He ran up the steps and through the door, letting out a cloud of smoke, the heat hitting him with force, and he coughed and spluttered. Great rafters were falling from above and he raised his hand against the heat to see if he could see any sign of her. Fighting off the raging flames, he went further into the building, as people were crawling on their hands and knees towards him, trying to get out.

Fear and flames choked him as he fought his way further into the inferno. He wanted her out of here. Now.

The building was being overtaken. But there was no

way he was leaving until he'd found her. He would die trying.

His arms smarted under the flickering flames, his chest burned with the heat. Then he saw a crumpled body under a fallen beam. Ædwen. His heart was in his mouth. He rushed over to her, scrambling over debris and tried to heave the beam off her battered legs.

'Ædwen,' he roared, bending over her, checking her pulse, stroking her hair out of her face. 'Ædwen, can you hear me?'

But she didn't respond.

He couldn't lose her.

Not now he'd got her back. Not without having the chance to tell her how he really felt. That he loved her. That he'd been a fool to let his hurt hold him back for so long.

He heaved again at the beam, using all his strength, and finally, it gave way. He gathered her into his arms and lifted her, carrying her through the blaze, sheltering her body from the flames using his own.

He made it back to the door just as there was an almighty rumble and avalanche of wood as the building began to give way. He stumbled out into the daylight and sank down on to his knees amid the chaos in the courtyard, cradling Ædwen, rocking her in his arms, praying for her to survive this.

'Help,' he cried, hoping someone would hear him. That the gods would answer his prayers.

'Save her,' he cried.

He couldn't live without her.

He loved her.

He wanted to spend the rest of his days with her.

# Chapter Fifteen

'Stefan!' Ædwen gasped, as she sat bolt upright in the bed. 'Ellan…'

'She's fine. Absolutely fine,' Sister Margaret said, plumping up the furs behind her and pushing her back down on to them, trying to keep her comfortable.

'Where is she? Can I see her?'

'She's asleep, dear. And you need yours.'

'How long have I been out?' she said.

'A couple of days.'

'A couple of days?' she gasped, echoing the older woman. 'Then I must get up,' she said, going to throw the furs off her and sit up. Then the pain lanced her. Excruciating pains in her legs. And she looked down to see they were black and blue, covered in bruises.

The woman pushed her back down. 'You're not going anywhere for a while.'

'Where am I?' Ædwen asked, looking round. Then she realised she was in Stefan's bed. That was something, at least. After all, there was nowhere else she'd rather be.

Where was he?

'What happened?' she asked.

'There was a big battle. Your father came. Do you remember?'

'Yes.' She nodded as the images of the attack came back to her.

'You got caught in the fire in the monastery. It tore right through the building. There's nothing left of it.' Sister Margaret sniffed, clearly upset. 'Your legs got trapped. Lord Stefan went in there, fought through the flames to find you. Put his life on the line, he did. Got badly burned himself. But he would not stop until he found you. He rescued you and carried you right out, the flames licking at his skin. They're all calling him a hero. For saving you. For stopping the fighting. But he's stubbornly having none of it, of course.'

Ædwen smiled. She could imagine. She lay back and shut her eyes, going over the events of the night and the battle the following morning, trying to remember as much as she could. Stefan making love to her. Meeting her mother. Stefan shunning her. The attack…and then the blaze. Her utter horror that the building she'd told people to take sanctuary in was going to burn. Fall. And she'd known she had to get them all out or she'd never forgive herself.

'You're very lucky,' Sister Margaret said. 'We were all worried you wouldn't walk again, but I think you will. You're strong. You're on the mend.'

'And Stefan?' she asked finally. 'Is he all right?'

'You gave him quite the fright. He's barely left your side. Barely eaten a thing. He hasn't been himself. Not at all.'

'Where is he now?' She was desperate to see him.

'I made him take Ellan for a walk to get her to sleep. I thought he needed some air. He's been cooped up in here for days. I know he thinks I'm mothering him, but… well, who else is going to do it?'

Ædwen smiled at the thought of Stefan being mothered. No, she didn't think he'd like that at all. She thought only Sister Margaret could get away with it.

'Would you like some water, dear, or ale?'

'Water, please,' she said, her throat parched. 'What happened with my father?'

'Lord Stefan fought him.'

'He did?' she gasped, her eyes wide.

'And he could have, well… Let's just say he won, but he was merciful. He let your father live.'

Ædwen swallowed. 'Why? I mean, I am pleased, of course I am, but there was nothing stopping him from taking his revenge.'

'Well, there was, dear. There was you. I imagine he didn't think you'd take kindly to him taking your father's life.'

'So where is my father now?'

Ædwen felt as if she was trying to piece everything together and it was making her head pound.

'He was called into the King's Great Hall and they spoke. I don't know what was said, mind. But he departed later on that night, back to Eastbury. But not until he'd sworn an oath of loyalty to the King. He left with a full pardon and he got to keep his settlement. That's something, after attacking the city, don't you think? Another round of Saxons and Danes united. I think your husband must have had something to do with that,' she said. 'I can't imagine the King giving him a full pardon otherwise, can you?'

'Was Stefan there? Did he speak with my father?'

'Not in the hall. But there are all kinds of stories about them speaking during the battle. But he kept away from the King and your father afterwards. He was far too pre-occupied with you. So bad tempered he was, until we told him you would be all right.'

Ædwen smiled. It sounded as if he cared and her heart lifted in hope.

'He let your father come to see you, though.'

'What?' Ædwen gasped. 'My father came here?'

'Yes, dear. He, too, seemed worried about you. He said he felt responsible for bringing this upon you and that he would now leave you in peace. He even told me he was glad I was here. And that he was pleased you had found contentment.'

Contentment… A huge lump grew in Ædwen's throat, because she still wasn't sure how Stefan truly felt about her. The last time she'd seen him, he'd given her that look…it had frozen her blood.

She heard the door open downstairs. 'Ah, that will be Lord Stefan now,' Sister Margaret said.

Ædwen's heart began to hammer in her chest. She was so desperate to see him again. And Ellan. She struggled to sit up in bed as Sister Margaret went to the top of the stairs.

'Is the baby asleep?'

'Yes, finally,' he said. 'Any change?'

'Come up here and see for yourself,' Sister Margaret said.

And Ædwen heard him take the steps, two at a time. She held her breath in anticipation.

He burst into the space and his eyes locked on hers. He took her in, sitting up in bed. His eyes swept over her and he crossed the distance towards her so quickly, she felt dizzy. 'Thank the gods,' he said and gripped her face between his hands hard and kissed her fully on the lips.

When he came up for air, his eyes were swimming. 'I thought I'd lost you,' he breathed. His eyes raked all over her, as if checking she was all right. 'It was more than I could bear.'

'I'll leave you two to it for a while. Come and get me if you need me,' Sister Margaret called, but Ædwen barely noticed, she was too busy drinking Stefan in, so happy to see him again.

He had a few scratches to his face, and some bandages wrapped around his forearms, but he looked to be all right. More gorgeous than ever.

She tried to get up, to get closer to him, but everything hurt.

'Don't move, just rest,' he said, sitting down carefully beside her on the bed, as if he didn't want to cause her any pain, and he leaned down and pressed a soft kiss to her forehead.

'Are you all right?' she asked, reaching out for his hand. 'Sister Margaret said you got burned in the fire.'

'I'm fine. It's nothing. Not compared to you. How do you feel? Are you in much pain?'

'I'm not too bad.' She felt all the better for seeing him. 'My legs are the worst. Sister Margaret said you rescued me. That I was trapped beneath a beam. And that you risked your life to save me. That was foolish of you! But thank you, Stefan.'

He shrugged. 'It was the least I could do. After all, I did get you into all this.'

And then she saw it. A flash of something. What was

it? Something was different. Wrong. Were his injuries worse than he was making out? It would be just like him to try to keep an injury hidden.

No…that wasn't it. There was a stern set to his generous mouth. Did he feel as if he was to blame? For what? For her getting hurt? Now that was foolish, too. It was her own fault for staying in a crumbling, burning building, trying to get every last person out.

'What happened out there, with my father?' she said. 'Sister Margaret said you fought.'

He shook his head. 'We don't need to talk about this now. You've only just woken up.'

'Stefan,' she warned. 'I want to know.'

He sighed. He kicked off his boots and brought his legs up on the bed. Leaning back against the wall, and wrapping his arm around her shoulder, he pulled her close.

'I've been so worried about you,' he said, sighing. 'I can't tell you how good it is to see you awake. When I saw you lying there with that beam on top of you, I couldn't breathe. I thought I'd lost you.' He shuddered. 'I prayed to both the Christian and Norse gods for them to bring you back to me. I wasn't taking any chances.'

She smiled. 'Well, it worked,' she said. She rested her head on his shoulder. 'I'm sorry I worried you.' And then she pulled away and looked up at him. 'You know, it almost sounds as if you care…'

He sat upright, releasing her, and turned to look into her eyes, serious. He took her hand in his.

'Ædwen, I owe you an apology,' he said. 'We should have talked the other day, like you said, like you wanted to, before I took you to bed. I have so much to tell you, so much I want to say… But we can do this another time if you're tired.'

'No,' she said, squeezing his fingers in hers. 'Tell me now. Tell me what happened.'

'I asked your father for a truce.'

'Sister Margaret said you bested him.'

'I asked him for a truce after I bested him.' He grinned, before he sobered again. 'I remembered what you said about Lord Werian. And that thief in the streets the day we got here. That everyone deserved a second chance. I told him I wanted to reconcile our differences and he agreed to stop the conflict.'

'That was good of you.'

He brought her hand up to his lips. 'I assured him he'd be pardoned if he bent the knee to the King and so he made an oath of fealty to Canute.'

'It was good of the King to let him go. I know you must have spoken with him—had a part in that—thank you.' She took a breath. 'Stefan… I don't want him and the things he has done to come between us. Not any more,' Ædwen said. 'I am truly sorry for all that he did. About what happened to your family. If I could take it back, I would. Stefan, I want to tell you about that day you first came here. When you landed on the beach at Eastbury. I want you to understand the background.'

He nodded then drew a hand over his face. 'It wasn't your fault, Ædwen,' he said. 'I know that you tried to stop him.'

'But when you woke up, I should have told you the truth right there and then. That my father was the one who ordered the attack. That he was the one who took your family from you—'

'Yes, you should have. But I understand why you didn't. You were afraid of what I'd do. You were afraid I'd take revenge.'

'No, that's not it,' she said, shaking her head. 'I didn't tell you because I liked you so much, I didn't want you to think badly of me, afraid it would change your feelings for me. I felt so guilty my father was responsible. But that was wrong. You deserved to know. You leaving me was my punishment. I felt that I wasn't enough for my mother to stay, or you either.'

He drew her towards him, shaking his head. 'That's not true.' He pressed another kiss to her forehead. 'I know that when I left you in Eastbury, I hurt you, Ædwen. Badly. I'm sorry. I should have realised, after your mother leaving you, that it was the worst thing I could have done.

'I was so overwhelmed by my own anger, when I saw you and your father together, when my memories came back. I realised he was the man who had slaughtered my family, and you were related to him, and I was shocked. Appalled. I did want vengeance. I was hurting… I couldn't look at you without thinking about it, so I knew I had to get away. I thought it had changed everything. The way I felt about you…but it didn't. Will you tell me—what happened to my family's bodies?'

'We gave them a proper ship burial in the sea.'

He nodded, taking that in. 'I was so furious I hadn't been given a chance to say goodbye. I felt as if I'd been denied my grief.'

'What were they like? Your father, your brothers… Will you tell me about them some time?' she said. 'And your memories. Some of the adventures you had.'

'Yes. I'm sorry, Ædwen. I never stopped to think

about the impact me leaving might have had on you. And the condition I left you in…to deal with that alone, I feel terrible about that now. I can't imagine how hard it must have been for you. I wish I had been there.'

'I wish you could have been, too.'

'I never wanted to be out of reach of you. Not really. And every day without you was agony. That's why I never took another woman; the only woman I ever wanted was you. When I found out we'd had a child, I thought you'd kept that from me, too, and I was even more angry with you. But I knew I'd love our daughter, instantly, because she was a part of you. Something we created through love.

'When I heard you were marrying Lord Werian… I knew I had to stop it, because in my heart, I believed you were mine. That you belonged with me.'

'And you couldn't have another failed marriage?' she queried.

'What happened with Dania, it affected me, badly. Her deceit, but what happened after, too.'

'You can tell me,' she said, so pleased he was finally opening up to her.

'We agreed to separate and she and Villads were a couple for a while. But then he found another woman and Dania was distraught. You'd think I might have been secretly pleased, glad it hadn't worked out for them, but I wasn't. I felt bad for her.'

'Because you're a good person, Stefan.'

'It made me feel hollow, though. It made me wonder if all relationships were the same. It made me believe if you cared for someone, you'll always get hurt eventually.'

'I'm sorry she hurt you,' she whispered. 'But do you still believe that?'

He stared down at her and grinned. 'No. You've changed my mind about everything. But I felt, if I had stuck by her, stayed with her after her betrayal, she might have been saved the same heartache. If I had just kept quiet, insisted their affair stopped and we remained a couple…'

She shook her head. 'But no one can live like that. In denial. Living a lie. And I don't want you to be with me out of duty, Stefan.'

'Is that what you really think?' He shook his head. 'It couldn't be further from the truth. I'm completely, utterly, totally in love with you, Ædwen,' he said, his eyes shining down on her. 'That's why I know this marriage will be successful. That's why I fought for those vows we made last winter. Why I stuck by them even when we were apart. Because I meant every word of them. I love and trust you. Wholly. With all my heart.

'And I was so worried I'd lost you out there in the monastery, without telling you what you meant to me, without you knowing how I felt. I want to be with you as you're all I think about, every waking moment. I wanted to reconcile the day, the very moment I left you, but I was far too stubborn, far too hurt, unable to make myself vulnerable again. It's why I withheld my forgiveness. And I'm sorry for the wasted time we've spent apart now. I don't want us to waste another moment. I want to make it up to you.'

'You already have.'

Stefan knelt down by the hearth and lit the kindling, lighting up the room in a soft glow, the crackling of the wood filling the silence as he came to sit down beside her on the furs on the floor. He'd carried Ædwen downstairs and made sure she was comfortable.

He knew that, outside, people were still clearing up the mess from the battle. The monastery, a symbol of their city, had been destroyed and people were mourning the loss. All that was left of it lay in a blackened heap of dust. But as Stefan had told the King, this was a chance to start over. To build something from scratch, as Saxons and Danes aligned. A new symbol of hope for a new, united people.

And it was that hope he held in his heart now, as he looked at Ædwen. He handed her a cup of ale and she sipped it slowly. Wearing one of his dark tunics that Sister Margaret had dressed her in, she looked beautiful, her eyes glowing in the firelight, her bruised legs tucked up beneath her.

Ædwen told him about meeting her mother, and he was pleased for her, delighted it was another wound that was starting to heal. She wanted him to meet her and he'd said he would love to, when she was ready to introduce them.

'Do you still care for your father?' he asked, a prickle of guilt assailing him.

A little crease appeared between her brows. 'He's never been the best father. He has ruled my life for so long. Dictated how I should live. It finally feels as if I might be free of him.' She smiled sadly. 'I cannot forgive the things he has done. But he is still my father. Ridiculously, I feel guilty that I have ruined his life. If he'd had a son, things would have been very different for him. And perhaps my mother. But the only way I could help my father was through an advantageous marriage—and I've shattered those dreams for him now.'

Stefan frowned. 'Am I not an advantageous marriage?' he asked, his lips curling upwards, letting her know he was teasing her.

'I'm not sure if he sees it that way.'

'Do you?'

She smiled. 'I don't feel I've done too badly for my-self,' she jested.

Having a daughter...imagining the world through her eyes, it was helping him to see Ædwen's perspective a bit more. That women had it tough. They didn't have as many choices as men did. But he would do anything for his daughter to have a happy life, to follow the path she wanted. Ædwen hadn't been given that. But he hoped he would be able to make her happy now.

'I was thinking about what you said, the other day, about our marriage not being a valid union. And I want to take away all your fears, all the uncertainty.' He wanted there to be no doubt in her mind, or anyone else's, about who she belonged to. And now he knew what he had to do. He would promise to be by her side for ever...again.

'By telling me you love me, you have.'

'But we should make sure there's no doubt,' he said. 'And that's why I've asked the King if I can be baptised, before we renew our wedding vows.'

She pulled away from him slightly, to look up into his eyes, her mouth falling open. 'What?' she asked, shocked.

'If we need a proper Christian wedding to make our union legitimate—and for the security of our child—then we'll have one. So there can be no doubt about us.'

'But, Stefan, you're a pagan, not a Christian!' she exclaimed.

'Can't I be both?'

'I don't know, can you?' she said, frowning, shaking her head.

'I was a pagan, for the first half of my life. But then I nearly died in a battle. When I woke up, I saw you…my *Hamingia.* I saw this,' he said, reaching out to take the little cross pendant around her neck between his fingers. 'I've seen how your religion can unite people, under our King. A king I look up to and respect.' He pulled her back towards him. 'Yes, I was born a pagan, but perhaps I can observe Christianity? I don't want there to be a difference between us, or our child, and the path we are on. Our beliefs…'

She frowned. 'Stefan…'

'This is something I have been thinking about for a while. Times are changing. The country is uniting. I don't see why I can't combine my beliefs.'

'You don't have to do this,' she said, shaking her head. 'Not for me. I love you as you are. For who you are.'

'I know that.' He smiled. 'But I want to. It won't change who I am as a person. But it will unite our family. I don't want Ellan to be forced to pick a side, to choose between us one day. I don't want her to be discriminated against because she has both Saxon and Dane blood flowing through her veins. I'm doing this because it's the right thing to do.'

And he needed that. After everything that had happened, he needed something to be right.

'I didn't believe in heaven until I met you, Ædwen,' he said, as he leaned in and placed a gentle kiss on her lips, and when he went to pull away, worried about hurting her, her hand came up to hold his jaw and she kissed him back.

He wrapped his arms around her and pulled him into his chest.

'You should get some rest now,' he said.

'Will you stay with me?' she asked.

'I will never leave you again.'

Stefan woke a while later to find the fire still burning, his hand casually anchored around Ædwen's waist, her legs entwined with his so he couldn't move. Not that he really wanted to.

He watched Ædwen sleeping and his heart was overflowing with love. He had never been so relieved as the moment he'd seen her awake and sitting up in bed. All his prayers had been answered and it had taken all his restraint not to strip her of her clothes and make love to her there and then.

He studied her features...her beautiful wavy blonde hair, her dark lashes resting on her cheekbones and her rosebud lips. Her chest was rising up and down, steadily, and he thought he could watch her for ever. She'd always fascinated him.

He thought about the evening, the week and month ahead with Ædwen and Ellan and couldn't believe he was thinking about the future when he had previously been unable to do so. Suddenly, the dark clouds that had been following him around for so long had cleared. Now the future was brighter than he had ever thought possible.

He could hear Ellan gurgling in her crib, so he gently

disentangled himself from Ædwen's arms, trying not to wake her, as he quietly went over to pick her up.

'Where are you going?' Ædwen asked, startling him. 'I thought you said you'd never leave me.'

He smiled. 'Ellan's awake. I was just going to get her.'

'All right then,' she said. 'You're allowed.'

He was back moments later, laying Ellan between him and his beautiful wife on the furs. Ædwen turned to face him.

'You know you've only been here a week and you've already turned this place upside down. Look at my room, covered in flowers and furs that people have brought for you,' he said.

Ædwen smiled, resting her hand on Ellan's stomach, and he placed his hand on top of hers.

'Can you believe we created something so perfect?' she asked him.

'I know…incredible. I want more, one day. Do you?'

'If you're offering me the chance to have more little Stefans running about the place, then, yes. Definitely I do.'

He smiled. 'But is it selfish of me to want to enjoy some time with you first? Practising.' He grinned.

'I'd like that,' she said, laughing.

'I do feel I missed out on seeing you with a big baby belly last time. I would have loved to have seen that and go through it all with you.'

'Next time, Stefan,' she said. 'You will.'

# *Chapter Sixteen*

That night, the King was hosting a feast in the Great Hall in honour of Stefan and his bravery. Stefan had said if Ædwen wasn't up to going, he would stay behind with her and look after her, but she didn't want him to miss his honorary meal and she wanted to see the praise he deserved bestowed upon him.

He helped her walk down the corridors, towards the grand doors, and she realised she was nervous, just like the first time she'd approached the King's hall. It was the first time she'd seen anyone since the battle and she hoped they didn't hold it against her. But at least this time, she knew Stefan was wholeheartedly on her side.

As the doors swung open and they stepped inside, a huge cheer erupted, men and women banging their tankards on the table and stamping their feet on the floor in support of Stefan and herself. They were chanting both their names. She couldn't believe it. She was astounded. She could feel the love in the room.

She looked around and saw her mother and Ethelred sat at one table and Maccus and Kendra at another. Sister Margaret and Ellan were up in one corner and King

Canute and Queen Emma were rising out of their seats, coming to welcome them.

'Your Majesties. You honour us with this feast,' Stefan said.

'And you honour us with your presence, Lord Stefan and Lady Ædwen,' King Canute said.

Queen Emma leaned in. 'We hope you are not in too much pain from your injuries, Lady Ædwen.'

'I am making a quick recovery, thank you. And I wish to apologise once more for the behaviour of my father. I am deeply saddened about the loss of the monastery and all those many lives.'

'We are stronger now because of it. Do not trouble yourself about it. We have united our lands, once and for all.'

They took their seats at the table with Maccus and Kendra and the woman instantly came over and gave her a hug. Then King Canute was out of his seat once more, ready to make a toast.

'I would like to remind you all of the obstacles we have overcome these past few days. But we have done it standing together, side by side, Saxon and Dane. We have already started rebuilding and we will rise from the ashes, greater than ever before.

'And I should like to thank my chief commander, my friend and right-hand man, Lord Stefan. He single-handedly put a stop to the fighting and united our peoples. But he said he owes this glory to his wife, Lady Ædwen. For his love for you is so great, it healed a rift and ended a war.'

*Ours is a love that has always gone beyond our countries, language and faith*, she thought.

'And now a toast to my Queen, who I am delighted to say is with child. An heir for the throne of England. May we wish her a healthy and happy pregnancy. *Skol.*'

And the whole room stood and cheered in unison.

*'Skol,'* all the people in the hall repeated.

It was a wonderful feast of wild boar and vegetables. And Ædwen loved being surrounded by friends and family. She knew this was where she and Stefan, and Ellan, and any future children they might have together, belonged. She felt happy. Content. At last.

Her mother came over to speak to her and introduced her to Ethelred, and Ædwen introduced her family to Stefan.

'I shall look forward to getting to know you better,' she said to her brother, before turning to her mother. 'And you.'

Her mother swiped a tear from her eye. 'Thank you.' Then Ædwen wrapped her arms around her mother, for she knew the torment the woman must have gone through all these many winters, as she had gone through it when Ellan had been taken. And she could not deny this woman her child. Herself.

The celebrations were raucous and the men were getting carried away, just as they had in the alehouse that night, but Stefan slipped his arm around her waist and leaned in, whispering that he was ready to leave when she was. She nodded.

Once back in their rooms, he laid her down in bed and got in next to her, and she felt warm and safe, nestled into his gently rising and falling chest. She turned to look at his face, taking him in. He was so handsome. She had always thought so, from the first moment she saw him, but he'd grown into a man to be admired. She studied his ruffled hair, his wide jaw, covered in a thick beard.

She loved him. She was completely in love with him. She always had been. And she would be for all time.

Her hand came up to hold his jaw and he rolled towards her.

She curled her hand around his head and drew him to her, kissing his lips, passionately. But as her tongue tangled with his, he pulled back.

'What are you doing? You're supposed to be recovering.'

'You're the perfect cure,' she said, pressing her body against him.

'Ædwen, you need your strength to focus on getting better,' he said, removing her hand from around his neck.

She frowned, frustrated. 'This will make me feel better.'

She didn't understand it. Did he not want her, like she wanted him? It was all she could think about. But he was being very careful with her, too careful, treating her like some precious trinket, and it was maddening. She wanted him to put his hands on her. All over her. Like he had the other day.

'And have you forgotten about Ellan?'

'No…'

'We don't want to wake her.'

And she lay back and sighed. 'You're right, she'll wake and then she'll want milk and then she'll never get back to sleep.'

Stefan grinned. 'You're a good mother, Ædwen.'

A warm glow infused her body.

She realised in just the short space of the week she

was beginning to anticipate her daughter's needs…like Stefan usually anticipated hers. She delighted in the mundane, everyday tasks of being a mother. She had discovered her wifely duties weren't a hardship either, yet Stefan seemed to be thwarting her attempts to seduce him at every step. He seemed to be refraining from touching her and it was infuriating.

She turned to look at him, frustrated.

'I won't take you again until you're better, Ædwen. I don't want to hurt you.'

'And if I'm not better by our wedding…?'

He grinned. 'Then we'll just have to delay it by a few days.'


Ædwen couldn't believe Stefan had agreed to be baptised at a great ceremony. And she couldn't believe that ceremony, and their wedding, was finally happening today.

She was standing in the palace courtyard, with all of the King's subjects, waiting for Stefan to come out of the remains of the monastery in the procession with the priests. A huge barrel had been erected outside, not dissimilar to the one she used to bathe in in Eastbury, and she was still in shock that he was doing this. For the King. For Ellan. For her…

Would he come to regret it?

The drums started to roll and she gripped Ellan tighter in her arms, hoping she wouldn't cry. She glanced up and saw the priests and nuns leading the line and Stefan in the middle of them all, dressed in a dark robe.

He looked up and met her gaze, then he smiled at her. She felt a rush in her blood. Would it always be this way?

she wondered. Would he always have this impact on her? It hadn't lessened over the months they'd been apart.

Her stomach fluttered with nerves. She had bathed with the Queen in the palace baths this morning and dressed in the beautiful blue silk tunic Stefan had bought her. The Queen had organised for her attendants to fix her hair and crown her with a wedding wreath. She looked every inch the bride. And she knew there was no other man she would ever want to wed. She knew she wanted to be with Stefan.

The baptism service began and she listened, attentively, as the priest read his words and Stefan swore his allegiance to the King and God.

But she felt a lump grow in her throat.

She rushed forward, unable to help herself. 'Stefan,' she said.

He turned and looked at her, then retreated down the steps to pull her to one side.

'What is it?' he whispered, glancing around at the people looking on.

'I don't want you to change who you are to be with me. I just want you to know that. That I love you the way you are. After all, our daughter is half of you.'

He smiled down at her.

'Thank you, Ædwen. But don't you see that's one of the reasons I am willing to be baptised? I want our beliefs to be aligned, in this life and the next. If I remain a pagan, I would go to Valhalla when I die, whereas you and Ellan would go to heaven. And I so desperately want to see you there. Because I want you for ever, Ædwen, in this life and the next. I never want to be parted from you.'

'Or I you,' she said, bringing her hand up to rest on his

cheek, her tears falling. 'I love you, Stefan. Everything you've just said, I want that, too.'

Stefan then climbed back up the steps and was welcomed into the pool. He shrugged off his robe and he was naked, apart from a pair of dark breeches. He looked magnificent and her throat dried.

He dropped down into the water and the priest gently pushed his head beneath the surface, immersing his entire body, saying he was being cleansed of his sins and being reborn.

Afterwards, they all made their way back into the church for their wedding.

Sister Margaret took Ellan off Ædwen's hands and she met Stefan at the altar. She couldn't believe this was her second wedding in as many weeks. Only this time, it didn't fill her with dread. Instead, flutters of excitement filled her stomach as Stefan stared down into her eyes. She couldn't wait to spend her future with him.

'You look beautiful,' he said.

'So do you.'

He had changed into his uniform, his dark hair neat, his Royal mail coat immaculate, with dark breeches and boots. He was her dream man. He always had been.

The priest asked Stefan to hand over his ancestral sword and he did so, his brow a dark line, his lips pressed together. She wondered what he was thinking, but she couldn't read his face. The moment felt huge. That he was giving her his father's blade, as if he had truly forgiven her for all that had happened in the past.

But this time, it was Stefan's turn to halt the proceedings. He took her hand and pulled her close, whispering in her ear. 'Ædwen, there's something I need to tell you before you go through with this.'

She looked up at him. 'There's nothing you can tell me that will make me love you any less,' she said and he smiled, repeating the words he had once told her.

'Nevertheless... I think I must.'

The priest paused the service and Stefan took her to one side, as the congregation whispered in excitement among themselves.

'I haven't been entirely truthful with you. And I want there to be no secrets between us.'

'All right.' Her heart was in her throat.

He took a deep breath and began. 'Ædwen, when you told me about the atrocities carried out by Danes on your lands, I never thought my own people could be capable of that... But Canute, before the battle...he told me he knew my father. I was shocked. He told me my father had come here, not in peace, as I'd always believed, but to attack these lands. To help Canute in his conquest of England.'

He combed his fingers through his hair with his other hand. 'I'm so ashamed... I'd always believed he was innocent. That your father had attacked our people, whereas, in fact, he was just defending his lands, what was his. *You.*' He shook his head. 'I've been afraid to tell you. I don't want you to think I'm the monster that you and your father always thought Danes were.'

She shook her head, placing a hand on his arm. 'I don't, Stefan.' She gripped his hands with hers. 'I never did. You weren't to know what he was planning... And would you go back and change it? Would you wish for him to be successful, if you had known, and if we could relive it?'

'No, of course not,' he said. 'Because if my father had been successful with his raid, what might have happened to you?' He shuddered. 'I was out there, fighting the men from Eastbury, and I came up against your father. I realised he had just been defending his home. His family. And how could I be cross with him for protecting you?'

She took his hands in hers. 'We have both made mistakes and so have our parents. We have suffered for their shortcomings. I just hope we don't make such bad mistakes with Ellan. But whatever errors we make, we shall make them and fix them together. Side by side.'

'May we proceed now?' the priest asked, coughing, interrupting them.

'Yes,' they agreed in unison.

Taking each other's hands, they repeated the vows the priest asked them to make, this time in front of a huge audience.

'I take you, as my husband,' Ædwen said.

'I take you, as my wife,' Stefan declared. 'Again,' he whispered, so only she could hear.

And she couldn't help but smile.

It was what she had always wanted.


The King and Queen had put on a huge feast for them back in the Great Hall and Ædwen was in awe. It was more spectacular than she could ever have imagined. A wedding anyone would dream of. She had to pinch herself it was happening. And so why was she willing for it to be over, wishing to be alone with Stefan again?

As if he could sense that, too, he leaned in and whispered into her ear, 'How soon do you think we can slip away?'

'I thought you were a patient man?' she jested. She leaned back in her own seat, enjoying the fact he now needed her, wanted her, as much as she did him, knowing the torture he was going through.

'We all have our limits. And seeing you in that dress, knowing you're mine, it's pushing me to the brink.'

She liked the fact she was driving him crazy. Because she felt the same. He had been making her feel like this for days and she couldn't wait any longer.

'Do you want your wedding gift?' Ædwen asked him.

'What, something other than you in my bed?' he said. 'What is it? I hope you didn't go to the market again on your own.'

'I wouldn't dare.'

'Good.'

'Come and see,' she said, taking his hand and leading him out of the hall.

They walked down the corridors of the palace, her leading the way, her legs almost totally recovered. 'You know, we could just head back to my room now we've escaped from the crowd, while we have the chance…'

'You have to have your present first,' she said.

He growled in frustration. 'Where are you taking me?' he asked, and he realised they were heading outside through the cloisters, into the courtyard, to the storage barns at the back of the square.

'All right, close your eyes,' she said, stopping outside some large wooden doors.

He gave her a look, but did as he was told.

She opened the wooden door, and he rolled on the balls of his feet, waiting to be told he could see the surprise she had planned for him.

'Ædwen, I really didn't need anything other than you.'

She came behind him and wrapped her hands over his eyes. 'Ready?' she asked, ignoring his comment.

'Yes.'

And then she released her hands. 'Surprise!'

It seemed to take a moment for his eyes to adjust to the light and he peered inside the shed. And then his eyes went wide when he saw it. 'A boat? No, not a boat, a longship?' he gasped.

'I know how much you miss the sea,' she said. 'I asked the King if he had a boat I could buy…and he said he would give you some days off other than the usual one day a year, so we can go on a little trip. See the seals… go swimming…sleep on the beach under the moon like we used to…'

He looked at her without moving for a few seconds.

'Do you like it?' she asked, holding her breath.

He took her in his arms, eradicating the distance between them, his hands coming up through her hair to hold her head, and he kissed her so fiercely it took her breath away.

He pulled away to look down at her.

'I'll take that as a yes,' she whispered.

He grinned against her mouth. 'I love it,' he said and kissed her again. A deep, open-mouthed kiss. He pulled her closer, conveying his desire and need. 'Thank you, Ædwen. You know me well… But now I want to know you again. All of you. I just can't wait any longer.'


'I want to show you how much I've missed you,' she said, as they fell through the door to their room and, within moments, she had dispensed of his coat, his tunic, her hand reaching down to unfasten the tie at his waist-band. She slid her hand beneath the material and took hold of him. 'You've had your reward from the King. But I have a reward for you also.'

She pushed him against the door and sank to her knees, tugging his breeches down. She trailed her fingers over his taut, muscular stomach and down.

Staring up at him, she took his length in her palm and he gazed down at her, his eyes wide, as if he didn't want to miss a moment of what he now knew she was about to do to him. 'I'm determined you will finish inside me, one way or another...' She smiled.

Then she drew him into her mouth, wrapping her lips around him.

He sucked in a ragged breath and gripped the wall with his one hand, the other coming up to hold the back of her head.

'Ædwen,' he whispered.

His hands twisted into her hair, and he pulled her closer, bringing her mouth down on to him, and she flicked her tongue over the tip, kissing him, licking him, gently sucking him. He bucked and she took him further into her mouth. He groaned, wildly, grappling with the wall, her hair, his strong thighs trembling.

Ædwen had no idea what she was doing, whether she was doing it right, she just knew she wanted to give him something incredible, as he had given to her the other day, when he'd kissed her so intimately. She dragged her teeth along the length of him, wanting to see if he trusted her, before taking him deeply again.

'Ædwen,' he choked. 'Oh, Ædwen.'

She knew when he bit out her name, the muscles in

his arms straining, his fingers tightening around her head, that he was about to lose all control. She heard him roar out his climax and felt the powerful rush of his orgasm on her tongue, tasted water, salt and spice… he tasted of Stefan.

And when he had finished, she sat back, looking up at him, glad she'd given him the satisfaction he deserved.

'That was…something else,' he said. 'Incredible. You're incredible,' he said, pulling her up to her feet. 'But I want to come inside your body next time. I want to give you my legacy.'

Her breath hitched.

'I thought you weren't ready.'

'I was just being greedy, wanting to keep you all to myself,' he said. 'But I also want us to be the family we should have been all along, Ædwen. A big family, so I'm thinking we'd better get started right away. And obviously, a big family means doing this a lot.'

He stripped off her pinafore and tunic, before removing his own, and kissed her long and slow on the lips, making it last. Just standing there together, naked, there was an honest truth to their feelings. She had washed him clean of all his sins, just like in his baptism, and he had been born a new man. And he was ready to start the rest of his new life with her, right here, right now.

He picked her up by her bottom and she wrapped her legs around him, and he carried her upstairs to their bed. He laid her back on the furs and she reached for him, opening herself up to him, showing him she wanted him, just as he did her. His need for this wonderful woman was insatiable. It always had been. And as the tip of him pushed all too easily into her entrance, their bodies knowing each other intimately, she whimpered, telling him that she couldn't wait to be joined with him any longer either.

As he stared into her beautiful eyes, he asked her if she was ready. Ready for the onslaught of pleasure he was about to inflict on her. Because he planned to take her deeper and harder than he ever had before.

She kissed him, saying yes. 'Please, Stefan, now.'

And with one hard, slick thrust, he plunged inside her body, all the way in, and she cried out into his shoulder, biting down on his skin. She wrapped her arms around his neck, clinging on.

And he wickedly did it again, wanting to be buried inside her, as if he was a part of her, and shudders of ecstasy racked her body.

'Will it always be like this?' she whispered, as he gave her a moment to ready herself before the next surge.

'This good, you mean?' he asked, his voice unsteady, stroking his hands over her bottom, tugging her closer still, as his lips found her neck. 'Yes. Because every time I make love to you, I'm showing you how much I love you, Ædwen. Promising to love you was something I decided when I first met you, and when I said those vows in Eastbury. And I'm never going to stop. And as my love for you is still growing deeper all the time, I'm going to show you how much I care, how much you move me, every night, every morning and all the times I can in between, for the rest of our lives.'

And as he soared intimately inside her again, he knew he was where he wanted to be, for the rest of his days.

And this time, he gave her everything. He began to

move harder, faster, sliding all the way in and out, pounding them both into an insane spiral of pleasure that had them both crying out in unison and euphoria, him burying his seed deep inside her, the place where he called home.

# *Epilogue*

⁂

Ædwen seated Ellan and their son, Aksel, on the bench in the longship, as Stefan pushed them away from the shore. They had travelled along the coast for a week or so now and were finally heading inland, along the river back towards Wintancaester. Their adventure of a lifetime was over and they would be home before nightfall.

This time together as a family had been special, whiling away their days on undiscovered beaches, fishing, seal-spotting and swimming in the ocean. They had seen so much, laughed so much, but she was ready to get her babies home. She had missed being away from all their friends and family and she had missed her nights alone with Stefan in their bed.

'Tell me the story again, Father. The one about the angel.' Ellan giggled as Stefan began to row the oars. He grinned and started to relay his favourite tale. The one about how he'd travelled from another island across the sea to come here and, when he'd washed up on these shores, he'd been met by a guardian angel, smiling down on him.

Ædwen didn't think she'd ever tire of hearing that tale, for it had such a happy ending.

She couldn't believe she had been blessed with a healthy son, as well as Ellan. Stefan had given her all that she'd dreamed of and more. But she wondered what he would think if she told him she wanted one more.

He had been overjoyed when her belly had swelled with Aksel. A devoted husband and always a wonderful father. He had lovingly pressed his ear up to her swollen stomach, listening for any sounds of a heartbeat, waiting for the little kick of a protruding foot. And his son looked like him. Aksel had his dark hair, his smile and his beautiful blue eyes.

Stefan had been talking about getting a new ink design on his skin, to represent his son, and she'd said they should look into it together when they got back to Wintancaester.

As they drew closer to the city, she could see the new roof of the monastery had been finished and it looked magnificent. Better than ever before. She felt as if everything that had been wrong had been put right.

They had sent a messenger ahead and, when they eventually pulled up on the banks of the river, there was a welcome party to greet them. They scrambled out of the boat to excitedly reunite with Ædwen's mother, Ethelred, Sister Margaret and Kendra, and everyone embraced each other. 'The King has prepared a huge feast for your return tonight,' they announced.

Later, when they had filled their stomachs and drunk their fill of wine, sitting around talking with their King and Queen, and everyone they cared about in the world, the children playing, running around in the Grand Hall, Ædwen felt content, in a way she never had before.

As she leaned back into Stefan's shoulder, he placed his arm around her, tugging her close.

'Do you think anyone will miss us if we head back to our room?'

Ædwen raised an eyebrow. 'Whatever for?'

He groaned. 'I need you. Badly.'

And she knew she couldn't deny him. She had never been able to.

'It's just as well I asked Sister Margaret to look after the children for us tonight then.' She smiled.

'I told you, you were an angel,' he said.

And when he finally carried her upstairs to his bed, deftly removing her clothes, soaring inside her, he whispered over and again, 'Ædwen, you're my heaven.'

At some point, they must have fallen asleep, as the next time Stefan woke, Ædwen was tugging at his shoulder and he dragged open his eyes to see her rearing over him, kissing him, flicking her tongue over the swirls of ink on his chest.

'Again?' he asked, grinning. 'Ædwen, you're insatiable.' He was weary from their long night of lovemaking, and yet he still felt the stirrings of desire in his groin. How did she do that? She had always made him feel this way. He could never, ever get enough of her.

She writhed against him, taking him in her hand, sending all his blood to his groin, and he groaned. 'What are you doing to me?'

'Is now a good time to tell you a secret?' she said, her lips curling upwards suggestively.

'I thought we didn't have secrets,' he told her.

'That's why I'm going to share it with you.'

'Go on then,' he said, as her lips stole lower, over his stomach, and his breath hitched.

'I want another baby, Stefan. I can't have enough of them. They're just so perfect. Like you.'

His eyebrows shot up. 'You want another?' he asked, surprised. 'Already?'

'Yes,' she said, moving lower still.

And he grinned, laughing. 'All right, Ædwen.'

He would give her the world if she asked.

In one swift movement, he pulled her up, ruthlessly rolled her over on to her stomach, spreading her legs wide with his own, stretching her arms out above their heads, as she wildly grappled with the furs. It was a total surrender, her sprawled out beneath him, whimpering, waiting for the pleasure she knew he would bestow upon her. And he surged inside her from behind, hard, completely and utterly impaling her with his big body. There was nothing between them, just skin pressed against skin. And he stormed her body, willing to leave another legacy inside her, the very essence of him behind. Ædwen was the only woman he'd ever want to create a child with. The only woman he trusted enough with his heart and his secrets. And as he heard her muffled, orgasmic screams against the furs, taking him with her over the edge, he knew he would always be her everything, as she was his. His heaven and his home.

\* \* \* \* \*

*If you enjoyed this story,
why not check out one of
Sarah Rodi's other great reads?*

The Viking and the Runaway Empress
Chosen as the Warrior's Wife
*in* 'Convenient Vows with a Viking'
Second Chance with His Viking Wife
Claimed by the Viking Chief
One Night with Her Viking Warrior

# HARLEQUIN
### Reader Service

# Enjoyed your book?

Try the perfect subscription for Romance readers and get more great books like this delivered right to your door.

See why over 10+ million readers have tried Harlequin Reader Service.

**Start with a Free Welcome Collection with free books and a gift—valued over $20.**

Choose any series in print or ebook. See website for details and order today:

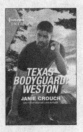

## TryReaderService.com/subscriptions